THE LAST THING
HE EVER EXPECTED TO DO
WAS TO KISS HER.

All Nick had wanted was for Callie not to get hurt when she fell off that crazy mare, not to get trampled or killed. But as he caught her in mid-air and felt the sweet weight of her in his arms, he instantly turned greedy for more.

There she was, still wild-eyed with fear, gasping with relief, her luscious lips parted and her breasts rising and falling against his chest with her hard breathing. Then she buried her face in his neck.

"Oh, thank God," she said, her lips hot against his skin. "I thought . . . I'd die . . . before I could get to you."

The words wrapped themselves around Nick's heart. He crushed her closer, and, still struggling for breath, she lifted her face and looked at him as if he were the most wonderful thing she'd ever seen.

"Callie," he said, "you have got to learn to ride."

Then he kissed her, long and hard.

Other **AVON ROMANCES**

THE ABDUCTION OF JULIA *by Karen Hawkins*
BRIT'S LADY *by Kit Dee*
DONOVAN'S BED *by Debra Mullins*
HIGHLAND BRIDES: HIGHLAND HAWK *by Lois Greiman*
MAIL-ORDER BRIDE *by Maureen McKade*
A ROGUE'S EMBRACE *by Margaret Moore*
WITH THIS RING: REFORMING A RAKE *by Suzanne Enoch*

Coming Soon

THE MACKENZIES: JOSH *by Ana Leigh*
ON A NIGHT LONG AGO *by Susan Sizemore*

And Don't Miss These
ROMANTIC TREASURES
from Avon Books

THE DANGEROUS LORD *by Sabrina Jeffries*
THE MAIDEN BRIDE *by Linda Needham*
MY TRUE LOVE *by Karen Ranney*

THE RENEGADES

NICK

GENELL DELLIN

AVON BOOKS ◆ NEW YORK

This is a work of fiction. Names, characters, places, and incidents either are the product of the author's imagination or are used fictitiously. Any resemblance to actual events, locales, organizations, or persons, living or dead, is entirely coincidental and beyond the intent of either the author or the publisher.

AVON BOOKS, INC.
An Imprint of HarperCollins*Publishers*
10 East 53rd Street
New York, New York 10022-5299

Copyright © 2000 by Genell Smith Dellin
Inside cover author photo by Loy's Photography
Published by arrangement with the author
Library of Congress Catalog Card Number: 99-96445
ISBN: 0-380-80353-4
www.harpercollins.com

First Avon Books Printing: April 2000

AVON TRADEMARK REG. U.S. PAT. OFF. AND IN OTHER COUNTRIES, MARCA REGISTRADA, HECHO EN U.S.A.

Printed in the U.S.A.

WCD 10 9 8 7 6 5 4 3 2 1

Chapter 1

September 16, 1893
Opening of the Cherokee Strip

Damn! The wild stallion's whinnying was going to bring every horse-hungry homesteader who'd sneaked into the Strip ahead of the Run—as he had—straight to this spot. Nickajack stepped out of his hiding place, intending to run the mustang off.

But his two penned mares immediately started neighing a warm welcome, and his own stallion, the Shapeshifter, went into a fit of shrill, jealous warnings loud enough to bring half the U. S. Army riding up this valley. An ironic grin tugged at Nick's lips in spite of his frustration. There was no hope for it. The mating dance would go on, no matter how big a horde of barbarians was about to swoop down upon them.

He kept to the meager cover of the dry-leaved cottonwoods and ran to the Shifter.

"Hey, it's downright dangerous to work yourself into a lather over the women," he told him, stroking the horse's neck. "Didn't you learn that at Pretty Water Creek, when I did?"

Nick had tied his mount back under a ledge, out of sight in the side of the draw, saddled and ready to pretend that they'd been in the Run. Good thing, too, since just fifteen minutes ago three soldiers had paused on the prairie floor above his head to have a couple of quirlies. He could only hope they were well gone by now.

"A little sweat'll make you look your part," he told the big black stud horse, "but this's enough. Settle down and let me go send that broom-tailed stranger on his way."

Shifter trembled, snorted, pulled back on the tie rope, and demanded his freedom with a high, sharp nicker.

"Here, now, here. I hate to keep you tied, but he might mess up your pretty face if I let you get at him."

Shifter rumbled deep in his throat. He wasn't scared of the interloper.

Nickajack stroked the wet, muscled shoulder, soothing with his voice.

"We don't need any other studs around here; I agree. I'll run him off in just a minute."

Damn it, though, he hated to. The stallion's band of horses, especially the nursing mares, needed water badly.

He looked through the sparse leaves for another glimpse of the wild ones. The stallion, a short-coupled red roan with a surprisingly fine head, was not only handsome in spite of his gauntness, but nervy as hell. He paced back and forth right up there near the penned mares, in spite of Shifter's screams and the fact that Nickajack's scent was bound to be all over the place.

Behind the roan, his small band of wild mares and colts were drinking from the pool fed by the spring. They were all mighty thin and half-worn-out from ranging so far for water and graze in the relentless heat.

"Better move on," Nickajack muttered. "I don't have water for all of you and mine, too."

The endless drought had sapped the spring as it had every other water source in the country. The pool was lower than he'd ever seen it and the creek that usually flowed from it had gone bone dry a month ago. Yet he still didn't step out where the stud horse could see him and spook.

The mustangs were flesh and blood, and

they hadn't had enough. They were desperate, or they wouldn't have come in to water in the middle of the day—and God knew they were going to need their strength. A few minutes from now, no matter which way they ran, they would have to turn and run some more, because suddenly, at the sound of one shot on the border, a bunch of ignorant, plow-wielding greenhorns would be racing all over their range.

Everything that belonged on this land would be displaced then. Nickajack clamped his jaw so hard his teeth gritted. Only a few more minutes until the Strip would be torn into pieces.

To try to keep from thinking about that, he ran his horseman's eye over the mustangs. Not bad. The stallion definitely threw his head on the foals.

"If he'd only shut up, he'd be right pleasant to have around," he mused aloud.

Shifter snorted derisively. He pulled back and half-reared, pointed his nose at the sky, and screamed again.

Nickajack listened for hoofbeats above them, but he heard only the hot wind as it blew from the south. The stud hadn't caught his fresh man-scent yet, so he waited for the wild band to drink a few more gulps.

He couldn't tarry long now, though. The sun rode almost directly overhead and the

Run would start at noon. A man on a fast horse with plenty of bottom could be here from the Arkansas City starting point within half an hour. Thirsty mustangs or no, he'd better drive his stake on his claim before some clodhopper did.

Nickajack finally slipped off the handwoven halter he'd put on top of the bridle, and let it drop to swing against the trunk of the tree. Gathering the reins, he stepped around and stuck one boot toe into the stirrup.

Instead of swinging up into the saddle, though, he acted on a sudden impulse. He set both heels to the ground and undid the latigo, unbuckling the cinch.

"Damn if riding bareback makes them call us Indian," he told the black. "Any man calls our hand, it's his funeral."

Suddenly the anger beat in his veins like a war song. He wished he could defy somebody, if the truth be told. Just like that desperate roan stud horse out there, his blood ran hot now, and his breath was moving, sure and strong, in and out of his body. It was a foolish wish, though, to expect a challenge—half the white-man riders in the race would be bareback for speed, no doubt, and he wouldn't look any more Indian than the rest.

Quick as thought, he jerked the saddle off anyhow, threw it over a low limb, mounted in one running leap, and rode the Shapeshifter, who reared a little as a warning to the wild horse, out through the grove of trees. The roan startled at the sight of them and whinnied the alarm to his band.

The next instant the mustang was rounding up the mamas and babies, setting the lead mare in motion while he kept one eye peeled toward Nickajack and Shifter. With the next heartbeat they were all gone, running toward the mouth of the narrow valley, reaching with their long legs for the open plains.

The Shifter plunged to follow, but Nickajack sat back and used his hands and voice to slow him.

"Settle down, old son. You can't catch him now—but you're still the best horse in the country."

It was true. He owed his life to the black a dozen times over.

During that long, wild year when he called himself Goingsnake and rode every inch of the Nation with his blood pounding hard in hopes of stopping the sale of the Strip, he and the Shapeshifter had risked it all, over and over again. But to no avail.

Tragically, to no avail. For not only had they not been able to save the Strip, they had caused killings while trying—with the help of one beautiful, treacherous woman. The only thing they could accomplish now was to keep this one quarter-section of this proud, beautiful land the way the Apportioner had meant it to be. Just this one.

First, the soldiers had ridden across the face of the Earth Mother as if they owned it. Soon the pumpkin-piling farmers would do the same. Then they would tear its face open with their plows.

The old rage rose higher and wilder in his sinews and his blood, rage enough to wreck the world. He clasped his legs tighter against Shifter's wet, hot flesh and smooched him into a run.

Blowing his breath out hard, trying to control the onslaught of fury and hatred, Nickajack shot past his mares, past the pond, then past the long, narrow mound marked by a weathered stone. His Cherokee mother's grave.

He touched the flag stuck into his belt beside the six-gun he wore, threw back his head, and sent the ancient wild-turkey war cry gobbling out onto the wind.

He didn't give a rip who saw him now.

If a wreck didn't kill her, the heat would.

Or it might be that she'd already died and gone to hell, as Papa had predicted when she'd announced she was carrying Vance Harlan's baby in her belly. Hell or the Cherokee Strip, it was hard to tell the difference here on the border on the day of the Run.

Callie Sloane lifted one shoulder enough to wipe the sweat off her face. She moved slowly, carefully, so as not to stir up her team any further. Her arm muscles burned like fire from the effort of holding in the raucous pair, but she didn't dare let up. The rule was that anyone jumping the gun and rushing out into the Strip before the signal would be shot, and she most certainly did not intend to die now—not after all the hardships she'd endured in the last two months.

She set her jaw, tightened her grip on the lines, and forced her mind away from the scary thought of her sorry team, her only transportation.

It surely was hot enough out here on the prairie for Old Ned himself. Maybe he was the one who'd thought up the idea of people waiting in the sun, crushed into line until their brains cooked and their arms broke from holding their horses, all for the chance to risk their necks in a mad race for a piece of free land.

"Hey, Lady! Can you holler 'gee' and move your team over just a hair?"

The man's loud voice came from directly beneath her feet.

Amazed, Callie looked down. A man on a bicycle, of all things, had by some miracle wedged himself in between her wagon and the heavyset man on the big horse who had two fresh mounts tied to his saddle rings.

"You'll get run over," she cried. "Get away from here. You're right in front of my wheel!"

"That's why you need to scoot your team over. Just a hair. Holler 'Gee.' Please, ma'am?"

"I know what 'gee' means!" she yelled. "If I could move this team over just a hair, I could make them dance the schottische."

The silly little person whose voice was bigger than he was wore a bowler hat made out of a heavy winter material with hardly enough brim to keep a candle's light out of his eyes, much less this blinding sun. In spite of her misery, Callie had to smile at the picture he made.

"May I?" he said.

He rolled right on up to Joe's head without waiting for her permission, took hold of his bridle, and pushed until the mule and the mare called Judy stepped sideways a couple of feet. The man with the three horses shifted too, but not without a shouted protest.

"Let go of him," Callie yelled to the fool on the bicycle. "Don't hold him. They'll fire the signal shot in just a minute."

The noise all around her quieted at her words, as if she knew something no one else did about the starting signal. The man did as she told him, and incredibly, her team stood still even after he dropped his hand. He turned and smiled at her.

"I'm good with them. Maybe I could trade you for my bicycle."

Callie smiled back. It made her feel less lonely somehow, even if he was a dangerous nuisance. Not a soul had spoken to her since Dora, her one friend in this border camp, had left at dawn for the place on the line that her husband chose. It made her feel better, though, to remember Dora's promises to send out inquiries for Callie's location as soon as she knew her own.

Dizziness left over from her morning sickness swirled through her again, and since the team was quiet, Callie let her knees collapse. She dropped down to sit on the wagon seat, made herself breathe deeply, and tried not to think about how truly alone she was. She must concentrate on the task at hand.

In a minute she'd have to drive like she'd never driven in her life. She, Callie Sloane, who'd walked everywhere she ever went for eighteen years, except for an occasional ride on a plowing mule. Until that day two weeks ago when she boarded the westbound train in Somerset and let it carry her out of the Cumberlands and out of Kentucky.

She could drive this team. There was nothing she couldn't do if she had to, for the baby's sake, and the love of its daddy and his memory. Drive she would, and find them a home she would.

Shifting both leather lines to one hand, she laid the other on her abdomen to see if she could feel the baby. Nothing yet. Her belly was as flat as ever and nothing moved inside her. One of these days she would feel it, though, like a little fish in water, and she would be so happy that she'd stayed true to the vision she and Vance had dreamed together.

"Hurry and grow," she whispered. "Kick and move around so you can keep Mama company."

At that moment, the hateful mule Joe twisted in his harness and cow-kicked at the man on the bicycle. The little man dodged the flying hoof without even looking. Callie couldn't keep back a laugh because the man seemed so nonchalant, as if he tamed bad mules every day of the week and was not at all impressed with Joe.

"He'll try again," she called.

"I don't doubt it," the man yelled back, twisting to look at her over his shoulder, "but he don't have much time left."

She could barely hear him for the noise rising again; it sounded like the biggest swarm of angry yellowjackets in the world, with a bunch of crazy people thrown in. Way too many people for the number of claims up for grabs.

The noise of the crowd roared even louder

for one instant and then a strange silence came, moving down the line from east to west. A soldier carrying a signal flag high above his head appeared out of the dust and rode out into the Strip. Callie's whole body froze and she couldn't get her breath.

"Five minutes 'til," somebody said.

"Steady now, steady," someone else answered.

That quiet command echoed on down the line.

Her heart racketing in her chest, Callie strained to hear the gunshot that would turn them all loose. The sun beat down hot enough to blister her scalp through her straw hat and her piled-up hair, the dust fogged in a cloud, and the smell of charred earth and grass from the government-set fires filled her nose. In this tinder-dry place, it was a wonder the flames meant to drive out the cattlemen hadn't taken hold and burned the settlers all to death.

Five minutes could be an eternity. The flag moved, swayed.

Suddenly the crack of a pistol shot ripped the air, at least four minutes too soon. The whole world exploded into a swirling mist of blurred ground and flying dust, cursing voices and cracking whips, train whistles and cheering spectators. They were off!

Callie got a glimpse of mounted soldiers dashing out, holding up their hands for people to stop. But no one did, not even when one pointed a gun.

The dust and ashes thickened until she couldn't see the ears of her team, much less what lay in front of them. They had leapt from nearly a standstill to a flat-out gallop, but she could feel and hear horses flying past her as if she weren't even moving.

They were a fleeting worry, though, because she had too much to do just trying to breathe the strangling air and hold onto the lines and stay in the wagon. It was tearing over the rough ground, bouncing like a plow behind a runaway. How could any land look so flat and be so rough?

Gunfire sounded somewhere off to her left and a long, shrill train whistle wailed. It gave her a chill. She'd forgotten about the hundreds more people crammed into the train and clinging to its sides. Most of them were headed for town lots, though, and not competing with her for a homestead.

She mustn't think about anyone else. All she had to do was spot a government marker on a piece of land that nobody else had claimed, and then drive in her stake.

Her team swerved suddenly and she saw it was to miss a cookstove, of all things, dumped on its back in the middle of the plains to lighten a load. The sight gave her goosebumps as the lurch of the wagon sent her sliding halfway off the end of the seat. It was awfully early in the race for such a sacrifice. It meant her competitors would stop at nothing to get a claim.

Righting herself, she lifted the lines and slapped them down.

"You've been trying to run all morning," she yelled, "so run!"

Dimly, as she flew past, she saw a man leap from his horse and reach for the stake on his saddle. A moment earlier, and she could've had that claim.

If she could've stopped this team. The way they were running now, they'd take her to Texas before they even slowed.

Gradually, working them with light tugs on the lines while she scanned the horizon the best she could, she got enough control to head Joe and Judy to the east, southeast. Somehow she had to get out of this press of dust-raising runners, so she could at least see a marker if one appeared. If she didn't make a choice soon, every claim would be gone.

"Sooner! You're nothin' but a sneakin' Sooner!"

The wind carried the angry shout clearly.

"Shoot the s. o. b.! Shoot him!"

Gunshots rang out, three or four of them, and then Callie heard nothing more except the noise of her own wheels. She shivered. Not only could a wreck or the heat kill her today, so could her fellow homesteaders.

The people in the border camp had talked incessantly of Sooners who slipped into the Strip to hide on choice pieces of land, ready to pretend they'd arrived in the Run, and many a man had threatened to shoot such cheaters on sight. Now it seemed that one of them had.

A dozen feet in front of her, the shape of a running horse formed in the middle of a cloud of dust, then the man clinging to his back. At that instant, they fell in a wild, tumbling roll forward onto the ground. The man landed free, past the horse's head and as she rushed on past and looked back, he got up. The horse didn't. A moment later, it let out a high, terrified scream that pierced Callie's heart.

But she couldn't go back, however much she wanted to help. With what she'd learned from Granny about doctoring both people and animals, she might do something for the poor thing, but she'd lose all chance of a homestead. She had to think of her baby and keep going while she had this wild team of hers halfway under control. Yet the hard decision brought tears to her eyes.

The wind blew away a great cloud of dust and showed her two people near a claim marker—a woman driving in her stake, a man on horseback. After a moment of apparent conversation, the man touched his hatbrim, whirled his horse and raced away. As he disappeared, the "woman" removed her skirts and sunbonnet. "She" was a man!

"What a low trick!" Callie cried aloud.

Joe chose to take that as an order and turned firmly to the left, dragging Judy with him. Callie sawed on the lines but he ignored her. In front of her the dust thickened, began to swirl, then formed a dustdevil that spun crazily away and cleared another path through the heavy air. She looked frantically for a marker, but saw none.

Farther to the east, the land was more broken and rolling. It rose and fell into some canyons and she could glimpse the tops of some trees down in a long draw, their leaves already brown from the drought. Trees would be wonderful, and even though these were tiny hills, this land would comfort her eyes every morning—much more than the flat, flat plains.

Best of all, a creek was probably the reason the trees grew there! Water on her land would be a gift from God, especially when she grew big and awkward right before her confinement, and was weak and tired following the birth. Dora would have enough to do when she came to help her birth the baby without hauling water, too. Yes! This was meant to be her claim!

She glimpsed a stone marker near the mouth of the draw and pulled the team to the right, urging them to race in that direction. They rushed up onto the edge of a deep ditch and down into it before she even saw it, nearly jolting her off the seat and over the side. Her box of precious books hurtled forward and slammed into the backs of her legs. She grasped it between her feet despite the pain and held it in the wagon.

That was one thing she couldn't lose, no matter what. Books could get her a teaching post when nothing else could.

The crack of a gunshot sounded faintly, way in the distance, and she saw fresh smoke rising on the horizon. Callie's heart leapt into her throat. People were thick as dust out here. This was her first and last chance—she had to stake this claim and be ready to hold it!

She bent sideways a little so she could feel the pistol in her skirt pocket and know it was still there. Considering that she'd bought it from the same man who'd sold her this wild team of animals, she could only pray that it would work better than they did. There'd been too few bullets to try it out more than twice.

The team carried her up a gradual slope and then down again, running straight toward the stone marker. Her heart beat even faster than the wagon was rolling, so fast that she had a sudden urge to jump off onto the ground and drive in her stake. It'd be better to get closer to the marker, though.

She was no more than a stone's throw from it when a loud cracking noise split her ears and a terrible shaking rippled through the wagon. The back end shook, and the rim of one of her wheels rolled past her, wobbling crazily before it fell over. *Stop!* She had to stop before the rough ground tore up her wooden wheel.

Shock froze her hands to the lines for a breath or two, but she hollered, "Whoa," got her team stopped, and then heard hoofbeats thundering somewhere near, growing louder by the minute. An instinct far older than she was forced her legs and arms to move. Now was her only chance.

She threw the lines in opposite directions and slid to the edge of the seat, grabbing her flag from beneath it as she went. She hit the ground running, racing for the marker with her skirts blowing ahead of her in the wind. As the noise of hoofbeats came closer, she plunged the slender stick that held her flag into the ground.

It wouldn't even stand. The earth was too dry. She snatched the gun from her pocket, turned it around, and pounded the stake with the butt. The stick sank in enough to stay upright. She had a claim!

Oh, praise God, she had done it! After all this agony, and all these miles, she had staked a claim!

Exhilaration nearly pulled her up into the air. She'd done it—she had a homeplace for her baby, a home of her very own! Papa couldn't banish her from here!

She bent over the flag, making sure it would stand, dragging air into her lungs, trying to catch a deep breath after her run. Only when the stick stayed straight and strong did she turn to look toward the sound of hoofbeats.

A big black horse was galloping at her, carrying a man in a cowboy hat and a blue shirt. For one hopeful heartbeat she let herself think that he would run on past, that the rider had his eye on something behind her—but the very bones in her body knew better.

The magnificent animal slid to a stop within an arm's length of her and reared high, reaching for the sky. Its cooling shadow fell across her but her blood blazed up hot, as hot as the ground searing the soles of her shoes. This man was trying to scare her with his horse's shod hooves threatening to crush her skull like a melon.

Callie kept her spine stiff and summoned the courage to look the bully in the face. His thighs bulged with saddle muscles that threatened the seams of his worn jeans; his powerful calves glued themselves to the horse's sweaty hide as if they shared a skin. He could ride, all right.

Finally, she looked up into his face.

He was handsome as sin, but that didn't help her any. His granite-gray eyes were the kind that gave no quarter.

Chapter 2

The horse and the man towered over her, like some huge, vengeful centaur of the desert. Any minute they'd come back down and crush her. A scream tore at her throat but she sealed her lips and held it in, fighting the urge to turn and run. Although every nerve in her body was cringing and cowering, she didn't even fold her arms over her head and close her eyes.

Instead, she stood her ground and stared into his gray eyes, which glittered in his sun-darkened face, while she placed one hand over her baby and turned her gun around in the other. She kept it hidden behind her skirts.

The horse dropped its front feet back to

earth with a soft thud, missing Callie by a good yard's length. A sigh of relief filled her chest but she held that in, too.

"You're jumping my claim," the man said in a flat tone that brooked no contradiction. "Move on."

His gaze pierced her. It dried out her mouth and paralyzed her tongue.

"No," she managed to say. "This is my claim."

"You've still got a chance," he said, as if she hadn't spoken. "Hurry and you can stake the next one."

Somebody shouted, not too far off into the distance. Hooves beat on the earth.

"You're mounted," she told him, narrowing her eyes against the dust and wind. "You go. I've lost a wheel rim, I got here first, and I'm not giving over to you."

"Big talk from a little woman," he said, an undertone of amusement in the words.

He looked her up and down, then his gray eyes came to rest on her face again. The look in them made her think of a slow-burning fire. He sat watching her, one hand resting on his muscled thigh, as still as if he never intended to move any more.

She couldn't move, either, for looking back at him.

Finally, her pulse pounding in double time,

she brought her gun out and lifted it in both hands, pointed it at him.

"I'll shoot you right down off that animal if you'd like to be buried on this claim," she said, holding her voice steady, "but that's the only way you're going to get possession of it."

The corners of his mouth twitched, as if he wanted to grin, but he didn't.

"You made a good decision not to laugh at me," she said. "I come from a long line of feuding mountain folks and I'm a dead shot."

"Well," he drawled, "it's downright refreshing to meet a woman who'll fight her own battles."

Callie thought she detected sarcasm in his wry tone but he still looked at her solemnly and she decided to take the remark at face value.

"You've met one, all right. I've come over a thousand miles for this claim, I staked it fair and square, and I intend to keep it, so you'd do just as well to ride right on out of here."

He glanced at the gun once more, then looked over his shoulder toward the sounds of hoofbeats, louder now. People were coming closer. His powerful leg tightened on the horse, and they plunged forward into an instant running lope.

Callie's heart leapt with joy. It worked!

Until he leaned down and pulled her hard-driven flag up out of the ground.

"Hey!" she yelled. "Leave that alone!"

He didn't even slow, only wheeled the horse and came at her again. A huge knot in her throat nearly choked her. He was robbing her! He was taking away her claim, the one with water and trees meant to be hers, the claim she'd suffered so much to find!

The flagrant injustice if it set her free. She lifted the pistol again, aimed it at his chest, steadied it in both her hands, and pulled the trigger. Nothing happened.

"Stop! Bring that back!" she yelled, as the thief thundered past her.

She swung around to keep the gun pointed at him and tried again to shoot the useless piece of trash.

He kept going, not even glancing over his shoulder, as if he'd known all along the rotten thing wouldn't fire.

She hurled it at him with all her strength, picked up her skirts with both hands, and gave chase.

"You'll not get away with this! I won't let you! Give me my flag!"

A few yards in front of her, his body shifted position on the horse, sliding so quickly sideways she thought he was falling off. He wasn't. As the big horse slowed and began to circle back toward her, the man hung low off one side, as easily as if he did such a thing every day, reached down, and with one sure thrust, planted her flag.

She ran faster.

"Don't bother to throw me a sop," she cried. "I won't have it! The other claim is better and it's mine by rights, and you know it, you filthy robber!"

He righted himself on the horse and rode toward her but without even looking at her. Not from shame, though, because he was staring at something over her head. Suddenly, she heard the hoofbeats right behind her and whirled to see who was there.

"Hey! You! I seen what you done. Pull up that flag!"

The challenger was so close that Callie veered to the right to get out of his path. A wild-eyed, bearded man riding a mule raced right up to her tormentor to face him down.

"Pull up that second flag, I say."

"Get out of here."

Her flag thief's eyes had turned so hard that one look could strike flint and make fire.

He is a dangerous man.

The thought hit her in the pit of the stomach. Somehow she hadn't known that quite so surely until now. It was a wonder he hadn't drawn his own pistol and shot her dead.

But the bearded man didn't seem intimidated in the least.

"Ain't right fer one couple to take two claims," he declared.

"You're way out of line, stranger. Ride on."

The cold order didn't faze the man on the mule.

"I'm willing to bet that you'uns ain't got two permits to make the Run," he said. "Wanna show me?"

Couple. You'uns.

It took another breath for Callie to realize that he meant the two of them. He thought they were together.

"We're not a couple!" she cried. "I don't even know him."

He just stole my claim from me—I never saw him before that.

But she shut her mouth before she said it. This bearded man wasn't going to help her get her land back; he wanted it for himself. He flicked his white-rimmed eyes at her.

"You don't know him. Whar's yore man, then?"

"I'm a widow."

He dismissed her with a scornful flick of his hand.

"Widder! Widder woman cain't prove up no claim."

He bore down on the man on the black horse again.

"Me and two brothers got families to work a farm. Seventeen young'uns amongst us. I'm layin' claim to this here quarter-section."

"It's taken. Hit the trail."

The man on the mule froze in his ratty saddle. Callie could see his skin whiten, even through the beard and the coating of dust on his face. He looked pretty dangerous himself. She wished she had her gun back, even if all she could do with it was bluff.

As if he'd shared the thought, the handsome man who'd stolen her claim drew his pistol, quicker than a squirrel stealing acorns. He rested its butt on his saddle horn and stared at the other man.

"You've got the drop on me, now," the muleback man said, his words coming cold and slow, "but Baxter is my name and I want you to know that sooner or later, that's the name the Land Office will write on the deed to this quarter-section right here."

"Ride," the land-thief said.

"You're protectin' her interests," Baxter said, flicking a scorn-filled look at Callie, "and in my book that says y'all are together, wed or not. I aim to go to the law with this."

The threat made no impression on her flag-thief.

"Then go," he drawled. "Ride or die."

This time his words held an edge so keen that Baxter pulled his mule around and started moving away.

"I'll be back when you least expect it," he

shouted, "and my brothers with me."

He clattered away, raising a storm cloud of dust.

New voices and noises of hooves and vehicles immediately drowned out the sound of the mule. The man on the black horse glanced around in all directions, then he holstered his gun.

"Run's over," he said. "The intruders from the south have met up with you locusts from the north. You got the last claim."

A storm of disappointment swept through Callie, a bitter wind that shook her right down to the bone.

"The Run may be over," she said, no longer even caring how dangerous he was, "but not between the two of us. I want the first claim I staked. I'm guessing by the trees that it has water, and this one doesn't."

"You guess right."

His eyes showed not one scrap of remorse, only a quick gleam of interest.

Most likely, he thought her a curious, amusing and pitiful specimen—a small woman, her old gun and her ragtag wagon useless, flinging foolish challenges at a muscular man wielding a fine pistol aboard a fine, fast horse.

A muscular man who had her at his mercy out in the middle of the prairie wilderness.

Her tongue went right on talking anyway.

"Then you've stolen my water from me. You

had no right. Give it back." A flash of irritation showed in his face, then, and one corner of his mouth lifted. He had beautiful, full lips that were very expressive when he released them from that hard, straight line.

But why would she even notice that? He was a ruthless, overbearing bully of the first order.

Suddenly, she was overcome with fury and disappointment so strong she trembled all over and got dizzy again. Her survival and her baby's were at stake, and the only weapon she had left was sheer determination.

"Admit it," she said. "I was first on that claim. You pulled up my stake."

He nailed her with one hot, sharp look.

"You must not have seen mine," he said. "It was there first."

"Hah! Now you're lying on top of stealing! This is an exceptional piece of reprehensible behavior on your part, Mr. . . ."

"Smith."

"Of course. Smith," she said sarcastically. "Well, you're hardly a gentleman, Mr. Smith. On the way out here I saw a gallant man give up a claim to a lady."

She didn't have one prick of conscience for keeping quiet about the fact that the lady wasn't a lady at all, but she did feel ashamed of sinking so low as to trade on her gender. It was a last-ditch effort, for sure, because Smith

could say the same as Baxter about a woman
alone not being able to prove up a claim.

Instead, he said, "It'd be hard for me to do
that, wouldn't it?"

"What do you mean?"

"I don't reckon a lady would draw down on
a man and try to shoot him without a word of
warning . . ."

He gave her a crooked grin that must've
melted many a silly girl's heart. It changed his
whole face, and sent a strange thrill racing
along her skin.

". . . Or call him a liar for no reason, either."

"For no reason! I certainly didn't see another
stake on that claim . . ."

His grin vanished.

"Maybe because you were trying not to see
it. I beat you to that claim by a good ten or
fifteen minutes."

"Prove it."

"Look for yourself. My stake's still there."

Panic shot through her, bringing back the
nausea with a vengeance, making her sick to
her soul. He surely wouldn't lie about something so easily proven. Oh, dear Lord, had his
stake been there all the time?

All of her insides went cold, in spite of the
heat, because he was telling the truth and she
knew it. But she *wouldn't* believe it—not yet.
She couldn't.

She wheeled and ran back the way she had

come, desperate to prove him wrong, but only a few strides later she saw it—a flag in the ground on the opposite side of the stone marker from where she'd driven hers. Her gaze skittered past it as if the sight of the windblown white cloth burned her eyes.

It might be a mirage.

It wasn't, though. Hadn't she learned in these past two months, when she'd lost her one true love and her home and family and all of the life she'd always known, that wishing did not change a thing? Ever?

Another step or two, and she stopped dead in her tracks. It was plain as the sun overhead that was boiling her brain: she would have a claim with no water, or no claim at all. When she was huge with child and barely able to bend and fill a bucket, she would have to drive those frenzied animals of hers no telling how far to get water.

The knowledge held her where she stood. She'd been a foolish dreamer to think the treed claim with water was meant for her and her child. It actually did belong to the ruthless man on the black horse.

His voice came from right behind her.

"You've had me in sight since you drove your stake, so you know that mine was already there."

He was at her shoulder, on foot now, leading the horse—they had come up behind her as silently as ghosts. She had let her feelings consume her watchfulness, and in this terrible desert, that way lay disaster for her and her baby. She had to be more careful!

She whirled on him.

"All right! I can see. I admit it!"

The words came out in a banshee scream and she clapped her hands over her mouth. Her blood was roaring in her head, the sickness rising again in her belly to steal what little was left of her strength. She set her mind against it, but it came anyway.

Never, ever could she let him see it; never would she tell him she was expecting a baby. That would make her completely vulnerable and he'd try to take the second claim, too.

Suddenly she couldn't even think anymore. The rest of the heat drained out of her face, her mouth went stiff with grief.

"I'm sorry," he said, really looking at her now. "I had no call to interfere in your life and get that last claim for you. Proving up a homestead is too much of a job for a woman alone."

"A hysterical woman, you mean?"

"Any woman," he said, almost gently. "I never should've done that."

"Why did you, then, if you knew you could prove this claim was already rightfully yours?"

"You were holding a gun on me," he snapped. "Remember? What was I supposed to do—shoot a woman?"

Now he was as hard and angry as ever.

"That's a good enough reason right there that a lone woman ought not be out here," he said.

"I'm not asking to be treated different from a man, in spite of what I said earlier," Callie snapped back. "Go ahead and shoot."

They stared at each other, the ridiculous words hanging in the air between them. Neither could resist a smile as hard as they tried.

"But not until I get a gun that works," she added quickly.

His smile vanished.

"A woman who won't give up," he said. "That makes what I've done even worse. If it hadn't been for my meddling, you'd be on your way out of the Strip right now."

"No, I'd be searching for a claim on foot or trying to ride my hateful horse to find one. I'd camp out here for days if I had to, waiting for somebody to give up and go back home."

"Let me buy you out, and you can get a place in town."

"No! I can't live in town. It'd kill my spirit."

"You can't survive alone out here. Go home, now, before you blister your hands and break your back trying to farm this ground."

"I can never go back to the Cumberlands," she said, her throat tightening with unshed tears.

He hesitated for a moment, waiting for her to say why. Somehow, somewhere in the back of her mind, that made her want to smile again, in spite of all. She would never have guessed he'd be interested enough to be curious.

"Well, I can't take care of you," he said finally, irritation flooding his voice. "I won't. I hate it that I tied you to this land."

"You didn't," she said, pulling herself up to her full five foot, three inches. "I would've staked a claim come hell or high water. It was Vance's . . . my . . . husband's . . . and my dream. We planned it from the minute we read about the Run in the newspapers."

He held her gaze although she tried to look away, and he saw her tears for Vance.

"Well, you've reached that goal in his memory," he said. "Now let me buy you out, Mrs. . . ."

"Sloane."

"Let me buy you out, Mrs. Sloane," he said again, in a soft voice so full of pity that she couldn't believe this was the same man who'd ordered her off his claim. "I'll pay enough for you to get a nice place with a well."

If there was anything she hated, it was being pitied.

"I'll soon have a well right there on my claim," she said, in a tone so bitterly fierce that it surprised her and him, too, from the look of him. "Until then, I can haul water however far it takes. If I have to do it a dipperful at a time."

The sharp gray eyes never left hers, the hard, handsome face never changed, yet something shifted behind it.

"I have a spring that never goes dry," he said. "You can haul it from there if you don't tell anyone."

Her meager breakfast of water and half a biscuit roiled in her stomach.

"No, thank you," she said. "I don't hold with secret obligations."

He said nothing, only shrugged. She could not understand him at all. One minute he was not going to take care of her, and the next he was offering her water from his spring. One minute he was angry, the next gentle.

"Besides, who would I tell?" she said, throwing a sarcastic glance to the left and to the right.

"Pilgrims like Baxter," he snapped. "And the pumpkin-rollers who did get claims and are hunting the closest water source at this very minute. Half of 'em will try to camp on a creek or at a spring until they get their shelters built."

"But it's heartless to deny people water when you have it!"

The more she thought about it, the more shocked she was.

"Why, you're worse than those vultures on the border, going up and down the line selling water for a dollar a glass!"

He gave a bitter chuckle.

"I'm worse than anybody you ever met, Mountain Girl."

He looked at her hard.

"Hold your tongue about the spring on my place," he said, "whether you come there for water or not."

He turned and threw himself onto his horse's bare back in a fast, fluid motion that reminded her of a panther pouncing.

"I'm not having anybody come onto my place," he said. "Except you, if you should decide to accept my offer."

"I feel very strange about withholding information that could keep someone from dying."

"Getting shot for trespassing could *cause* them to die."

"Well, that sounds familiar," she said wearily. "Next thing you know, we'll have a real mountain feud out here on the prairie."

"No," he said, "no feuds, just facts. This can be a dry country, and anybody stupid enough to think he can tear up this ground and farm it might as well learn that right now."

He sounded just like Papa in one of his rages against the Harlans.

"And you're the one mean enough to teach 'em," she gibed.

"Damn straight I am," he shot back, "and don't you forget it."

He was mean as a snake, but, she realized suddenly, her days of being afraid of meanness were long gone. He needed to know he couldn't bully her. They would be neighbors, after all, and neighbors did have to do things together sometimes, whether they wanted to or not.

She gave him a narrowed look.

"I'm no more afraid of you than a bear is of a squirrel."

That made him laugh for real. Then he sobered.

"If there's another weapon in that wagon, go get it," he said. "I'm leaving you now."

"Well, thank the good Lord. I was commencing to fear I'd never see the back of you."

That bit of sassiness made him grin.

"You might thank me, instead," he said.

"For what?"

"For seeing your flag flying over a claim, any claim. And for running Baxter off."

Wasn't that just like a man? He was sorry he'd got her a claim, but now he wanted thanks for it.

"I refuse to be obligated," she said. "I know! I'll repay you in pumpkins when I gather my first crop."

He clearly didn't think that was funny.

"You'll be obligated, all right, when the blue northers blow and you only have to haul your water half a mile instead of five."

Oh? And wasn't *that* like a man, too, assuming she had said yes when she hadn't.

"Seems to me you're so proud of your gallantry that you'll be likely to bring the water to me."

He looked her over, up and down, with a little smile tugging at the corners of his mouth again.

"I don't care to see anybody that often, not even a body as good-looking as yours."

She was glad that hot look didn't make her blush. At least, not so he could see it beneath her hat.

"Fine," she said. "Don't come back. You've already claimed my land; next thing I know, you'll be trying to claim my wagon, too."

"But not your team," he said. "Never that team."

That made them both laugh. Their eyes held for a long heartbeat.

Then he smooched to his horse, surged past her, and was gone.

Callie was still smiling as she turned and walked slowly down the slope toward her wagon. The dizziness had left her, and she didn't feel sick at her stomach anymore, either.

That little bit of verbal jousting had been fun—it had made her feel almost connected to someone again, after all these days and nights of loneliness just past.

Even in the border camp, when she'd met Dora and her family, she had still felt like such an outsider, so cast out. Which she was. It was hard to believe that she would never see or be a part of her own big family again.

But how could she feel connected to that man who called himself Smith?

She reached the wagon and climbed inside to get a drink of water and a towel to wipe her face—for all the good that would do. Sweat and dust would attack her again as soon as she went back out to work on the wheel. But at least there weren't as many ashes from the government's burning flying around here, as there had been on the border.

Her arms and legs trembled, and she sat down on the trunk that Granny had sent with her all the way from home. She longed, suddenly, to open it up and take out the photograph of Vance, but she couldn't afford the time. It would be dark in a few hours and she had to fix that wheel and drive onto her own place before then.

She had to find a spot to park the wagon that would be halfway defensible if Baxter did come back.

Worry swept through her; it sucked the strength right out of her muscles and sinews. The pistol she'd bought from that cheating, swindling, lying reprobate in the border camp might never work again. She had no other weapon except a butcher knife.

She wasn't afraid of meanness, true—but that was if she saw it coming, had a chance to face it down. A sneak attack in the dark was different.

Callie slowed her breathing and listened. The only sounds besides the wind were the squeals of Joe and Judy, who had never stopped kicking and biting at each other the whole time they'd stood there, she guessed. The next chore was to unhitch and hobble them and let them graze, while she tried to get the wheel off the wagon and the rim back onto it. Even driving no farther than her claim could break the wheel, and then she'd be in truly desperate straits.

Her stubborn mind left the necessary planning and jumped back to Baxter.

The crowbar might make a decent weapon, but as her brother Josh used to say, "If somebody's close enough to hit with a stick, he's close enough to take it away from you." The same was true of her knife.

Baxter alone could cause her no end of grief, and much more, if he brought his brothers. He had not seemed to be a principled man.

Terrifying scenes came boiling up out of her imagination, possibilities that stopped her breath. She had to protect her baby at all costs!

Hot as it was inside the canvas-roofed wagon, she kept on sitting there, limp with dread of what she might meet outside. Thin cloth and rickety wood though it was, it seemed as secure as a fortress compared to the endless mountainless desert where there was no cover.

It took more strength than any movement she had ever made in all her eighteen years, but she forced her body up and onto her feet. She had not, as God was her witness, traveled a thousand miles without friend or kin beside her, then stuck to her purpose through the hell that was the border camp and the chaos that was the Run, to sit still in a wagon and bake.

Or to let winter find her there without shelter and freeze her. She had a baby to provide for and a home to build.

Pushing her box of books and some of her other heaviest possessions toward the back of the wagon bed, she prepared to unload them to lighten the wagon for removing the wheel. She didn't know exactly how, but she could do it. She must.

She would not be dependent on or beholden to anyone. The home she would build here, no matter how humble, would belong to her and the baby, and no one else would have any say in it. No one would have the power to throw her and the baby out of this home.

The first thought that hit her, though, as soon as she stepped out into the open, scared her more than Baxter's threats.

She wished for Smith; she wished with all her heart that he would come back. Not to protect her, not to fix the wheel—but to keep her company, here in this wide, lonesome land.

Chapter 3

The young Widow Sloane was finding out that homesteading wasn't easy.

Nick sat his horse and watched her struggle to loosen the hub and get the wheel off the wagon; keep the crowbar propped under the box—as if it would hold the weight when the wheel came off, if it ever did; keep the sweat out of her eyes; and try to stay behind the petticoat she had rigged up for shade all at the same time. Good. Maybe after she got her wagon rolling again, she'd drive it right on out of the Strip.

But she'd said she could never go back to the Cumberlands. Now, how could that possibly be? You'd think she'd killed somebody.

He'd been wondering all day why she couldn't go home, studying on it with a sharp curiosity that wasn't really in his nature. Generally he gave no thought to another person's business, but when she'd said that, he'd wanted to ask her why so bad he could taste it.

But that was why people came West—to lose the past—and nobody had a right to ask any questions.

He pulled down his hat, squinted his eyes against the glare, and followed every move she made. It was a big job for someone so little—a small-boned woman who stood barely over five feet and wouldn't weigh a hundred pounds soaking wet. But she wasn't backing down from it any, attacking that hub with all the vinegar she'd poured into trying to jump his claim.

She was a woman of deep feelings, all right, and from a feuding family, so she might have killed somebody back in the mountains. That would've been no reason to run, though, if such was their custom.

Mrs. Sloane had clearly been hard at it ever since he left her. Those snuffy animals of hers were hobbled and grazing, and it looked like half the wagon's contents were unloaded. Great. Now she was *camped* on his claim.

Maybe she couldn't go back to the Cumberlands because it hurt too much when her husband died. Maybe the pain when she even thought about returning was so stabbing keen that it felt as if it would kill her. Maybe it was the same as his own hurt when he thought about ever going back to the Cherokee Nation.

Well, one thing about it: she was the opposite of Matilda Copeland in actions and looks, too, so she wouldn't always be reminding him of the sly, inscrutable dark-haired beauty.

He brushed the gray gelding's sides with the dull rowels of his spurs and started down the slope. What did he mean, "always"? This little woman wouldn't last until winter, no matter how much grit she showed.

But this had been hers and Vance's dream, she'd said, to homestead in the Cherokee Strip. There had been unmistakable love in her voice when she'd said his name.

What kind of man had Vance Sloane been?

The gray he rode had settled down a lot in the last few days. He'd learned to trust Nickajack, which left him free to use his smooth, natural way of going. Mrs. Sloane didn't hear him coming, didn't know when he stopped behind her. She was making so much noise flailing away with some rusty tool that she wouldn't have heard a shotgun blast.

"Mrs. Sloane."

She stood up and whirled around in an instant, the tool ready in her upraised right hand, her green eyes fierce. A woman warrior.

Her hat was hung on the side of the wagon, and her pinned-up hair looked like a red-gold crown. A crown that was melting in the sun—wisps of gleaming hair fell all around her face.

Lord, she was in a bad spot out here! Any high-line rider could've come up behind her just as he had done.

"I told you to keep a lookout," he said.

"I told *you* not to come back."

They stared into each other's faces and he couldn't slow his heart's sudden, fast beating. He'd scared the life out of her and he was sorry—that was the reason.

"You'd be in a fine fix if I hadn't."

"I can do this! I can take care of myself! Go away."

"I'm at home," he said. "This is my claim, if you recall."

"And I'll be on my own place, too, in a little while, if you'll stop interrupting my work."

He glanced from her to the wagon and back again to her face.

"Maybe. But you'll be on your place on foot and with no more of your supplies than you can carry, if you don't have some help."

He stepped off his horse.

"Isn't there a custom in the Cherokee Strip of waiting to be asked before a visitor dismounts?"

"I just told you—I'm not a visitor." He strode to the wagon.

That took her back a little, but she covered it quickly.

"Well, uninvited visitor or lord of the land, go on and leave me to it. I don't intend to be obligated to you."

He dropped to his haunches in front of the wheel, looked it over carefully, and whistled for the horse to come to him, bringing tools in the saddlebags.

"Too late," he said, throwing the words over his shoulder. "You're already in my debt, Mrs. Sloane, remember?"

"For my dry-land claim," she said hotly.

"Sell it to me, if that's how you feel," he said, "and go find one with water."

"Don't start that again."

He stood up and started taking what he needed from the bags. "Then stop complaining about not coming out of the Run empty-handed."

"I'm not!"

"Sounds like whining to me."

He left the gelding ground-tied and went to the pitiful little bunch of belongings she'd managed to wrestle out of the wagon, chose a cask of about the right height, and carried it over to prop up the wagon's box.

"Look," she said, wearily wiping the sweat from her face with her sleeve, "maybe I'm not strong enough to do what you're doing. But I want you to know that I'll pay you, and I won't take no for an answer."

"Fine," he said. "Bring me those pumpkins you promised."

"No! I mean now. Money. I have a small amount left . . ."

He frowned at her. "You're more worried about obligations than anybody I ever saw."

"Owing someone a debt gives that person power over me. I won't have that, ever again."

Her tone held a dozen feelings all mixed together, with only one of them clear: experience. She had suffered from someone's power over her, that much was sure.

Nickajack stole a sharp look at her, wondering. *Was* that love he'd heard in her voice when she'd said Vance's name? Could her husband have been heavy-handed and overbearing with her?

"I don't want power over you," he said. "Don't get all wire-edged over that."

"You said you weren't going to take care of me."

Frustration at that truth prickled along his nerves as he dropped down and began pulling off the wheel.

"I'm not," he said. "I'm just trying to get you off my land."

"And out of the country," she said. "You want to fix my wheel thinking that then I'll be so grateful or so beholden that I'll do what you say."

Damn. The woman would raise the temper in a sleeping baby.

"There's as much chance of that as sunshine in a snowstorm," she huffed.

She had an endless supply of grit, that was for sure.

"Well, if it's to assuage your guilt about taking the best claim, forget it. It won't work."

That made him so mad he shot to his feet, whirled to look at her, and grabbed her by the arms, all in the same motion.

"What I feel guilty about is getting you any claim at all," he said through clenched teeth. "You need to try to prove up a claim like a pig needs a hat."

Her face paled with anger until the faint dusting of freckles stood out across her nose. He caught the light scent of flowers and powder beneath the dust and sweat.

"I can prove it up." Her teeth werc clenched, too. "And I'm not accepting help today or any other day. I will *not* be beholden to you, Mr. Smith, so you can climb right back up on your big, black high-horse—"

She tore loose from his grasp to turn and look at his mount.

"You've changed horses."

"Yep."

"This horse was nowhere in sight the first

time I saw you," she said. "Nor the saddle."

He didn't answer.

"Mr. Smith," she said, in a voice filled with surprising authority, "where was this horse during the Run?"

He laughed. He couldn't help it. "You sound like my teacher at the Dwight Mission Schoolhouse when I was seven years old."

He sat on his haunches again and went back to work on the wheel.

"That's because I am a teacher."

He cocked his head and shot a glance at her. She'd pulled herself up to her full height and set her fists on her hips, looking for all the world like she was ready to challenge the big eighth-grade boys in the back of the one-room schoolhouse. Her dress was sweated through at the neck and down nearly to the waist in a vee-shape between her high, beautiful breasts. The big boys would be forgetting what they were in trouble about, right about now.

Desire knifed through him, even stronger than the anger had been. What was happening to him? He was losing his grip. No other human being had so much as *nearly* touched any of his emotions for many moons now. Yet he was letting the Widow Sloane jerk him from one end of the row to the other. This had to stop.

"Hm," he said, pulling the wheel off into his hands, "a teacher. Where's your school?"

"It'll be built next spring, or we'll hold it in my house. I can make it through the winter without a salary."

That last didn't sound quite as sure as the first.

"Maybe not after you pay me back for fixing your wheel."

She startled a little at that, but covered it nicely.

"Don't try to change the subject on me," she said. "Where'd you have that horse and saddle stashed?"

Then it really hit her.

"And those tools!"

She went to his horse and lifted one of the saddle bags.

"You've got ten pounds of hardware in here and ten more there on the ground," she said. "Don't even try to tell me you made the Run with all that slowing you down. You're a Sooner, aren't you?"

He stood up and went to get the wheel rim. "Do you think I'd admit to that? And if I did, what would you do? Challenge my claim at the Land Office?"

She narrowed her big green eyes and stared at him from between thick rows of curling auburn lashes that hid her thoughts as well as a mask would've. It was her eyes that always betrayed her deep feelings. That face, with its turned-up nose and lush, strong mouth, could belong to a champion poker player, that was certain sure.

"That'd be right ungrateful of me, now, wouldn't it?" she said. "That's probably your reason for being such a Helpful Henry. I just now realized it."

"Hey, little lady," he said, leaning the rim and wheel against the side of the wagon, "you're the one always trying not to be obligated. I haven't asked for any payment."

She gave him an even harder look.

"Don't be calling me 'little lady'. My name is Callie. Or . . . Mrs. Sloane, if you prefer."

"Callie."

"Yes. Short for Calladonia."

"I'm Nick."

"Well," she said sarcastically, "Nick's not quite so run-of-the-mill. I was expecting Tom or Joe or Bill or Jim, Mr. Smith."

"The Smith's real."

"Well, then, what am I going to owe you when you get my wheel fixed, Mr. Nick Smith?"

A kiss. One kiss from those lush red lips . . .

He slapped that thought away.

"You can pay me back tonight," he said.

Her eyes opened wide. She must've mind-read his first, unspoken answer.

"Tonight?"

"We need to watch each other's backs tonight, here on the border between our land.

There'll be plenty of claim-jumpers prowling around."

"All night?"

He nodded. "I doubt they'll have any rules about what time they can backshoot a man . . . uh, a person."

"But that certainly wouldn't be proper," she said. "I'm a . . . I have no husband. You're . . . unmarried, I assume."

"That's right. But hard times make strange bedfellows, I've always heard."

There it was again—that flicker of shocked surprise in her big, green eyes.

"I hardly think we'll be *bedfellows*."

She was using her teacher voice again, prim and proper.

He couldn't resist teasing her a little.

"Oh, I don't know," he said, "we're liable to doze off along about mornin', after such a hard day as we've had."

"I *do* know. We will not."

Nickajack chuckled and gave a little shrug. "We'll see."

Her fists went back to her hips, then she took a step toward him.

"Now, Mr. Smith, I intend to be the schoolteacher for this part of the country, and I can't have it said that . . ."

He held up a hand to hush her.

"Don't come unwound on me, Callie. Nobody knows us tonight. Nobody'll know where we'll sleep or whether we will. Nobody cares. Besides, there'll be plenty of neighbors camped on their common borders tonight."

He took a step toward her and looked her straight in the eye.

"If you aim to prove up a claim like a man, then there's times you have to forget you're a woman," he said. "You're a homesteader now."

As always, she didn't miss the implication.

"So you've given up on trying to buy me out? You realize that I'm going to hold down this claim no matter what may happen?"

Such gratitude, such a . . . vindication, appeared in her eyes that he couldn't help but bask in it. For some reason, his opinion meant something to her. A whole new warmth moved through him.

He couldn't summon the strength to contradict her.

"Baxter and his kind'll multiply in the dark, since nobody's claim is registered yet," he said.

She put one hand to her throat.

"I hate to admit it, but Baxter did throw a fright into me," she said. "He . . . well, he's too wild-eyed. He may not be quite right in the head."

"Could be. He didn't scare much." He felt his lips curve in a grin. "But then, neither did you."

She grinned back and it was a wonderful sight, with her wide, luscious mouth. Her smile was bright as sun on a signal mirror.

"And I'm not sure if I'm right in the head, agreeing to turn my back on you in the dark."

Her voice held a teasing tone that drew him like a warm fire in winter. He teased her back.

"You said I was no gentleman, but do you take me for a man with no honor at all?"

"We-e-ll, that remains to be seen. My main worry is not my virtue but my breath, since you want me gone so badly," she said, with a little grin. "Or at least, you did. What if you're only pretending to accept me as your neighbor?"

"The black marks on my reputation have never included shooting a woman in the back," he said, smiling, holding her gaze. "I'll even furnish you with a gun that works, so we'll be on level ground."

That made her laugh out loud. She had a hearty laugh that surprised him, since there was sadness deep in her eyes.

"Level ground is exactly right," she said, glancing around her at the prairie. "I've never seen such level ground."

Some of the sadness had crept into her voice. He felt an urgent need to cheer her, to hold onto the warmth of their jesting.

"Anyhow, I'm the one who ought to be worried about turning my back," he said. "You're the one who's already taken a shot at me."

She narrowed her eyes and threw his own words back at him in a fair imitation of his own voice.

"Damn straight I'm mean, and don't you forget it."

That made him laugh, too. She was a good mimic.

When she was being playful, she was beautiful. Not beautiful in that tall, sleek, dark-haired, majestic way that Matilda had been beautiful, but beautiful in her spirit. She was as different from Matilda as a honeysuckle blossom from a rose. A blood-red rose, as it happened.

They stopped laughing at the same moment because he tensed and turned to look to the south. He'd heard hoofbeats.

"What? What is it?"

He shook his head and held up his hand for quiet.

"Riders coming," he said, when he was sure. "Two horses."

Amazement in her eyes, she stared at him.

"I don't hear anything but the wind."

"You'll have to learn to hear if you stay."

A flash of hurt and then anger crossed her face.

"I'm staying. You can count on that, Nick Smith. Before I'm done with the Cherokee Strip, every pig you see will be wearing a hat."

That made him laugh again. He might as well laugh as cry or throw rocks, because this woman plainly intended to stick here. At least for now. She and the two riding toward them, and hundreds of others besides.

He spoke to her straight.

"If these riders stop here," he said, "don't breathe a word about water."

He went to his horse, drew the long gun from its saddle scabbard, and stood in the shade of the wagon to wait. Callie walked to her stack of belongings and pulled out a cast-iron skillet. He tried, but he couldn't keep from smiling a little.

"Your new weapon?"

"Don't laugh," she said. "Unlike the gun, I know this will work."

"You'd have to get mighty close to a man to hit him with it."

"That's your job," she said. "You distract him. Or them, if this is Baxter and his brother."

He shook his head at the determined look on her face. God help her, out here by herself.

"I can see right now I'll have to get you a gun."

He held up his hand for silence when she opened her mouth.

"No obligation. A loan, only a loan. You can cook my supper tonight for payment."

The visitors proved to be a man and a woman on separate horses, with a child up in front of the woman. They rode in a straight line toward Callie's wagon, so they obviously did intend to stop.

"A woman!" Callie said. "Oh, I hope they're our neighbors."

Nick's gut tightened. She'd better not be telling the other woman everything she knew.

"Remember not to mention my spring."

She cut her eyes at him as her only answer before she laid her skillet down and walked out to meet the new people. Damn his flapping tongue! It had been totally unlike him to let slip his source of water to her in the first place.

"Hello, there, Sir, Missus," the man called. "We're your neighbors to the south. Our name is Peck."

He had a mellow voice with an educated tone to it. In that way, at least, he was not another lout like Baxter. And as any man with any manners would do, he was looking at Nick, politely speaking to the man of the place instead of to a woman he'd never met. Miss Callie, however, took it upon herself to reply.

"Welcome, neighbors, come on in and get down."

Damn! She didn't have to say that!

The Pecks immediately accepted both invitations.

"Cool a bit and rest awhile," she babbled on, as if this were her place instead of his. "I'm

Callie Sloane, and this is Nick Smith."

If only she'd keep quiet about the water, all this hospitality would be fine.

"I'm Jacob Peck," the man said, going to the other horse and lifting the child to the ground, then helping the woman dismount. "This is my wife, Sophronia, and our little girl, Hope."

Callie instantly engaged the woman and child in conversation while Peck strode purposefully to Nick with his hand outstretched.

"Good to meet you, Mr. Smith," he boomed.

He had a firm handshake and a direct, honest look in his eye which, under other circumstances, would have caused Nick to like him well enough. Now he wished the man right back where he came from.

"So you're one of the lucky ones," he said, nearly choking on the words. "You got a claim."

"Well, I suppose it remains to be seen whether that's lucky or not," Jacob Peck said heartily.

Nick smiled a bit in spite of himself.

"That's a common sense remark."

"Common sense and the good Lord will carry us through," Peck said. "And good neighbors. That's why we're here."

Oh, great. A regular social animal.

"I was just taking off this wagon wheel," Nick said, gesturing toward the wagon, hoping to discourage a long visit.

Peck evidently was a generous man, too. He turned and looked at the work.

"Need a hand?" he asked. "I'd be glad to give you some help with it."

"No. Thanks anyway."

"Do you have enough water to soak it to get the rim back on?"

What a busybody! And what a loudmouth! He'd spoken loud enough to stop the women's conversation. Nick held his breath at what Callie might say.

"Mr. Smith is being good enough to help me," she said, strolling over to join them with Mrs. Peck and the child in tow. "This is his claim right here, where my rig broke down, and that next quarter-section over to the east is mine."

Nick's gut tightened. That was what came of having the world full of people—feeling the need to explain things which were nobody else's business.

Mr. Peck turned, smiled at her and tipped his hat.

"Will your husband be joining you soon, ma'am?"

"I'm a widow, sir," she said.

"Well, we wish you all the best with proving up your claim, ma'am," he said. "Please don't hesitate to send to us if you need help. Our claim is the one directly south of yours."

Mrs. Peck was beaming at Callie.

"I'm so glad you'll be near us, Mrs. Sloane," she said. "It's so nice to have another woman in visiting distance."

"Come by any time," Mr. Peck said. "Our latchstring is always out."

"And mine," Callie said eagerly. "Please don't pass by without stopping."

Foolish girl. She didn't know the first thing about these people.

Nick threw her a sharp glance. She'd better not try to include him in this neighborhood social club, and none of them had better be dropping by his cabin.

"Mama," the little girl piped up, "where's the water?"

"We don't know yet, dear."

"I'm thirsty."

Nick stared hard at Callie's profile, willing her to look at him. Stubbornly, she wouldn't.

"Papa has the canteen on his horse. Come with me and I'll give you a drink."

Thank goodness, these people really did have common sense. But Callie couldn't let sleeping dogs lie.

"Oh, no," she said, "you may need your water on the way back. This heat is so fierce."

He set his jaw and waited, helpless. The only thing worse than this makeshift, neighborly homesteaders social would be dozens of them camped at his spring.

"I have water in the wagon," Callie said.

"Come here, Hope, and let me give you a drink."

Neither of the Peck adults insisted on using their own supply, so Callie climbed into the wagon and brought out a cup filled with water. The little girl took it in both hands and drank thirstily.

"Thank you, Mrs. Sloane," Peck said.

"Yes, thank you," Mrs. Peck echoed.

Incredibly, a silence actually did fall, even between the chattering women. And, of course, Peck chose that moment to inquire about a water source.

"We haven't found any water on our place, at least not so far," Mr. Peck said. "Do you have any information about the nearest spring or creek or river, Mr. Smith?"

Nick felt Callie's glance, but he didn't return it.

"Chikaskia Creek's about five miles due south-southwest," he said, gesturing. "You'll be riding into the wind, so you'll have to hustle to get there and back before night."

Peck turned to look in that direction.

"I'm thinking there'll be more claim-jumping trouble after dark," Nick said. "Somebody's liable to come along and rip up your flag and plant their own while you're gone."

Unfortunately, that didn't worry Peck one bit.

"We have four grown sons holding the

claim," he said. "They're plenty capable."

"We've already had trouble with one man trying to take my claim," Callie said. "Baxter is his name. He has a black beard and he's riding a mule. Watch out for him."

Mrs. Peck gasped.

"Oh, we will. Thank you for the warning."

For another long moment, no one spoke. Nick hoped they were thinking about the dangers out here on the prairie. Maybe they'd go back where they came from.

Then Callie and Mrs. Peck resumed their chattering and Nick kept trying to overhear them. He had no idea why—if Callie said the wrong thing, the harm would already be done and there'd be no way he could undo it.

"How low is the creek?" Jacob Peck was saying, for the second time.

"Running less than half full, somebody said right before the Run. I haven't been over there yet."

Callie gave him another look, one which plainly said that the least he could do, as a sneaking Sooner, was to save these nice people the long trek to the creek.

Imperceptibly, he shook his head. His spring probably could supply the Pecks, him and Callie, too, but the Pecks had too many family members. Word was sure to get out to the whole countryside once they all knew. Besides, damn it, he had intended to keep it secret from everyone.

"So would you say that we need to start digging our well soon? Even with the ground so dry?"

"Four grown sons are a lot of help," Nick said.

It wasn't his responsibility to advise these people. He'd already taken on one charity case too many.

"I hope you don't have any trouble finding the creek," he said. "Just keep watching the southwest horizon for a line of trees."

He turned back toward the disabled wagon.

"You've been so kind, I feel I should help you with that," Mr. Peck boomed.

"No, thanks. You need to be on your way."

Rude behavior he knew, but he'd pretended to be sociable for as long as he had patience.

He softened it a little by adding, "You don't want to be too late in getting back. There'll be some murders tonight. And some bad beatings meant to intimidate people into leaving the choicest claims."

Mrs. Peck overheard that, although he couldn't imagine how, considering the fact that she and Callie were both talking at once.

"Let's go, Mr. Peck," she said, taking the cup from the child and giving it to Callie. "I hate to leave the boys for too long."

Finally, after what seemed another hour,

they took their leave, with the women squeezing each other's hands and exchanging promises to visit very soon.

When Callie had waved them out of sight, she turned to him.

"They're nice people and they would help either one of us any way they could," she said. "Do you think your spring would run dry if you shared it with them?"

"No, but it would with a couple of dozen families camped around it. Six adults and one child are too many tongues to wag."

He went to the blasted wheel.

"Why didn't you let Mr. Peck help you with that?" she said, following his every step.

"Because I didn't want to be obligated," he roared, turning on her. "Surely you can understand that."

A stabbing pain of aggravation hit him right between the eyes.

"You are all the neighbor I can handle," he said, managing to lower his voice—but not much. "I don't want to be visiting with people, I don't want them dropping by to see me, I don't care if I never see another homesteader for as long as I live. I'll stay on my own land and they can stay on theirs."

Her eyes widened and sparked with anger.

"That attitude is downright . . . inhuman!"

"The human race is the one to stay clear of," he snapped. "You're better off living with the deer or the wild horses or the prairie dogs. They're a whole lot more civilized."

A shadow crossed her face, bringing the sadness back into her eyes. It invaded all the lines of her body, wilting her in an instant before his very eyes. Angry as he was, true as his words were, he could kick himself all the way to Texas for saying them.

"You have a point," she said finally. "I certainly . . . know what . . ."

Nick held his breath, waiting for her to finish.

What? What has your short life taught you about the cruelties of your own kind?

She only stood there, lost in memories, staring at a spot in the far distance, silent as if he had vanished from the earth. He hurt to see the pain so raw in her eyes. She looked so lone-wolfing sad.

"However . . . ," he said.

His portentous tone made her look at him.

". . . There are some exceptions to every rule."

He flicked a significant glance at her grazing animals.

After a moment, she took his meaning.

The sparkle returned to her eyes. "You're right," she said, "even you couldn't find a civilized thing about those two."

The sadness vanished from her eyes while

they laughed together, and he felt ten feet tall and bulletproof.

Then panic sliced through him.

What the hell was he doing, being so proud of his power? Callie Sloane was the one with the power. In the last ten minutes, hadn't she dragged him through every feeling there was? Hadn't she made him lose his temper and even want to cry real tears? That made him a pitiable creature, in anybody's tally book.

If he couldn't get a grip on himself he'd better stay away from her. And he would.

After tonight.

Chapter 4

~~~~~~∞∞∞~~~~~~

Nick built Callie a small fire pit in spite of her insistence that she could do it herself, and snaked in enough wood from the deadfall around the trees on her claim to cook supper. Then he left her rustling around in the wagon gathering up something to cook. She wouldn't hear of letting him bring something from his own supplies, although hers looked pretty darn meager. Meager enough that, unless she had more than the "small amount" of money that she had mentioned, she would never make it to spring. Damn it all, she ought to just move to town and get a job if she could never go back to Kentucky.

He smooched to the gray and, with no spurs

and no leg, the two-year-old responded like a seasoned mount. Nick patted his neck.

"You'll do," he said, "now let's go home to put this wheel in the water."

He was determined to see to his chores and get back to Callie's little wagon camp before dusk. Dark was the natural time for bad men to do whatever mischief they'd planned while hiding out in the day. Any no-good sidewinder in the country could come riding right up on her, as the Peck family had done.

Of course, he knew he couldn't protect her all the time. He didn't *want* to, for that matter. But tonight would be full of short-trigger situations she'd not be able to handle.

"I'll take her a gun," he told the gray. "And if she's really such a dead shot, she'll be all right. After tonight."

As soon as they reached the pond, he set the wheel to soak, carried the rim on up to the cabin, and did the chores. Then, acting on an instinct he didn't even notice until the gray was unsaddled, brushed, and turned loose into the canyon pasture trap, he whistled up the Shifter.

"I might need you this time, old pal," he muttered, and took a long minute to slip his arm around the black's neck and stand with his cheek against him.

The Shifter rumbled at him, contented as a cat full of cream.

Any time there might be danger, he didn't feel ready unless it was the Shapeshifter between his legs. The big black was the only one, horse or human, he'd trusted for a long time now.

The only one he'd talked to who'd talked back.

That was the most likely reason he was so curious about Callie Sloane, and always wagging his chin at her. He'd been talkative as a old woman ever since she'd taken a run at his claim.

Loneliness had never gotten to him before, but it could happen. The voices of those soldiers on the canyon rim this morning had sounded as strange as the call of a parrot to him. Come to think of it, those were the first human voices he'd heard for at least two moons, since that Bar X cowboy had brought the warning note from Fox. Maybe he was so curious about the Widow Sloane because he was going soft in the head.

"Reckon that's so, Shaper?" he said as he threw on the blanket and saddle. "Must be, 'cause we're not about to get all tangled up with some woman, now, are we?"

Just the thought of how tangled he already was with Callie Sloane was enough to make a man downright daunsy, as his old boss used to say about anyone downcast or moody. But he didn't really feel downcast, getting ready

to ride back to sand-in-her-craw little Mrs.
Sloane. Must be the prospect of eating somebody's cooking besides his own.

He went to the cabin for a handgun to loan
her, and then washed up and put on a clean
shirt. No sense smelling like a skunk if he
didn't have to—and besides, it was nothing
but polite to slick back your hair before sitting
down to a lady's table for dinner.

The first thing he noticed when he rode out
of the mouth of the draw and up to her campfire was that she, too, had changed clothes. She
wore a dress with no collar, and the front was
cut low enough to show the pretty curve of
her neck into the hollow of her collarbone. Her
shape sure was womanly for her being only a
girl.

"It'll be ready, soon," she said, looking at his
fresh shirt. "Seems we both cleaned up for Mr.
Baxter, if he should decide to drop by this evening."

"Wouldn't want to be rude," he said, as he
swung down.

"No, I can testify to that," she said wryly,
bending over to turn something in the skillet.

Her breasts swelled beneath the cloth, her
skin pale as milk against the green calico that
reminded him of spring apples. Her freshly
combed hair rested in a neat coil on the top of
her head, but stubborn wisps of it still escaped
the pins. One lazy strand curved around and

cupped her face, brushing at her jawline, which he'd love to trace.

He tried to make himself look away, but at that moment he couldn't. It wasn't that he'd been too long without seeing another human; it must be that he'd been too long without seeing a *woman*. Now he wanted to touch her.

After Matilda he had sworn off women forever, and he intended to keep that vow. He reached for his old rage, willed it to rise and drown out the desire.

God knew, and so did all the cattlemen and Indians who'd ever roamed here, that the Strip was a land that could bring a longhorn to its knees and make a wolf hunt a hole. A woman alone had no more chance than a chunk of ice in hell of surviving either a cold season or a hot one on this prairie, even if she had shelter.

She looked to be intelligent; she was a schoolteacher, damn it. Why didn't she have sense enough to know that this land would pull that iron determination out of her, one endless day at a time, and beat her small bones to bits against it? Why didn't she see that this sky would arch above her and draw the spirit out of her, one endless, lonesome night at a time, and make her feel like a speck of dust on a grass blade against its vastness? Why didn't she leave here before the Strip got hold of her and hollowed her out until she never

felt like flashing that blinding smile, ever
again?

He ought to be hanged for ever offering her
water. It was an invitation given out of guilt,
and so was everything else he'd done to help
her this whole day. He was lower than an egg-
sucking dog for staking her a claim in the first
place, and the only way to redeem himself was
to make her see reality and go.

Nick turned to stride to her wagon, then began rudely pawing through her things, looking for tools, looking for supplies, looking for
ways to make her see the true insanity of this
venture. That Vance character must not've had
the sense God gave a wooden goose, or during
all their dreaming and planning he'd have told
her the thousand reasons not to try homesteading without help.

"What are you doing now?"

She sounded mad, suspicious—as if she
couldn't trust him not to steal some of this pitiful stuff. That fed his anger.

Five tools. Count them. Old and rusty and
dull as a case knife. Five pathetic tools to build
a shelter before the blizzards blew, five cheap-
made tools to tear open the face of the Earth
Mother and force food from her before this
cask of flour and barrel of beans ran out.

"Have you tried this plow?"

Frowning, she walked toward him.

"You don't have the muscle to hold this plow point in the ground."

"What do you know about my muscle? What do you know about what I can do?"

She walked up to him, bristling like a porcupine.

"I haven't tried it yet, no. I haven't exactly moved onto my claim yet, much less laid out a garden plot."

"Oh, you'll have to plow a whole lot more than a garden," he said. "With as few trees as you have, you'll have to build your house out of sod. Think you can keep that wild team of yours hitched for all that ground-breaking?"

She stared at him, clearly furious, one eyebrow raised.

"I reckon," she said dryly, "since I did keep Joe and Judy both hitched for the Run."

He shrugged.

"Hope you've got a sharpening blade in here somewhere," he said. "The point of this thing'd be hard to stick in a bowl of butter, much less the drought-hard earth."

Callie answered with a distinctly unladylike snort and turned away.

"You certainly know how to ruin a supper," she said as she stalked back to the fire. "I thought we'd have a civilized conversation and a nice meal."

Strangely, that touched him. She had been looking forward to this supper.

Well, why not? No doubt she was doubly lonesome, being so far from home and he, no doubt, was the person she knew best west of the Mississippi—it wasn't that she'd especially been looking forward to supper with him.

Then the fact that he'd even had that thought made him furious with himself again. Her loneliness was not his responsibility.

"Look, Callie," he snapped, striding toward her, "supper's not important. Plowing is, if you're staying. Have some sense!"

"*You* have some!" she shouted, wheeling to face him. "I won't be running to you for help if my plow is dull; I won't be begging you to feed me. You're not going to be put out in any way by my presence on the next claim!"

Except in one way: wondering how you're faring.

She stopped short, drawing a long, trembling breath to calm herself. He saw that she was much angrier than he'd realized.

"I didn't ask you to fix my wheel."

She brushed the curving strand of hair away from her face. Her hand shook.

"True," he said, trying not to yell how stupid it was for her to stay here and die. "I'd just hate to ride by your place someday and find your body—frozen or starved or dried to a husk or overcome by the heat."

He took a step toward her and stared into her huge green eyes.

"Listen to me, Callie Sloane. You don't know this country. You're a strong, smart woman or you'd never have made it this far, but you need to go back to Kentucky. Go back to your folks and your home."

"I can never go back to my folks and my home," she said in a low, quiet voice that tore at him.

Sadness flooded into her eyes.

"Papa said never to come back as long as I live."

He waited and waited.

Finally she continued.

"Vance . . . was from the other side of the feud. My kin and his have been fighting for a hundred years."

"Why?"

She shrugged.

"Who knows? Nobody even asks. It's the way it is, like the sumac turning red in the fall."

Callie turned her face away to hide her tears, and he badly wanted to comfort her. But what comfort could there be for banishment from the land you belonged to? He would feel cut loose from the earth if he had to leave this prairie forever.

"We have sumac out here, too," he said awkwardly. "That'll be one thing that's the same."

She looked at him, her huge green eyes glistening, thanking him for trying to help. A man would always know where he stood with her, because, unlike Matilda, she was one who couldn't lie worth shucks. Her eyes told the truth.

"Look, Nick," she said finally, "let's forget about everything and eat this good food. I haven't eaten all day, have you?"

"No."

Food had seemed a travesty this morning, the day of the Run. Now that day was over, and he was eating with the enemy.

"Pull up two barrels," she said, "and I'll fill our plates."

So he did, and she did, and they began the meal of fried cured ham and sourdough biscuits and dried apples he had smelled simmering. Suddenly he felt starved.

"I made fresh, strong tea," she said, "to keep us awake."

He nodded. Poor girl. Didn't she even have any coffee?

"Where's the conversation?" she said, teasing him with a small grin. "Tell me a story."

He shook his head.

"Too many years as a cowboy on this range," he said. "You eat when you get a chance and do it fast. Talk's for afterward, if you don't have to get in the saddle again."

"All right," she said. "Sorry there's no butter

for the biscuits, but I've got honey in the wagon."

She started to get up, but he stopped her with an upraised hand.

"Save it," he said. "It'll be mighty fine this winter."

"Will you come over and share it with me?"

He looked at her for a long time. God knew, she was one brave girl.

"I will," he said, "and I'll bring the butter if you'll tell all your other visitors not to ride up into my canyon."

She gasped with delight.

"You have a milch cow, besides two horses?"

He nodded. "One thing I always hated about the cow camps was no cream, no milk, no butter."

"Wonderful!" she said. "Next time I go to town I intend to trade for some chickens, and then we'll have eggs, too!"

A strange feeling twisted his gut. Not only was he eating with the enemy, he was making plans to keep it up all winter. With a woman he was trying to run out of the Strip. He was losing his mind.

"Did you hear what I said about the neighbors?"

"Yes. I'll explain that you're an ill-tempered, churlish, shameless, bold-faced Sooner who shoots first and asks questions later."

She picked up her tin cup and looked at him over the rim.

"You don't want them to see your place? You already built a cabin?"

"Anybody can see that cabin's been there since long before I could be called a Sooner."

Then, from some impulse he couldn't explain, he added, "My daddy built it when I was a little boy."

She stared at him, transfixed.

"Then you're right to be a Sooner," she cried. "If it was my homeplace, I'd take no chances with it, either!"

He could see her thinking about it, perhaps trying to imagine this land when the cabin was new.

"Was he one of the cattlemen who used to lease grazing land in the Strip?"

"No. He came out here to catch wild horses and never went back to the Nation."

"The Nation? Was he a Cherokee?"

He nodded.

"An eighth or so. My mother was nearly fullblood."

He clamped his mouth shut. Nothing like confessing to being a Sooner and an Indian to a rank stranger. What was it about Callie Sloane that had loosened his tongue?

"No need to noise the word 'Indian' around any more than the word 'water,' " he said. "Only eighty allotments were set aside for

Cherokees, and my claim wasn't one."

She answered him with a solemn, thoughtful nod. Her eyes were darker than usual and
her face more pale in the deepening dusk. Its
shape was so pure, its look so full of light
against the night, that he wanted to gaze at
her forever.

If he did, the fact that he'd just handed her
enough information to cause him to lose his
home would never again cross his mind. He
wouldn't be able to think of anything but her.

Such a storm of feelings rose in him, he
couldn't have sorted them out if there'd been
a gun at his head. He put down his fork and
stood up.

"I need to see to my horse," he said, and left
her.

He walked out past his horse and then hers
and her mule, all the way to the edge of the
arroyo that the creek deepened with every
flash flood. His heart kept on pounding hard
and fast, rolling in his chest like ominous
thunder.

Looking out across his beloved prairie made
it worse. Campfire lights glowed everywhere,
sparkling with a taunting cheerfulness that
tore him up. Why, he could even hear voices
and faint faraway music on the night breeze!

Last night he'd been the only human being
for miles as the grass waved in the wind and
the wild animals settled into their dens.

This night, people were everywhere, their plows in hand. Soon the face of Mother Earth would blow away.

Fences would be next. Lots of fences—more, many more than the cattlemen who'd leased the land had ever built. There'd be enough fences to pile the wild horses up against them when the snow and sleet flew, enough to prevent them from drifting to shelter in the hollows of the land.

He had known this and he had fought it and he had hated it for so long that the bitterness ran wild in his blood. Nickajack waited for the old rage to rise in him.

Instead came a despair that spread deeper into his bones with every breath he took. How could the sun have set as always? Why hadn't it blazed down and burned the earth to a crisp? How could the wind die down into a breeze tonight instead of growing into a curling, twisting tornado that would clean the ignorant farmers off this land and blow them back to wherever they had come from?

But the most mysterious question of all was how could one of those ignorant farmers, on this sorry, devil-spawned day of the Run, reach out and touch him in the heart?

They carried his saddle blanket and her quilt, both of his handguns and his long gun, and a canteen of water up to a rolling rise.

Nick got them situated at the feet of the few scraggly trees so they wouldn't be silhouetted against the horizon in the moonlight.

"We can see your flag and your marker from here," he said, keeping his voice quiet so it wouldn't carry out into the night. "Imagine a circle around us, take that half of it, and watch for movement against the sky."

They settled in, carefully sitting far enough apart that they weren't touching. Callie looked east and north, he west and south. He handed over the extra gun.

"Here's a handgun you can use," he said, "but I'm hesitating to let you have it."

"Why? I told you I can shoot."

"That's what I'm afraid of," he drawled. "I know you'll at least try, and *this* gun works."

They chuckled very quietly, like conspirators up to no good.

"Proper or not, I'm glad you stayed here tonight," she blurted, as if she, too, felt the camaraderie. "I've never spent a night alone in my life, and out here in this huge, open place with claim jumpers prowling around it wouldn't be a good time to start."

It sounded so preposterous, he laughed.

"You what?"

"Never spent a night alone. On the train, there were other people in the car. At Arkansas City, Dora took me in and let me camp with her family until I bought my own outfit. Besides, there were thousands of people camped all up and down the line."

"But before that. In Kentucky."

"Some of my kin was always with me. I shared a room with my Aunt Janey and my littlest brothers."

"Where'd your husband sleep? With your big brothers?"

She hesitated. He thought he'd offended her with such a direct reference to the marriage bed.

"Oh, well, of course, after I married . . ."

Her soft voice trailed off for a moment.

". . . Vance never did leave me, never was gone at night. Until he . . . passed on."

Then, hastily, as if to change the subject, she said, "I don't think we have to worry about getting through the winter, Nick. If this land can be this hot after the sun's gone down, it's too hot to ever be cold."

He chuckled.

"Tell me that again come January. It'll be just as cold then as it is hot now."

"Surely not!"

"Surely so. And that same week in January it can turn warm enough to spawn a cyclone."

"What a place! Does it feel so huge to you that it seems you're no bigger than an ant?"

"No. I feel part of it."

"What feels natural to me are the mountains, wrapping their arms around me. They

make me feel safe and this makes me feel ...
exposed, I guess. Like a chicken about to be
caught by a hawk."

"You'll get used to it."

If you can survive it.

"Back home, nobody leaves the mountains
without some of their kin going with them. I
guess everybody feels the same way I do."

"Sounds like mountain people don't trust
outsiders."

"Flatlanders," she said. "We don't. And especially not the government."

"Then you've come to the right place," he
said. "I have a lot of trouble with that myself.
Any kind of government, tribal or ..."

The Shifter's soft whinny called to him
through the dark.

Nickajack sensed Callie freezing in place.

"Baxter?" she whispered.

"Maybe."

But they waited and listened for a long time
and heard nothing else. Finally Callie let out
her breath in a long sigh.

"Don't be scared," Nick teased her, in a
whisper. "Fear's your worst enemy."

"I'm not scared!" she whispered back.

"In a pig's eye!"

"Pigs! Why do I always make you think of
pigs? If you keep this up, I'm going to start a
pig farm right here on the line between your
claim and mine."

"Go ahead. The wind's usually out of the south or southwest, so all the smell will blow to your place instead of mine."

That made her laugh. Her laugh made him go warm in the pit of his belly.

They waited a long time more without a single word and without moving, but they heard nothing else except some faraway singing.

"The horses are settled," he said, at last. "Nobody's sneaking around."

"I'm going to get the school," she said fiercely, right out of the blue. "I won't let anyone else have it. And nobody, sneaking or not, is going to get this claim, either."

His jaw clenched. *Damn* the minute he'd jammed her stake into this ground. And damn the fact she had such a one-track mind.

"I thought you planned to raise pigs," he said, keeping his voice light.

She made an unladylike noise of derision.

"Only if you drive me to it."

There was something so trusting, so companionable, in her voice that he felt like the most treacherous snake in the world. He shouldn't even be here, shouldn't have been pretending that the connection between them was real and that they'd be riding back and forth sharing supper all winter.

"No," she said, "I've been thinking that Mr. Peck might want to teach the school in this district. It's plain he's an educated man, and he has all those sons to do his farm work."

She sounded so disconsolate that he searched for a way to cheer her. Usually he never bothered to think what another person was feeling, much less try to help. What was it about her?

"He didn't strike me as the kind to want to fool with a bunch of young ones, though," he said.

She thought about that.

"I believe you're right," she said, more hopefully.

It scared him, the way she believed him and the way he tried to glean what she wanted, what she meant, what she was thinking inside. He had to stop it.

"Maybe you'll get the school, even if he wants it," he said. "After all, they'd have to pay more to a man."

"Well, thank you so much, Nick, for cheering me up."

He had to laugh, she went from worried to hopeful to tartly sarcastic so fast.

"Just trying to help."

"Well, don't try anymore."

"Then don't cry anymore."

That silliness brought a low chuckle from her, and then she was silent. Suddenly she spoke, her tone so low and calm it made the hair stand up on the back of his neck.

"If I ever let myself cry, my tears would wash away the world."

The words struck him like an arrow in the heart. They held the bald, honest truth and not the slightest shred of self-pity.

"You're too young for that," he snapped.

Had she loved her husband, that Vance fellow, so much?

"Young has nothing to do with it," she said.

They both fell quiet then, as if speech had no more power.

He felt the same way, he realized, but he hadn't known it until she said it. Not that he had actually cried since his mother's death nor ever expected to, but that was exactly the way he felt.

She was in the Strip tonight because sorrow had chased her there. He was in the Strip tonight not only because it was his home, but because he was running from the past as hard as Callie Sloane or any other homesteader. If he weren't, he'd still be back in the Nation, meddling in other people's affairs and mixing his life up with theirs.

Getting young men into situations that guaranteed they would never grow old.

And now, God help him, he'd done the same thing to this gallant girl who would be on her way out of the Strip right now if he hadn't idiotically staked her a claim.

She seemed to have moved nearer, although

he didn't turn to look. And she still smelled of flowers, somehow. That ought to be impossible, clean dress or not, for even with the sun down and the night breeze up, the heat remained fierce.

The silence kept on growing more comfortable. It stretched out between them and pulled them together until it made as mysterious a bond between them as words had done. After a long while, Callie gave a feathery sigh and he felt her small shoulders lean against his back.

The night came on, laying more darkness across the sky and pulling more stars out to glitter, as if nothing had changed in the whole universe. The new fires gleamed everywhere he looked. He waited for his legs to move, his arms to reach for Callie Sloane and lay her down so she could truly rest, perhaps carry her into the wagon—except in there, out of the breeze, the air would be stifling. He had to do something so he could move away from her.

And he would. After a while.

Chapter 5

Callie opened her eyes. She started to wake, but the sweet smell of woodsmoke pulled her down into the dream again. The aroma floated in the heavy summer air, and wandered along the creek to find her and her little brothers picking blackberries up in Tall Pine Cove. They were having a good time because nobody was mad at her, the boys weren't crying and calling her a traitor through their tears, and her fingers were flying to gather the ripest sweet berries. It was during the good days, before any of them knew about her and Vance.

Then she drifted into believing that the smoky aroma came from the cookstove in the

kitchen, the day after she'd told Papa about
the baby. Not one of her kin was speaking to
her except Granny and Mama. Today she had
to leave the mountains and the Sloane Valley
forever. She was banished, and only Granny
and Mama were trying to help her—with their
eyes red and tear-swollen and their sadness
cutting them in two, right down to the bone.
She felt the same way, like she couldn't hold
her body together to walk out of there.

Helpless, she sank deep into her bed and
listened to Mama's cast-iron skillet clattering
against the stove lid and the rolling pin
thumping on the worktable, ready to roll the
biscuit dough for the last breakfast Callie
would ever eat with her family. She ought to
get up and help, but instead, she snuggled her
head into the crook of her arm and tried to get
back into the berrypicking dream with her
brothers.

"Callie, I'm leaving now."

A man's voice, not Mama's. It woke her immediately.

Nick Smith's voice.

A frightening feeling washed through her.
Even dreaming about Kentucky, she hadn't
thought the man speaking was Vance. Or
Papa. How had she known so fast that it was
Nick?

He was leaving now.

She sat up, pulling the rough blanket up

over her breasts with both hands. It smelled of horse sweat and dirt and it was way too hot, but she huddled under it anyway. He must have covered her sometime in the night.

A stronger smell, the smell of coffee, began drifting into her nostrils beneath the sweetness of the smoke. Her stomach roiled. Ever since she'd started this baby, coffee in the morning made her sicker than anything.

"I have to saddle up," Nick said abruptly, striding toward her.

Oh, Lord, he had to go away—fast! If she threw up in front of him, he might guess the reason and haul her off to town, slung over his saddle. If he was worried about riding by her place someday and finding her body frozen or starved, he'd certainly refuse to live next door to her *and* a baby!

She held her breath against the coffee smell and pulled down her skirts, which had bunched up around her thighs beneath the blanket. Then she held it up to him.

"Thanks for the use of it," she said thickly, wanting to get to her feet but not daring to move.

He just stood there, all easy and loose, with his saddle slung over his shoulder, holding it with one hand as if it were a feather. He stared down at her as if judging her, somehow.

"It got right cool before sunup," he said, sounding angry, as if she had demanded an explanation of why he'd covered her.

"Thank you," she said again, then didn't dare say another word.

He grabbed the blanket, then turned and strode quickly toward his black horse, which was patiently waiting. He stopped and turned back.

"I made coffee. I'll bring back your wheel when it's done. After that, you'll have to take care of yourself."

She waved him on, afraid to open her mouth to speak.

He went to the horse again, but took what seemed to be an age to saddle and mount. Finally he turned to ride away. The horse took a couple of strides, then stopped.

"Make a show of possession," he called, "and forget the socializing."

"I *know*!"

She did all right with that one, so she gulped in another breath.

"And I'll never say the word 'water,' and I'll throw my body across the entrance to your canyon if anyone comes near it."

He threw her an exasperated look, as if she were being completely unreasonable, and rode off without a word of good-bye. Yes, after meddling freely in her affairs to his heart's content, Nick Smith rode away and left her.

Thank goodness.

As soon as he had disappeared into the

mouth of the tree-lined draw, Callie leapt to her feet and ran in the other direction, over a small rise and down it, where she emptied the meager contents of her stomach into the sand. Shakily, she walked back to the wagon, bathed her face in the tepid water in the barrel, and managed to take the coffeepot off the fire.

She walked away from it while it cooled and lost its scent, and went to sit on the tailgate of her three-wheeled wagon. Well, she would see him again, because he'd bring back her fourth wheel.

Shocked at that thought, she pushed it away. She had come out here alone and she could take care of herself. She could get used to being lonely, too. The wheel was the only reason she cared whether she ever saw Nick Smith again or not.

Callie scooted back to lean against the corner of the wagon bed, pulled up her knees, wrapped her arms around them, and stared out at her new home. A show of possession. Today, she supposed it'd have to be a few furrows plowed, because she had no idea how to build a sod house. Sod, for heaven's sake! Whoever heard of building a house out of dirt?

And Nick thought her plow too dull. Well, for his information, there was a file in that box of old tools that came with the wagon.

He certainly hadn't been very companionable this morning. No doubt he was mad at himself, for fear she would think he had taken her to raise, no matter what she'd said last night.

She knew how men's minds worked. From raising seven brothers she knew it was much the same as little boys' minds worked. That knowledge might come in handy for more than teaching school.

Immediately, shame washed through her. She didn't need to know anything about men, because she was never getting involved with another one. Vance was her true love and he always would be, for there was only one for everybody in the world. She would make their dream become real for the sake of their little one, and she could do it by herself.

Callie got up and got busy, going to the tool box for the file, then jumping down to the ground to sharpen the plow. She didn't dare even consider eating breakfast, so she might as well get on with her day's work. Simply surviving out here would take all her strength and common sense, so she needed to keep her wits about her and start finding out how to make a shelter for her babe.

Plus, at the border camp, everyone had talked about rushing to register at the Land Office as soon as they could after staking the claim and finding its legal description. She glanced at her wagon with its missing wheel, hoping Nick would return with it today. This was her only transportation.

Riding away with the wheel and the rim held out from the horse as if they weighed no more than the saddle he'd carried this morning, he had looked like a legendary hero out of a book, a man powerful enough to do anything. Just remembering how his muscles had knotted and flowed under his thin, sweat-soaked shirt and how broad his shoulders had looked above his slim waist and hips, sitting so easily in the saddle, made her go all tight inside all over again.

She gave the plowshare a hard, swift swipe with the rasp. That was the last time, the very last time, she would allow herself to think about Nick today. She must put her mind to sharpening this plow, making enough furrows that anyone could see this claim belonged to someone, and finding the legal description marker so she could write that down.

As always, she had a folded leaf of paper or two in her reticule. If she finished plowing before Nick . . . before her wheel came back, she would walk around her claim for a while with paper and pencil and a canteen of water looking for that information.

She dropped the rasp. After she'd watered Joe and Judy! Good heavens, how could she have forgotten to take care of her animals?

"I forgot you even existed," she told them,

leading them one at a time in their hobbles to the bucket she'd filled from her barrel. "Doesn't that seem impossible, as awful as you are?"

Once they'd drunk their fill and gone back to grazing, she rushed back to work on the plow. At the rate this was taking, the sun would be saying high noon before she had a single inch of ground plowed.

Nick surely was against plowing. So then, how did he expect to make a living on his claim? How had he been doing it all this time? Had he lived there steadily since he was a boy?

No, because he'd mentioned cowboying and eating with other men. Surely that hadn't happened on his claim he liked to keep so private.

Settlers hadn't been allowed to live in the Strip before yesterday; only cattlemen had leased it for grazing. So how had Nick's family made a home here?

She let the rasp go still and turned to look toward the mouth of his draw as if he would be there waiting to answer her question. The faint sound of hoofbeats immediately turned her head in the opposite direction. She listened. Someone was coming. From the south.

Quietly, as if whoever was about to ride up to her wagon was already within hearing distance, she laid down her tools and climbed back into the wagon. Sure enough, the extra handgun that Nick had brought her was there, carefully placed on top of the flour barrel, where she'd see it. He had not left her defenseless.

She took the gun, checked the load, and slipped it into her pocket before she returned to the tailgate and jumped to the ground. Hiding at the side of the wagon, she listened again. Maybe the rider was coming from the east.

No, whoever it was seemed to be coming from the south—but sound didn't travel out here the same as in the mountains. She cocked her head to listen harder.

Yes. From the south. So it surely wasn't Nick. Yet it could be, if he'd left his claim by some other way.

Her heart stopped. What about Baxter? Could he be coming back with his brothers in tow? With Nick gone, and her alone?

With a hard, fast lurch, her heart beat again.

Maybe something was wrong at the Pecks' place. But it was hard to believe that with all those men there, they would be coming to her for help.

This definitely was trouble, though. Whoever it was was riding in such a tearing hurry that her heart began to beat in triple time. That kind of speed on a hot day like this—on any day—could only mean an alarm.

She stepped out from behind the wagon,

shielded her eyes with her hand, and squinted into the distance. A cloud of dust formed as she watched. She couldn't yet tell what made it, so she turned back to see where Joe and Judy were. This galloping visitor might inspire them to try to take off in spite of their hobbles.

They were remarkably calm, grazing away as if they would never be influenced by what another horse or mule might do. Since they were very near the wagon, she turned her attention back to the dust cloud, which was now much bigger.

Once again, she walked around to the far side of the wagon to wait. She curled her hand around the butt of the gun in her pocket. This could prove to be an enemy.

The thought chilled her in spite of the heat, which was already unbearable this early in the morning. If only Nick hadn't been in such a hurry to leave!

She brought up short. Hadn't she told him she could take care of herself? She could. And unless this was Baxter on a wild tear to shoot her as he passed by at a gallop, it wasn't an enemy. Enemies sneaked up on people. Enemies ambushed each other. Why, this person's horse wouldn't have enough wind left to carry him in an escape.

The common-sense lecture made her feel much better, and she looked around the corner of the wagon. A horse and rider materialized out of the fog of dirt, but it took a minute more before she could make out much about them. They wore such a layer of dust that she couldn't see it was a boy on a bright sorrel horse until they slid to a stop a few feet from her.

The lad slumped in his saddle, gasping for breath, as she ran to him. He was no more than ten, about the same size as her brother Adam. In the midst of her panic, a blade of homesickness stabbed her in the heart. Adam had been more upset than any of her kin, except Papa, that she had consorted with a Harlan.

She turned loose of the gun in her pocket and reached up with both hands.

"Get down," she said, "rest your horse."

She looked at the horse standing splay-legged and trembling, lather dripping from its muzzle.

The boy shook his head.

"Fire!" he croaked.

He cleared his throat and spat.

"Prairie fire!"

Goosebumps broke out on Callie's arms. She looked behind the boy, then glanced over her shoulder at her wagon. If it burned, she'd lose everything she owned and her hope of survival. How could she have felt helpless only minutes ago, with all that at her disposal? At least with it, she had a fighting chance.

"Where?"

She scrambled up onto the tailgate to get water for the boy. When she went back and held it up to him she noticed that her hands were shaking.

"South of our claim," he said, "Pecks. I'm a Peck."

He took the water and gulped it all.

"Some neighbors come told us," he said. "Them and my pa don't know what to do. Pa says there was a man here named Smith who seems to know the country."

"He's gone back to his own claim."

"Pa give me orders to find him," the boy said, handing the cup back to her, then pulling on the reins. "Tell me where."

Callie's blood rushed to her head. She couldn't send him to Nick, who had left her to guard the entrance to his lair. And she couldn't let him ride that horse to death.

"Get down," she said. "Stay with my wagon. I'll go get Mr. Smith."

"No, I will. Pa thinks we've got time to do something if the wind don't pick up too much. He wants that man Smith to help us know where to set a backfire and judge the distance and all."

"Get down."

Eighteen years of ordering younger brothers around had given her an authority not to be challenged. The boy half-fell off his mount.

"What's your name? Besides Peck?"

"Danny."

"Well, Danny, you and your mount are both about played out," she said. "Stay here and wait for me to come back with Mr. Smith. If you rest a bit, maybe you can plow a firebreak around my wagon."

While she talked, Callie's mind raced as fast as her heart, trying to think how to handle this situation now that she had taken control—this situation of saving all her belongings and those of no telling how many other people's. Not to mention their very lives. She had no earthly idea how to fight a fire except with water, and that was something they'd have to do without.

"Help me," she said, rudely ripping the bridle off the Peck horse. "Hold that mare over there until I can get on her."

Staggering, the boy ran to Judy and put his arm around her neck. Callie came right behind him with the bridle, and he looped the reins around and held them where his arm had been.

Awkwardly, she stuffed the bit into the surprised mare's mouth, her arms shaking the whole time. She could count on the fingers of one hand the times she'd ever ridden horseback—and never bareback.

But she wouldn't let herself think about that.

"Give me a hand up," she said, as soon as

she and the boy got the strap buckled and the reins straightened out.

He held out his hands, she stepped into them, and suddenly she sat astride the grumpy mare. She pulled her skirts out of the way as best she could and tried to hold on with her legs, the way Nick had done on the black horse.

"Take off the hobbles," she said, tying a knot in the reins, "and pray I can stay on."

His dust-covered face fell into lines of shocked astonishment—and that was the last thing she saw clearly. From then on, it was Katie-bar-the-door, because Judy did not intend to waste this chance at freedom. Callie pulled on the reins and got her headed in the right direction, and as they plunged into the long, tree-lined draw, she had to drop them onto Judy's neck so she could hold on with both hands. She twisted her fingers deep into the shaggy mane and prayed.

Dear Lord above, help her stop bouncing and sliding around in every direction. She should've taken time to get the boy's saddle, too, for this mare's back was slick as ice on a mountainside.

Her skirts bunched and tangled again, and although she squeezed her legs harder, her position felt more precarious by the second. She glanced down at the rocky, dry creekbed, but only for an instant. Too far, it was way too far to the ground. She was used to traveling on her own two feet, not even in a wagon, and certainly not on a horse. All her family had ever owned were mules for plowing.

Danny's face and that of his little sister, Hope, flashed through her mind. She thought she could smell smoke; thought she could feel the heat from the flames on her back. It was the sun, the merciless Western sun—it had to be. She tried to look over her shoulder, anyway.

All of a sudden, the horse plunged ahead so fast that Callie's body whipped backward from the force. She slipped way to one side and fear pulled all the breath out of her body while the strain threatened to tear her muscles.

But she wouldn't let go. She couldn't. Only Nick would know what to do about the fire, and she had to get to him. Nick could save them all.

She clawed her way back to the top of the mare and struggled into a precarious balance. She managed to bend closer to Judy's neck and take a new grip on her mane before the mare flattened out into a gallop.

Nickajack paused with the bundle of hay held high in both hands over the fence of the rock pen. He held his breath to listen. It was hoofbeats, all right: a horse moving fast. Callie?

His heart thudded hard. Maybe Baxter had come back and scared or even shot her. Maybe she was bleeding and trying to get to him for help.

Hot regret sliced through him. It had been insane to leave her alone!

Instantly, he was furious with himself. She had come here alone, hadn't she? If she had trouble, it was her trouble. He couldn't watch out for her all the time. And even if he had nothing else to do, that wasn't his job. He hadn't invited her to the Strip in the first place.

But without your help, she wouldn't still be here, now, would she?

He threw the hay into the pen with his mares, then turned and ran to the cabin for the rifle. Without even looking in, he grabbed it from the rack over the door and turned back, crossing the porch in two strides, leaping off the end of it, already running. He headed for the bend in the creek, where, in case the rider wasn't Callie, he could stop an intruder out of sight of his cabin and the spring and pond.

It must not be Callie, for surely she couldn't ride either one of her irascible animals. This was one horse coming up his creek, not two and a wagon.

Whoever it was, they were coming at an erratic rate: loping and long trotting, then galloping again. That made him think it was somebody hurt and trying to hang on. Or maybe trying to stay conscious.

Who else but Callie would know or even guess that somebody lived up this draw? Or was it an outlaw looking for a hideout?

Suddenly the pace doubled to a faster lope, which soon fell into a flat gallop. Why in the hell risk crippling a horse by galloping in that rough, rocky stretch where one wrong step could snap a cannon bone in a heartbeat?

Nickajack ran harder, but before he got to the bend below the low pool of water, they burst into view.

It was Callie! He stared, blinked, and looked again. She wore no hat, her hair flew loose and long behind her, whipping in the wind like a burnished silk banner, while the nasty-tempered mare did everything she could to unseat her rider. Callie was riding her, though.

Barely. Clinging desperately to the mane, she slid to one side and then the other, coming dangerously close to falling off twice in as many heartbeats. Her red-gold hair spilled over her shoulders in all directions, half the time nearly blinding her by flying across her face.

God help her, had she come all the way from her wagon like this? She must have. How had she even managed to mount the devil mare, in between her constant kicks and bites at the mule?

Then Callie's hair blew back and he got a glimpse of her huge eyes, which looked too frightened to see him. He ran even harder. If she fell off at this speed, on that ground, there was no way she'd be unhurt.

As he ran, he tried to think what to do. No wonder "Runaway!" was such a dreaded warning, second only to "Fire!" A man on foot coming at a horse that was already panicked out of its mind, or even a mounted man racing alongside it, basically only made the terror worse and the horse go faster.

He couldn't stand still and wait for this to play out, though—he couldn't.

Judy swerved hard to the right and ran under the low-hanging branch of a cottonwood, trying her best to scrape Callie off. At first, when Callie looked up, she raised one hand to try to ward off the blow, then, at the last second, she dropped low onto the mare's neck and passed underneath, unscathed.

Nick got to them just as they charged up onto the bank that encircled the pond, the mare's hooves slipping on the slope. Grabbing at the bridle proved futile, for the mare was quick as a cat and veered past him. But as she reached the top and saw the water, she hesitated.

He grabbed the near rein and pulled. She came around and started to circle, and he stepped to her side at the same moment she jerked her hindquarters around.

Callie came completely unseated.

Nick dropped the rifle and caught her in his arms.

Chapter 6

The last thing he ever expected to do was to kiss her. All he wanted was for her not to get killed, not to get hurt, not to fall off that damned crazy mare and get trampled. And as soon as he felt the sweet weight of her in his arms, he knew he'd been granted those wishes.

But he instantly turned greedy for more. There she was in his arms, still wild-eyed with fear, yet gasping with relief, her luscious lips parted and her breasts rising and falling against his chest with her hard breathing. He glimpsed the ghost of her smile before she buried her face in his neck.

"Oh, thank God," she said, her lips hot

against his skin. "I thought ... I'd die .... before I could get to you."

The words wrapped themselves around his heart. He crushed her closer, and, still struggling for breath, she lifted her face and looked at him as if he were the most beautiful thing she had ever seen.

"Callie," he said, "you have got to learn to ride."

Then he kissed her, long and hard.

She tasted of flowers and of honey, and she smelled of sweat and the horse and the dust, and he couldn't get enough of her. Her lips felt like velvet, hot and soft, and deep in her throat she made a little helpless sound of surprise that made his head go light.

He found the fit of their mouths as soon as they touched and fell into the kiss with never a thought, only a needing that was more than wanting, a needing that blotted out all the others. He didn't need air anymore, or the sunshine, because he was kissing Callie.

Callie. She wasn't hurt and here she was, melting against him, slipping her arms up around his neck.

Callie. All he could think was her name.

Suddenly she tore her mouth away, just as his tongue begged for entry, just at the instant that hers teased him back and started to welcome him in. She made an incoherent panicked sound.

"No, I can't," she said, gasping, "I'm forgetting; I have to tell you . . ."

He looked into her eyes.

"We'll talk later, Callic," he said, and tried to take her mouth again.

She looked straight at him and her eyes went soft, but she stiffened her arms and held him away.

"There's a prairie fire, Nick! We have to help fight it!"

The two terrible words cut through everything else in his head. Instantly, the kiss was past and the present was a whole world dry as dust, the grass and brush everywhere as combustible as guncotton.

"You have to tell the Pecks where to set the backfires—"

He went cold to the bone, furious in a heartbeat.

"God Almighty, why me? Who am I, the Governor?"

"You're the only one who knows the country."

"How does Peck know that?"

"By the way you talked about the Chikaskia Creek, I guess."

"Damn it, Callie, I'm not taking responsibility for those people!"

The terrible roaring conflict in his head started up again as if just yesterday Green Lightfoot and Austin Deer-in-the-Water had fallen off their horses with bullets in their backs, bullets meant for Nickajack himself. Bullets that never would have been flying if he hadn't set himself up as a leader, trying to persuade other people to do what he wanted.

"Why not help if you can? You're one of them, aren't you?"

"No!"

"They're locusts and intruders and ignorant pumpkin rollers, so you don't care if they burn to a crisp? Won't you burn up, too, if the fire gets past them and comes rolling up this canyon?"

"That's my lookout. I've got horses to see about. I won't be responsible for anybody else."

"You are, though," she said, giving him a narrowed look, "even if you stay right here all by yourself."

"How do you figure that?"

"If you're the only one who can save them, but if you don't, you're responsible."

He stared at her, his heartbeat a wild tumult. She stared back, fear a presence in her eyes.

"I have to get back," she said, turning to look for her wild mare.

Damn it all straight to hell, there was no hope for it.

Judy was grazing peacefully a stone's throw away. He strode toward her and she merely raised her head and looked at him, too tired to run anymore. He took hold of the reins, reached for the buckle, and gently stripped her bridle off.

"What are you doing?" Callie cried, running toward him, a bit unsteadily. "I'll never catch her now."

"I'm turning her loose," he snapped. "There's no sense in riding her to death."

Or killing your own meddling, foolhardy self.

"That bridle's from the Peck horse," she called.

"I'll return it, damn it! If they insist on trusting me with their lives, they can trust me with a piece of tack."

He glanced back at her.

"Go to my barn," he said. "Gather all the towsacks and saddle blankets you can find, except for the ones on top of the saddles, and tie them in rolls on the two saddles nearest the door."

She nodded assent.

He turned and ran for the cabin, whistling for the Shapeshifter as he went.

The light inside the barn was dim, but even in her haste, Callie paused to notice how neat Nick kept it. It felt homey and cared-for, like a barely-remembered place from the long-distant past, since it had four walls and a roof.

She hurried down the center aisle, glancing

both ways into all the stalls, and saw no extra
sacks or blankets. Then she noticed the shelves
above the feed bins, filled with folded towsacks, and saw an old saddle blanket covering
a stack of wooden buckets.

Still breathing hard, she gathered her finds
and ran to the saddles with them. A glance out
the wide door showed Nick running toward
the barn with two horses following, his big
black and a tall reddish-brown one.

Pray God this horse would be easier to ride
than Judy.

He'd be here in only a moment, so she began rolling the sacks tightly and tying them to
the first saddle in the row. No telling how far
the fire had come by now—it might even be
at the Peck place. Hers would be next.

Oh, how could she have wasted time with
a *kiss*, of all insane things?

And her treacherous lips still wanted more.
They'd tasted Nick's spicy-sweet, dark honey
man-taste, and they wanted to taste him again.
If she gave in to her selfish body, she'd run
out there to meet him right this minute and
throw herself into his arms again.

She jerked the second set of saddle strings
straight—so hard that she had a moment's
panic that she'd broken them—and wrapped
them around the sacks, her cheeks flaring with
heat. She had kissed him back, she truly had.
And that was a shameless, unforgivable thing

to have done, because she would never, could
never, love anyone but Vance. She shouldn't
be feeling even so much as the temptation of
kissing another man.

Especially not a man who'd drag his heels
about helping his neighbors fight fire, and
who'd refused to give them water!

Nick and the horses burst through the doorway.

"Good," he said, taking the saddle from her
hands, swooping to pick up the blanket she'd
found lying on it and had pushed aside. "Callie, this is Fast Girl, but don't let her name
scare you. All you have to do is keep your feet
in the stirrups and hold onto the horn."

Her temper, already rising in anger at herself, flared at him, too.

"If Judy couldn't scare me, I don't think Fast
Girl's name will," she said sarcastically.

He threw her a look over his shoulder as she
tied the first batch of strings on what would
evidently be her saddle, since he was swiftly
cinching the first one onto the black horse.

"You showed a lot of sand with that ride,
all right," he said. "Even to attempt it, much
less finish it."

She couldn't answer. Suddenly her throat
felt tight, and an overwhelming urge to weep
came over her. Reluctant or not, Nick was
helping her now, the way he'd been ever since
she'd come to a stop in the godforsaken,

danger-ridden Strip. He was going to take her back to her wagon at least, with a bunch of sacks for fighting the fire, whether he went to help the Pecks or not. She couldn't expect more than that from a man who only wanted to be left alone.

A man with a hot, sweet kiss that could enrapture her more than that of her true love.

Nick drew the Shifter's cinch tight, shot the tongue of the buckle into the hole, and looped the end of the latigo through the loop all in one motion. Then he went to saddle Fast Girl. Callie had the sacks tied on and she moved out of his way so as not to slow him down. When he held his hands out to give her a leg up, she was ready.

Maybe she would survive out here, after all, he thought. Her blood was pounding like his with the words "prairie fire" driving the quick beat of her heart; he could see the pulse jumping beneath the porcelain skin of her temple. Her breath was still coming fast and her hands shook a little as he handed her the reins, but she was game. That hair-raising ride on Judy hadn't scared her into staying on the ground.

He threw himself onto his horse.

"She'll stay with the Shifter," he said, nodding at Fast Girl. "Take a deep seat and hang on."

He kept a sharp eye on her as they started down the creek, watching her slide a little in the seat and learn to grip with her thighs.

"I do much better with a saddle," she called.

"You'd do even better than that if we had time to adjust your stirrups."

When he knew she had her balance, he laid his heels to the Shifter and they pounded faster down the draw. Callie was tired—he could see it, and she was beat up from that nightmare ride to find him—but she didn't look back. She just clung to the saddle horn and faced whatever lay ahead.

But by the time they reached her wagon and the Peck boy, who had miraculously managed to take that sorry excuse for a plow and cut a shallow, crooked furrow halfway around the vehicle, her shoulders were sagging. She looked smaller and more fragile than she ever had, and she still had a fire to fight.

One glance at the boy's horse told Nick that it, too, was played out.

"Nick, this is Danny Peck," Callie said, as they stopped beside the wagon. "Danny, this is Mr. Smith, the man your Papa sent you to find."

The boy ran to him.

"We seen the smoke," he said breathlessly. "My pa says will you please help, 'cause it's a monstrous big fire on the claim south of us."

He turned toward his horse, then turned back to look at Nick with big eyes full of fear.

"Likely it's on our land by now."

Nick's gut contracted. Peck was dumping this kid's life into his hands, and no telling how many more, and the man didn't know Nick from Adam's off ox.

It was too late to get out of it, though. He had come back with Callie, the fire was eating up the grass on its way toward them, and he was in for it now.

"Here, you have to have a fresh mount," he said, trying not to look into the boy's trusting blue eyes or get to know his face. "Callie can ride with me."

Nick sidepassed the Shifter to Fast Girl's side and plucked Callie from the saddle.

He realized that second that he'd made a terrible mistake. All he wanted, fire or no fire, was to pull her into his arms and kiss her again.

For comfort. Only for that. It must be that he needed the comfort of her closeness, because he was trapped in this situation he'd sworn would never catch him again.

Now how weak and stupid was that?

"Ride behind me," he said, and helped her get settled astride on the blanket while the Peck boy clambered up into the saddle she'd just left.

She didn't put her arms around his waist or hold onto him at all. He glanced around as he smooched to the Shifter and saw she had hold of the cantle board with both hands.

"Straight south of here," the Peck boy shouted, and Nick rode out to lead the way.

He would've sworn he was in hell long before they rode anywhere near the smoke and the flames of the fire. The whole way, Callie kept sitting like that behind his saddle, trying to hold herself away from him. And that was good—since if she had her arms wrapped around his waist and her breasts pressed against his back, he would've felt wilder inside than he already did.

Something about it made him fighting mad, though. It seemed like a gesture of distrust or prissiness or some such damn thing. After she'd kissed him right back with a passion not half an hour ago!

It was his own fault. He should've taken the Peck boy up on his horse with him and left her on the mare. Now she'd probably fall off the Shifter after staying on Judy and Fast Girl, too. Well, it'd serve her right for being so schoolteacher-prim about not touching him.

"Hold on," he called irritably over his shoulder, without looking at her. "And keep your feet out of his flanks."

The Peck boy, riding Fast Girl beside them, looked over at Nick as he smooched to the Shifter again.

"Lope on," Danny yelled. "This mare can stay with you."

Nickajack ignored him. One thing he *didn't*

have to do was buddy up to the neighbor kids.

"Yes, she can," Callie called back, "she creates such a wind, I almost blew off her back."

The boy laughed and Nick's tension eased just a little. But it was a mistake to ask the Shifter for more speed, Nick realized, for it jerked Callie back and then forward, into him. She bumped him again and then finally, at long last, laid her arms around his waist.

Instantly, he wanted to turn and hold her. But at the very same time he wished he could push her away, set her onto the mare, and leave her behind. What the hell was happening to him?

He'd better get his mind off women and onto fires, if he was racing to this one as the savior of the Chikaskia settlers. His mind and his instincts had to be free to guide him right, or he was liable to have sodbusters with nothing but the clothes on their backs camped all over his place.

Now, *that* was a thought that should be sobering enough to do the trick.

About three miles later, they smelled smoke. The Peck boy stood in his stirrups a few yards ahead, waving to three riders galloping toward them from the east.

"There's my brother," the boy shouted, as Nick and Callie caught up with him. "He's brought some neighbors."

They all appeared to be greenhorns, by the way they were dressed. Nick nodded and waved for them to come on.

"Let's get to it," he shouted, as the newcomers rode within hearing distance. "Follow me." He lifted the Shifter into a long lope again.

At the wagons on Peck's claim, a small crowd was gathered. How many were Pecks, how many were other neighbors, Nickajack neither knew nor cared. All he wanted was for this fire to be conquered and the lot of them to be scattered to the winds.

Callie let go of him, slid to the ground before he could hand her down, and started helping Mrs. Peck untie the sacks on both his horses. He turned away from the glimpse of her from over his shoulder, her bright hair gleaming, her face so resolute that she looked curiously wise. Well, she had better be, damn it, or these people would die because she had brought the Goingsnake to lead them.

He slammed his mind against her again and sat his horse, feeling the wind. The flames were visible now on the horizon, leaning a little toward the west. They didn't look to be sweeping straight to the north, where they could get his place and Callie's.

But they could change direction in a heartbeat. They could blow straight east in the next minute and consume their bodies, and their claims wouldn't matter, then.

"We've got three barrels of water here," Mr. Peck shouted through the hubbub.

"Wet the sacks and blankets," Nick shouted back.

He sent Callie a glance meaning that she should oversee that. She replied with a straight look and a short, solemn nod that told him she would, then set to the task.

Nick swept his gaze around at the waiting settlers.

"As the women wet the blankets, you men go pick one up."

And then come with me. We've got to set a backfire, and now.

The words wouldn't come out of his mouth. He cleared his throat, but no voice would sound. What if the backfire turned on them?

Yet they had no other weapon. And three barrels of water was no more than a drop in the ocean.

His hands and feet wouldn't move. The Shapeshifter danced restlessly beneath him, throwing up his head to whinny his protest at the smell of smoke, fighting his instinct to run from fire while he waited for direction from his rider.

Yet Nick sat there with the reins frozen in his fingers and the sweat running down his spine. The boy who had come to fetch him couldn't be more than ten years old, yet he was lining up with the men for a wet towsack to fight the fire. What if he didn't live through it?

Everyone was doing exactly as he had said, obeying his instructions to the letter, each man looking to him as he picked up a wet blanket, waiting for the next words out of Nick's mouth as if he were Moses on the Mount. He had to do something, or sit here and let them all burn to ashes for sure.

Or do something wrong and cause them all to burn to ashes.

His mind's eye flashed to two sixteen-year-old boys' bodies on the ground, their handsome young faces already buried in the soft green grass of the Nation, their backs dotted with trickles of blood flowing from the bulletholes. He could hear the sudden, deadly cracks of the shots.

He'd looked to the screen of trees where the assassins were hiding in ambush, knowing even as he did so that he'd never see their faces, never be sure of their names. They would not face justice; they would get away with taking two young lives for no other reason than that the boys rode with him.

Or that he'd been the target and they'd missed him.

Either way, he was helpless to save them, helpless to do anything that would make a dime's worth of difference.

Something touched his leg. He jumped and

looked down to see Callie standing at his stirrup, her green eyes wide and deep.

"The wind's shifting to come out of the east,
don't you think?" she said.

Still frozen, he sat and looked down at her.

Her skin had gone so pale that the freckles
stood out across her nose, but not from fear.
Her eyes blazed with hope and trust. In him.

"Nick, you can do this," she said. "I'm sorry
that you must, but you can."

She believed it with all her heart.

He might as well believe it, too. He couldn't
very well turn and ride away, could he?

Wetting his finger, he lifted it into the wind.

"Pray it'll hold," he managed to say.

Then he tore his gaze from hers and swung
around in the saddle. He looked out across the
ragged bunch of neighbors he had never
wanted, held his hand high, and shouted,
"We're setting a backfire! Men, follow my
lead. Boys, form a line behind them. Women,
keep every cloth wet."

These were only Callie and Mrs. Peck and
her little girl, but they could do the job. As if
to prove it, Callie thrust a wet saddle blanket
into his hands and ran back to the wagon that
held the water.

He threw the blanket across his pommel and
began pushing the Shapeshifter toward the
flames. This fire *could* be turned: it was already
moving west. The wind was all that gave their

pathetic little bunch any chance at all against the flames. It blew right out of the east, steady and straight, bending the edges of the fire even more toward the west. The men and boys followed him toward it, some running on foot because their mounts were too scared for them to manage.

Nick stood in his stirrups, looked up and down the fire line, judging it one last time, then pulled some lucifers from his pocket and jumped off the Shapeshifter's back. Positioning the men and boys with gestures, handing out the few matches he had, he managed to open himself, body and soul, to the task at hand, the way he had always dealt with danger. No past, no future—only now and what had to be done filled his mind. For the first time since that day the boys died, they left him.

He scraped the head of one of the lucifers across the sole of his boot, bent and set the grass afire at his feet, his wet blanket ready in the other hand. Instantly, he had to use it, for the wind made a swirling shift. The others, watching, imitated him.

Somebody yelled a warning about the wind, and the frantic fight began. The stiff breeze grew stronger and helped them, then turned treacherous, then helpful again, then undecided, and the glimpses of arms lifted and lowered, the flash of orange flames, and the black of the burned grass became all he could see. The noise of sacks slapping against the earth and fire crackling in the air filled his ears. His body raised up and bent down, his hands held the blanket, and his arms beat at the fire with no direction from him.

Someone thrust a wet blanket at him and he realized that the Peck boy was running back to the water barrel to exchange dry blankets for wet for the other men, also. Everyone was working as hard as he was—but everything they could do, might not be enough.

Callie's face and her eyes full of trust appeared in his mind's eye to squelch that thought. He couldn't fail her. He would not.

In spite of their incessant beatings at the flames that tried to stray the wrong way, and his eternal vigilance at keeping track of where everyone was, a streak of fire raced toward the wagon and the women. Nick ran to beat it into submission, then glanced over his shoulder.

Callie didn't see him; she was busy fighting to make the Pecks' horses pull the wagon closer to the fire. Silently, he cursed his short-sightedness. He should've put one of the men on the wagon, someone with more brute strength, although no man was a match for the power of a horse.

His gut twisted with fear. Terrified horses had been known to run directly into a fire— sometimes to try to get to the barn where they felt safe, sometimes from pure, blind panic. Callie would be helpless if this team bolted.

Someone yelled and he had to turn back to the fire. The next time he let himself look, she had wrestled the wagon into place and was holding the team relatively still while Mrs. Peck dipped the sack that her small son brought her. Callie stood up and braced her feet a little bit apart, watching the team, lifting her chin in that determined way she had that made him smile.

The wind shifted firmly to come from the east once more, stronger now. Nickajack breathed a little prayer of thanks and slapped at another tongue of fire trying to creep to the east.

What about her dead husband, Mr. Sloane? What kind of man had he been? Had he loved her well?

The smoke thickened and swirled in the wind, which was dancing a little, threatening to change direction again, but the main danger had finally passed. Their line of burned grass had widened enough that not many sparks blew across it anymore.

God, please don't let the wind shift now.

He put out another tendril of flames, then turned toward the wagon to rewet his blanket while the boy was busy with someone else. Callie waved him away, shaking her head, and

Mrs. Peck tipped the barrel to show it was empty.

Somebody yelled from behind him, and he turned to see that the wind was shifting again. It steadied, strengthened—and the fire completely gave in to it in that instant. The trouble spots all burned back into the strip of charred grass they had created, and then the main body of the fire raced away to the west. It ate up everything in its path, dipping a little to the south again, heading southwest straight toward the low wall of Comanche Butte, which offered only rocks for fuel.

It was over. They had won.

Nobody killed, nobody hurt.

Suddenly Nick found himself standing still for the first time in what seemed hours, but was more likely only half of one, surrounded by weary, smoke-blackened men who were shaking his hand and pounding his shoulders. Every one of them was smiling.

Their first big danger had been defeated. They had survived their first night and now their first day in the Cherokee Strip.

"Great work, Smith," Peck said. "We appreciate your leadership more than you can know."

The others joined him in a grateful chorus of thanks.

Leadership . . . just what he didn't want. Now they were liable to be asking him for advice on everything from dryland farming to varmint killing. They weren't going anywhere, now. They would be here to stay.

"The wind was with us," Nick said.

He turned away and strode across the crackling, dry grass, stamping out a spark here and there, searching through the lingering smoke to find Callie. She was standing to one side, shading her eyes with her hand, staring out at the retreating fire, every muscle in her body still tensed for the fight.

Then she spun around.

"Nick!"

Running toward him, smiling that blinding smile of hers, she made him want to run to meet her.

But that didn't mean a thing. Nor did it mean anything that he had felt compelled to find her during and after the fire. Or that she had called up his courage when he couldn't find it for himself.

Kissing her hadn't been significant, either. He had done it out of relief that she hadn't been trampled beneath that wild-eyed mare's feet. That was all.

He had sworn a year ago never to trust another woman, never to even get entangled with one for more than a night. And he was going to keep that vow—come hell or high water, prairie fires or mountain girls.

He was going to leave Callie strictly alone.

After he got her back to her place.

After he returned her wheel and her damned horse.

He turned away and stalked toward the Shifter with a growl.

Chapter 7

Callie called to Nick again, and he stopped and waited for her to reach him, watching her with a little frown creasing his forehead. Surely he wasn't angry with her for bringing him here, since everything had turned out so well!

"We did it," she cried. "Oh, Nick, thanks for coming—you've saved all our stakes."

Mr. Peck, hurrying toward them with two of the other men on his heels, chimed in before Nick could answer her.

"Yes, yes, we're all grateful," he said in his booming voice. "Mr. Smith, we'd like to invite you to come by our camp on your way home. Mrs. Peck was frying dried fruit pies when we got the alarm, and we would take the greatest pleasure in sharing them with our neighbors."

"Thank you for the offer of hospitality," Nick said, and only then, when he turned to glance at Mr. Peck, did those fierce gray eyes let hers go. "But I must get back to my place at once."

"So must we all," Mr. Peck said, "but we'd like to treat you as thanks for your expert assistance."

"No thanks needed—that's what neighbors are for," Nick said brusquely. Then he added, "You can return the help someday."

He took Callie's arm and turned toward the horses again.

"We'll be glad to, but we hope it's not help returned in kind," Mr. Peck said, his tone positively jolly, now that the danger was past. "I think the people of Chikaskia Creek have fought enough fire."

A cheer went up all around.

Nick looked back and lifted his hand in acknowledgment, but he kept on walking. Callie looked back, too, feeling every inch of his long, strong fingers through her sleeve as if they were touching her skin. Everyone's eyes were on them.

"I don't mean to be dragging you away. Are you wanting to go to the fried pie social?" he demanded gruffly.

To her amazement, she realized that she had

no desire to stop by the Pecks' camp without Nick.

"No," she said, "and that's good, because you're furnishing my mount."

He shot her an annoyed glance.

"Somebody else can take you back to your claim."

In direct opposition to the words, his grip on her tightened.

"Or I could return Fast Girl to you later," she said lightly.

He gave her that look again, as if to judge whether or not she meant the remark seriously.

She looked at him with an innocent face.

"I ride her well enough to be on my own with her, don't you think?"

She saw the brief struggle between bald truth and thin tact in his eyes.

"Not well enough. To strike out alone, I mean. With the smell of smoke and all this fire excitement in the air."

Callie laughed.

"Come on, Nick, don't worry about my feelings. Tell me what you really think."

His jaw tightened.

"You've got to learn to ride if you aim to survive in this country," he said. "I've already told you that."

He sounded thoroughly irritated, which aggravated her no end.

"I do aim to survive out here," she snapped. "Count on it. And I will learn to ride, but so far I've only been here a day and a night and they've been pretty busy."

That made him smile. She tried, but she couldn't resist smiling, too.

"Besides," she said lightly, "Judy's the only horse I have, and I'm not sure she's the one for me."

His grin broadened as he slowed down to avoid startling the little group of horses who were alternately grazing and lifting their heads to look toward the now-vanished fire.

"You ought to trade her off to one of your neighbors," he drawled with a chuckle in his voice.

"But then I'd never get the Chikaskia school," she said, grinning back at him. "I'd have an enemy for life and the beginnings of a feud."

He laughed.

"Better saddle ol' Joe the mule, then."

Gathering the reins of both his horses, he led them away from the others and crossed Fast Girl's reins on her neck. He went to her side and held his hands for Callie to step into.

She steadied herself by holding onto his shoulder. It was broad and hard and strong as steel, and in spite of the ashes covering his shirt and the sweat soaking it, a powerful urge came over her to caress those muscles, to explore them with her fingertips and memorize them with her palm.

He lifted her as easily as if she weighed nothing at all. She managed her tangled skirts enough to throw her right leg over. Too soon, she had to let go of him as he set her onto the filly and stepped back.

"Nick," she said, as she settled into the saddle and he began shortening the stirrups to fit her, "will you teach me to ride?"

He glanced up at her quickly, then went back to his work.

"Callie," he drawled, "do you reckon that'd be such a good idea?"

She hesitated, but not because she was uncertain of his meaning. His tone was unmistakably sensual. He looked up again with those heart-stopping eyes, and they held her still and breathless.

So he felt it, too, this unreasoning desire that came over her sometimes when she was with him—this desire she must keep under control at all costs. Hadn't giving in to Vance destroyed her whole life?

No. It isn't a good idea. Spending time with you will make me want to kiss you again. It will make me want much more than that, I can already tell.

"I don't see why you shouldn't give me lessons," she said. "You're a wonderful rider and you have lots of horses for me to practice on."

"Aha," he said, walking around the mare to

adjust the other stirrup. "So you think you can work up a horsetrade with *me*. Remember, now, I've seen Judy at her worst."

That made Callie laugh again.

"I'll come up with something for boot," she said, watching his every move as he finished with the stirrup, then went to the Shapeshifter and mounted in one long, flowing motion full of masculine grace.

"If you trade with me, you'll have to offer something mighty fine," he said. "I wouldn't trade you Judy straight across for any animal on my place, including the old coyote who comes around in the Cold Month looking for handouts."

"What an insult!" she said, loving the boyish, mischievous expression that fell across his face as he entered so readily into the game. "Poor Judy. She'd be hurt if she heard you say that."

"No, she wouldn't. Judy doesn't care what anyone thinks of her. She shows you that every time you look at her."

When they started riding out, everyone waved and called to them. Nick returned the good-byes politely but briefly, never slowing the Shifter's pace.

"Come by to see us any time," Mr. Peck called. "If you need to, water your horses at our place before you start home."

"Much obliged," Nick called back, and lifted the Shifter into a short lope.

"You surely are leaving in a hurry for someone who told Mr. Peck what neighbors are for," Callie teased him.

He shot her such a fierce look that she laughed out loud. His scowl grew worse and she wished she hadn't. Evidently, he wasn't in quite such a good mood as she'd thought.

"I was talking about neighbors and trouble," he growled, "and I've had enough of both today to last me 'til spring."

He looked at her as accusingly as if she were the cause of the fire, as well as of his seeing his neighbors. Callie's temper flashed.

"You ought to thank me for bringing you down here," she said sharply. "If I hadn't, your cabin might be burning to ground along about now."

He ignored that.

"Don't be trying to pull me into any pie socials or box suppers or all-night shindigs," he warned.

How much gall could he have! As if she'd set her cap for him and then kidnapped him to go to the fire!

"Don't worry," she shot back. "I wouldn't go walking out with an old grouch like you! Not even to so much as a . . . a hog killing!"

He glared at her. She glared at him.

"*Now* who's bringing up the subject of hogs?" he said.

Callie stared him right in the eye and tried not to smile, tried not to let go of her anger, so the mysterious charm he held for her couldn't take hold. Her valiant efforts didn't do one whit of good. Nick's frown deepened, but the corners of his mouth turned up in spite of him, and all she wanted to do was laugh and reach out to touch him, to trace the shape of his sensual lips with her fingertip.

"I'm not bringing it up as a topic of conversation," she said, managing somehow to speak sharply. "I'm only using it as a figure of speech. It means I wouldn't go anywhere with you."

Liar, liar, pants on fire.

Mischief flashed in his eyes, paler and more mesmerizing than ever in the sooty rims that had formed around them in the sweat on his face.

"I know one place you'll go with me," he said.

"Where?"

"To running water. To a place where you can stand in the deep shade under cool running water and wash the ashes off your skin."

He looked her up and down, slowing his horse a little. Hers slowed, too, of course.

"How does that sound, Callie Sloane? Wouldn't it feel good to wash away that layer of grit and ash sticking to you all over, gluing you to your clothes, itching and stinging you and making you feel hotter than a poker in the fire?"

His low voice moved her like the touch of his hand.

"It sounds like you ought to get a job selling snake oil," she said. "I don't believe there's a place like that within five hundred miles of here."

He smiled a slow smile.

"There's your trouble," he drawled. "Lack of faith. I'll take you there straight as the crow flies."

She raised her eyebrows and fixed him with her schoolteacher stare.

"Did I say I wanted to go there?"

"I saw it in your eyes," he said, and kissed to the Shapeshifter, who went into a ground-eating long trot.

Her horse followed, of course. Callie probably couldn't have turned her if she'd tried.

Finally they rode out of the lingering haze created by smoke and dust to see Callie's wagon off in the distance, listing to one side, looking like a great white cloud fallen from the sky and stuck to the land. It seemed like a miracle to Callie, when she remembered how afraid she had been that it and everything in it would vanish in the fire.

Nick didn't even glance at it—he turned in

at the mouth of his treed canyon. Fast Girl stayed with the Shapeshifter.

"You're bluffing," Callie called. "Admit it, Nick, and take me home."

But I don't want to go home. I want to go with you.

"Nope. You as much as called me a liar. I have to prove I'm not."

They sounded like two little kids, and she felt like one. The fire danger had passed, Nick was her companion, and she had something to look forward to.

"Are you planning to conjure up a waterfall?" she teased. "Oh, I know! You'll pour a bucket of water over my head."

"Wrong and wrong."

"You're bluffing."

"And ought to be a poker player," he said, mimicking her voice. "Snake oil salesman, poker player. Which is it?"

"I'll have to see your running stream of cool water before I can tell you," she said. "Maybe I'll say you should witch water for a living."

"I haven't even got a peach tree to give me a forked branch to witch with," he said. "There's no magic to it."

"Hmmf," she said skeptically. "There will be if we stand under a shady, flowing stream that's cool in this parched country today."

"We will," he promised.

They trotted slowly alongside the rocky

creekbed with an easy silence between them. They passed the low-water pond and the treed pasture where Nick had some horses, then rode up the slope into his front yard, and across it to the barn.

"It seems a hundred years ago that we ran out through that doorway with the sacks tied onto our saddles," Callie said. She stood in one stirrup, held onto the horn while she kicked free of it, and half tumbled, half slid to the ground from Fast Girl's back. "Doesn't it?"

Nick had already dismounted and was coming back to help her. He was too late.

"At least you've learned to dismount," he said. "We can skip at least one of your riding lessons."

"Only after I've had a little more practice," she said, "or grown longer legs. I could break my neck if I don't do better than I did just now."

"Have you ever thought about a mounting block?"

His voice was dry and teasing.

"Thanks so much for the useful suggestion," she retorted in the same tone. "I'll just carry one around on the back of my horse, and if I need to get down and fight a fire or go into a store in town or anything, I can lower it on a rope."

He laughed. "Think about it. It might slow

Judy down if she had to carry the extra weight."

Callie grinned at him, suddenly feeling very close to him again.

"You're just trying to think of reasons for me to keep Judy," she said. "You're scared you're going to end up as her next proud owner."

"It'll never happen," he said, looking down at her with that slow smile she loved. "I'd have to be dead drunk, or she'd have to be the last piece of horseflesh in the Strip."

"I wish I had a barrel of Uncle Jasper's white lightning," she said.

"It would do you no good," he drawled. "I'm foolish, but not foolish enough to let any woman, much less you, fill me full of liquor."

He grinned at her, then turned to start unfastening the cinch on his mount.

"Wait in the shade," he said. "I'll take care of the horses."

"I'll help. That'll get us into the water that much quicker."

"Aha," he said. "You still don't believe there really is any cool water."

"I'll believe it when I feel it running over my skin."

"Go ahead," he said, over his shoulder, "the water's here. Start taking off your clothes."

"Nick!" she squealed in surprise.

Then she imitated his voice.

"I'm foolish, but not foolish enough to take off my clothes in front of any man, much less you."

He laughed.

"Well, at least we know we don't trust each other."

"Except with our lives in a prairie fire."

He turned, his head cocked to one side to study her. They exchanged a long, straight look.

Finally he narrowed his eyes and gave her the barest nod, an incisive gesture that somehow affirmed her words more emphatically than a shouted agreement would have done. Then he went back to work.

Now that they were no longer riding, the heat was worse. Every square inch of Callie's skin itched, and the smells of burned grass and charred earth filled her nostrils with every breath.

"Soon I'll be begging you for directions to your waterfall," she said, imitating him to unsaddle her own mount. "You'd better be telling me the truth, because right now a cool bath would be heaven on earth."

She pushed her bedraggled hair off her face and pulled her saddle off the mare, then started to carry it into the barn. Nick took it from her and carried one in each hand, as easily as if they weighed nothing at all. After he put them on their racks, he went back outside, stripped the bridles off, and slapped the horses on their rumps, sending them thundering away.

"They can stay in the pond the rest of the day if they want," he called to Callie over his shoulder. "They've earned it."

"So have we—I mean the rest of the day in the waterfall," she said, "but I'll go to the pond with the horses if I have to."

He laughed.

"Go with 'em now, if you don't trust me."

"Now, Nick, you know I trust you," she said lightly, "even if you are a flatlander."

"Only because you have no choice," he said wryly.

He came back into the homey barn to put up the rest of the tack. Callie watched him hang it neatly in place, then looked all around at the old building while she breathed in its rich aromas of horse, leather, hay, and manure. A person could live in here and be perfectly happy—it was more orderly than lots of people's houses.

"Oh, Nick, I'm so thankful this barn isn't a pile of ashes right now. You didn't want to, but you saved a lot of people's stakes today."

"Thanks to you."

"Well, yes, I did get you to the fire. I'm known for my persuasive powers," she said lightly, "for talking folks into doing things they don't want to do—like learning multiplication tables and practicing penmanship . . ."

"That's not what I mean."

He stiffened where he stood and turned to look at her, his gray eyes blazing like stars in his dark face.

"I froze," he said simply. "If it hadn't been for you, everything and everybody on the Chikaskia could be ashes by now."

It cost him a lot to say that, she could see. But at the same time, she could tell that he couldn't keep from saying it, that he needed to talk about it with her.

"How did you know?" he said. "And how'd you know what to say to jar me out of it?"

"It was the look in your eyes," she said slowly. "I could tell that whatever you were seeing off in the far distance was too much for one person to face."

"But how did you know that?"

She lifted her hands, palms up, and shrugged helplessly.

"I just did."

He searched her face, her eyes, as if she might be hiding a better answer there. She told him silently that she knew no more.

Finally she spoke. "What were you seeing, Nick?"

At first she thought he wasn't going to answer, but then he made a little gesture to say that she should come with him, and turned to leave the barn.

They started walking toward his cabin.

"When I was called Goingsnake," he said, in a voice so profoundly sad that it instantly took over her heart, "I rode all over the Nation trying to rouse feelings against the sale of the Strip. A bunch of boys began to ride with me. Two of them were killed—for no other reason than because they were doing what I told them."

The air went out of her in a quick, short rush.

"And you were afraid somebody would be killed in the fire? Doing what you told them to do?"

He gave a brusque nod.

"What I was seeing was those two fine, young bodies sprawled on the grass, bleeding."

Slowly, they walked on in silence.

"We rode into that ambush because of a woman."

His tone was studiedly neutral, but he gave her a slanting glance.

Callie caught and held it.

"You were thinking that you were at the fire because of me."

"I guess. I guess I was thinking that it was all about to happen again."

"Then how in the world did you ever . . ."

"I didn't," he said. "You did it. Whatever it was."

"Did she persuade you to go there? Into the ambush? That other woman, whoever she was?"

"Matilda," he snapped, his tone full of bitterness. "Matilda, who was considered the most beautiful woman in the Nation. She told my enemies what route I would take to the meeting of the Board of Governors."

They walked into the front yard of the cabin, its sunburned grass covered with withered leaves, fallen early because of the drought. Callie could hardly hear them crackling beneath her feet because her ears were filled with his voice, which was pure tortured regret.

He was seeing it all again, she could tell by the faraway look in his eyes—no, he was *living* it all again, and it was unspeakable. She couldn't bear to feel the pure pain emanating from him. It made her hurt for him and it stirred her own soul-searching sorrow.

She grabbed at the first topic that might distract him, even a little bit.

"What enemies did you have who were so dangerous?"

"Many. The Board of Governors wanted the money from the sale of the Strip for the People; some of the powerful tribal leaders believed it was the only way to keep the Nation itself from being opened to settlement; and some people thought I had no right to meddle in political decisions since I'd lived in the Strip nearly all my life."

"But that gave you more of a right!"

He shrugged. "That's what I thought."

He walked across the side yard and past the back of the cabin. Callie stayed beside him to a cut in the canyon's side where a spring came gurgling out, up above Nick's head. It ran down to the pond in a fairly strong stream.

"So this is the reason the pond isn't as dry as the creekbed and all the rest of the land," she said.

"Yes, but it's slowing down," he said. "Another moon with no rain and it'll be gone, too."

Nick picked up a piece of wood standing against the trunk of one of the cottonwood trees that grew along the water's edge. He stood on tiptoe and wedged the board into a slot dug in the earth beneath the spring, so that the water fell with more force after coming over its curved surface.

"If you'd rather go to the pond with the horses, you can," he said, with a fleeting ghost of his grin. "But this water's cooler."

Callie stepped beneath the water and closed her eyes as it washed over her like a cool, liquid blessing.

"I'll go to the house and get you some dry clothes—"

"No!"

"Callie," he said patiently, "I don't intend to get bold with you or take advantage of you in any way—"

Her cheeks flamed hot despite the cool water pouring over them. Looking up into his face, tilting her head out of the water so she could hold her eyes open, she said, "I know that. I know you, Nick."

His gaze burned into hers for a long minute, his face inscrutable.

"My real name is Nickajack," he said. "I want you to know that, too."

"Nickajack. I've never heard it before."

It felt good on her tongue.

"It's a common Cherokee name."

He had trusted her with his real name. It made her want to tell him her secrets in return.

"Nickajack," she said quickly, "I'll not need dry clothes. These need to be washed as much as I do, and they'll dry on me in a heartbeat."

I need my clothes on for my armor—for something to protect me, to stand between us in this closeness with you.

She needed to be far away from him, for her own good. She needed to flee back into her loneliness, much as she hated it, or she'd be wanting to be with him all the time.

Instead, she reached out and pulled him into the falling water. It was only to distract him from his memories, yet she had to force her hand to fall away from his arm.

"Let the cool water wash the worry out of you, Nick. There's nothing you can do now, so it's better not to think about the past."

Politely, he ignored that foolish remark. There wasn't much room for them both to be beneath the water, but she stood apart. If she touched him again, she'd throw herself into the comfort of his embrace. As it was, she was letting water run into her eyes so she could look at him.

"My name," he said. "Don't let anyone else hear it. Some white man would challenge my claim."

She nodded, then turned her back to him, afraid she couldn't keep fighting the urge to reach for him again. Guilt ran in her, just as it did in him. In the impossible advice she'd just given him she'd been talking to herself, too, hoping her own guilt would flow away in the spring's stream.

"I know exactly how you feel," she said, loud enough to be heard over the sound of the water.

"Don't tell me that," he said sharply. "How could you?"

She whirled to face him, wanting him to know she wasn't speaking lightly. His eyes pierced her to the core, then he tilted his head back and let the water stream through his hair and over his set, hard face turned up to the sky.

Now he was gone far away from her—and she couldn't stand that any more than she could his closeness.

"I was the cause of Vance's death," she said. "He wouldn't have died if I had agreed to run away with him penniless."

The muscles in his jaw relaxed a little bit.

"Because I thought we should have money to buy our homesteading outfit, Vance was working all the time at every job he could find," she said. "On a logging job, he slipped in the mud and a tree fell on him and killed him. I might as well have pushed him—it never would've happened if he'd been rested and not in such a hurry."

Nick looked down at her, water pouring off his chiseled cheekbones, his aristocratic nose, his square, strong jaw. His wet shirt clung to his skin and showed every muscle along his shoulders, across his broad, hard chest.

God help her, she wanted to throw her arms around his neck and glue herself just as tightly to him as that cloth. She wanted to kiss him again so much that her lips actually hurt. She must be a horrible person. How could she feel that way at the very same time she was mourning Vance?

And her the cause of his death!

"So that's why I can never love any other man," she said, looking up into Nick's gray eyes.

She dragged in a deep, full breath of air that smelled sweet and good and clean from the water passing through it.

He had told her his real name—which she immediately knew he told to very few people.

His kiss had shifted the very heart inside her breast, as Vance's never had done.

And now he was looking at her as if he and she were soulmates. His heavy-lidded gaze drifted to her mouth.

This had to stop.

"I gave up my whole family for Vance, and my leafy, green mountain home," she said impatiently. "The reason I'm going through all this misery out here is to fulfill my and Vance's dream. He's the only man I can ever love."

His look didn't change.

"Now I know exactly how *you* feel," he said, and lifted his face to the sky again. "I'll never trust another woman after Matilda."

She couldn't feel anything but desire and the fear of it. He wanted to kiss her, too, that much was plain.

This was misery, standing so close to Nick and not touching him. Looking into his eyes and wanting to kiss him so bad that her lips ached.

One thing for sure, though—the misery would be worse if she kissed him again, because another kiss would just make her want more, much more.

She turned her back to him and stepped out of the water.

Too late. Too late.

The words sounded over and over again in her head.

What she and Nickajack had already shared was more intimate than anything physical ever could be. This talk, and his name, and that moment when, frozen in the face of the fire, he couldn't speak.

How had she known that and known what to do to bring him out of it? Already, there were far too many deep feelings flowing between them to suit her.

She and Nick had better stay far, far apart.

Chapter 8

Callie drove into the raw, new town—called Santa Fe, like the old one in New Mexico, but named for the nearby railroad—with a great sigh of satisfaction. Alone, with nobody's help, she had hitched up her team and driven them straight from her claim to town, following the directions she'd asked from the Pecks yesterday.

It had been a godsend when they'd stopped by on their way home from registering their own claim, even if one part of her had been bitterly disappointed that they weren't Nick. She must, absolutely must, quit thinking about him. Any man who could go to the extreme of sneaking into her camp like a thief while she was away cutting sod did not want to see or talk to her.

And whose fault was that? Her own. She'd caused Nick to behave that way, because she'd insisted on coming home as soon as she got out of the shower and had barely talked to him at all on the way. He'd led Judy so she wouldn't run away again and made sure everything was all right at her camp before he left her there.

Nick didn't see or talk to her when he brought back her wheel and repaired her wagon, because he thought she didn't want to see or talk to him. That was for the best—and she was glad he'd decided to accede to her wishes.

It still made the bottom drop out of her heart, though, to remember coming back to the wagon to find it sitting on four wheels. Had she offended him so much that he'd never speak to her again?

She sighed again, in resignation this time, and made herself look around her. The Pecks would be her friends, and she might make more friends here today. And when the baby came it would be her constant companion. She had come out here to be independent and prove up a claim and she would do exactly that.

Santa Fe seemed like a metropolis after nearly a week alone on the prairie, and she'd started looking for the Land Office. She hoped that horrible Baxter hadn't somehow laid claim to her land—if only she hadn't taken so long at making a show of possession before she came to town!

She sat up straight, pulled on the lines to show her recalcitrant team that she was still there, and started searching the new buildings for signs. No Land Office yet, but there was a tent with a cross on it for a church, several tents with lawyers' shingles, most advertising skill in land disputes (which she might need, according to what Baxter did), a mercantile in a tent, and, farther down toward the east end of the street, the frame of a two-story building rising into the air.

There were lemonade joints, restaurants, cafes, dance halls, blacksmiths, and a livery stable in a wonderful spot beneath a big cottonwood, one of the few trees in sight. All were tents or rickety structures thrown together with an assortment of boards and canvas, except for one small building made of limestone which looked to have been there for awhile. It bore a crudely lettered sign, obviously new: JAIL.

That surprised her. Somebody here must be mightily concerned about law and order.

There was also a horrifying number of saloons and what must be brothels, all crowded together. This must be what the Pecks had called Hell's Half Acre. Probably the jail was already a necessity.

The other surprising thing was that Joe and Judy had begun walking docilely through the mixture of buggies, freight wagons, horses, and people hurrying along the main street of Santa Fe. It was a great relief to the sod-cutting blisters on her palms not to have to pull on the lines so much.

Then she saw what had to be the Land Office up ahead at the far end of the street: a small, rough shack with a long line of people snaking along for what seemed a mile. Callie stood up from the seat and, sure enough, saw a sign tacked above the little porch that proclaimed in large, crooked letters "LAND OFFICE." Her heart sank. There were so many claimants waiting to register that she'd never get back to her place tonight.

But suddenly, that wasn't the main reason her stomach tied itself into a knot. Was Nick standing in that line? Or had he already been here on another day?

She dropped back down onto the seat with a thud of disgust. Why did she keep on thinking about him, day and night?

Well, at least she had stopped thinking about his kiss.

Almost.

She had nearly forgotten how he'd kissed her with such a wild sweetness, how they'd shared that awful fear and the danger of fighting the flames, how they'd looked into each other's eyes and told each other secrets neither would say to anyone else. By the next time she drove into town, she would have completely forgotten all that.

Nickajack Smith meant nothing to her, and he shouldn't. She had come all this way to homestead in Vance's memory, and that was exactly what she would do.

Yet she ran a sharp eye over the line of claimants as she passed them, even looking over her shoulder as her wagon rolled in front of the soon-to-be two-story building. Nick wasn't there. No matter how big the crowd, he would've caught her eye in a heartbeat. Every part of her listened to the little voice of truth inside her that said that.

So she made her head turn and her eyes fix on the frame of the big two-story building going up only a few yards past the land office. Carpenters swarmed all over it like bees in a hollow tree, their hammering and sawing and shouting floating out to join all the noises in the street. It would seem really strange to come in to a brand-new town for supplies, a town that would make Pine Forks, Kentucky, seem two hundred years old.

She drove on past the construction with its sweet smell of new wood and its atmosphere of competence to turn the team under the neatly lettered hanging sign that proclaimed LIVERY STABLE AND WAGON YARD. This would be a safe place for her to sleep in the wagon, if it turned out that she must stay the night.

She made the arrangements to leave her team and wagon there all day and overnight, if necessary, took the small jar of water she'd stowed under the seat and put it into her reticule, removed her certificate permitting her to be in the Run so it wouldn't accidentally get wet, and hurried to the Land Office to stand at the end of the line. She had bread and ham in her pockets, so she would stay until she registered, if it took all day and into the night.

Dora was the one she needed to be looking for, not Nick. She examined the line again. Dora had promised to come help with the birthing, and Dora was the one who was her friend.

Yet her gaze stopped on the back of every tall man. None had shoulders wide enough.

A small group of people stood talking directly in front of her, gathered in a loose knot while they waited in line. Two couples, one a man and woman about the age of the Pecks, old enough to have grown children, and a man and woman about Callie's own age, were listening to a single man of about thirty who was holding forth in a lecture about the best methods of raising corn. The younger couple exchanged an amused glance as he drew a quick breath and rushed on to the next point of his spiel, then their eyes held and the look turned tender and hot.

It filled her with a throbbing ache.

For Vance. She missed him, still, more than words could say. She wanted Vance. It was Vance to whom she'd given her heart.

Staring off across the dusty street, Callie tried to see his face but it refused to come to her. Tears stung her eyes. Surely she couldn't forget him—she had to remember, so she could describe him to the baby!

"Well, well, if it ain't the little missus who ain't a missus after all!"

Cold fear shot through her as the familiar voice brought her whirling around on one heel. *Baxter*. With a sneer on his face that would be enough to rouse her fighting spirit even without the taunting remark.

Fear grew alongside her anger. He had walked up behind her with her totally unaware.

"My marital status is none of your business," she said.

The garrulous man fell silent and the two couples listening to him also turned toward Callie and the brewing confrontation.

"Here to try to register my claim, are ye?" Baxter said. "Well, I aim to counterfile."

"Get in line," Callie said. "And get yourself a lawyer."

Then she turned her back on him.

A man strode around the corner of the frame of the two-story building next to the Land Office. For an instant, she thought she'd imagined him.

Nickajack.

A huge relief filled her, much to her chagrin. She would not depend on anyone, especially not Nick, since she could easily fall into the snare of wanting to do so all the time.

She ought to turn her back on him, too, and not watch him.

But he moved like the mountain lion she'd seen up close that time on Old Baldy, as if he ruled every inch of the earth he set foot on and every mile of it he could see. He was coming toward her with the balls of his feet barely brushing the ground and his long, beautiful thigh muscles flexing against the worn cloth of his Levi Strauss pants.

And he had seen her already. There was not the slightest indication in his face or manner, but she knew it was true from something shimmering in the air between them.

Foolish as that was. She'd probably hurt his feelings so much that he wouldn't look at her, either.

Then something above him caught her eye, and she looked up to glimpse a thick board beginning to fall from the second story directly above his head.

"Nickajack!" she shrieked, cupping her hands at her mouth to try to make the sound carry over the noises of the carpenters and the street. "Look out! *Nickajack!*"

She started running toward him, as if she could reach him in time.

He whirled on his heel to look behind him instead of up, but he did take another step and it carried him out of danger. The board struck earth at his feet in an explosion of dust.

Callie kept running—somehow she couldn't stop until she reached him. The other end of the board landed in the soft dust and he looked down at it, then up.

Callie raced up to him, grabbed his huge arm and held onto it, even though she couldn't reach all the way around the hard muscles. Her body contracted deep inside.

"Sorry, partner," a man's voice called down. "It just slipped out of my hand. Glad it didn't hit you."

He was young and worried, peering down at them through the scaffolding, his hat pushed back on his sweaty hair to see them better, his blue eyes as sincere as his tone had been. Nickajack dismissed him with a nod and turned to Callie, who was still holding onto his arm.

She forced her fingers to uncurl; her arms to drop to her sides.

"I . . . I was scared you—"

"Hey, Nick-a-jack!" Baxter shouted. "I was wonderin' where you was when I seen yore woman standin' in line all by her lonesome."

Nickajack threw Callie a glance she couldn't read, then strode toward Baxter, escorting her swiftly with one huge hand at the small of her back.

"Shut up about me and the lady, Baxter."

"I got jist as much right to speak my mind as you."

"Do it someplace else."

"You and whose army gonna make me?" Baxter said. "And don't try t' tell me one more damn time that you two ain't together."

A clutching fear took hold of Callie's stomach. They would never be rid of this obnoxious man, and now he was making a scene in front of a hundred people.

"Watch your mouth," Nickajack snapped. "There are ladies present."

Some of the other men murmured agreement. Baxter wasn't daunted in the least.

"Listen to you," he drawled insolently, loudly, looking around him in hopes of drawing a crowd. "Protect the little redhead's dainty little ears, protect her claim, stand there with yore arm around her and then tell me again you ain't . . ."

Nick's face turned so fierce that Baxter did bite his tongue and hush.

Then a sneering smile spread over his mouth.

"Oh . . . *Nick-a-jack!*"

He spoke far more loudly than necessary, in a voice as full of taunt as a schoolboy's.

"Only other man I ever knowed with that name was a red-skinned Cherokee back in the Nations."

Some of the noises of the land office crowd lessened, Callie realized, and a few people walking by stopped to listen.

Nickajack glared at Baxter, watching his gun hand, but he kept it still and away from the handgun he wore in the waist of his pants. Nickajack's was in a holster at his hip.

Baxter took a belligerent step toward him.

"Let me tell you something, Blanket," he said. "You ought to've got you one of them Indian allotments, 'cause you ain't gonna get one meant for a white man. I aim to counterfile agin' you and your *woman* both."

"Go ahead."

The implied threat in Nick's level tone of voice made Baxter hesitate with his mouth open to speak. Then he recovered.

"*She,*" he said, flicking his eyes at Callie, "ought not have no second claim of her own, and you ought have none at all. The U. S. Government paid you Cherokees good money for this land, and it's white settlers they bought it for."

Nick stared at him, his right hand hovering over the gun he wore. Callie's breath caught and wouldn't come out of her throat.

"I'll see about this whenever it's my turn to register," Baxter bellowed, but he held his gun hand hard against his belly, clearly afraid to draw against Nickajack. "I'll get a lawyer if I have to."

"Go ahead and hire one," Callie said. "I intend to. I'm not about to give you my claim without a fight."

Baxter glared at her.

"You didn't stake that claim, Missy. He did," he said, jerking his thumb toward Nickajack. "And he already had one staked that he has no right to. My quarrel is with him."

"Not if you're talking about my land. This man is not my husband and my claim belongs only to me."

"There's no connection between us," Nickajack said, and a weird feeling shot through Callie, as if he'd betrayed her. "Leave her alone. If you want to counterfile, do it against me."

"I will," Baxter said nastily. "And my brother will counterfile against her."

Nickajack stared at him until Baxter turned and walked away.

The older man in the group ahead of Callie in line called to Baxter.

"You're a fool, man! He ain't no Indian; his eyes is as gray as mine."

"You never seen a blue-eyed Indian?" Baxter shot back, and marched indignantly on down the street.

Callie resumed her place in line, Nickajack right behind her. Her heart was beating a hundred times too fast and the same number of emotions pulled her heart in every direction.

"I told you," he muttered, in a low tone to the top of her head, "not to let anyone else know my name."

She whirled and glared up at him.

"You were about to be knocked senseless. How could I think?"

His gray eyes held hers. He was truly angry!

"Well, it's your own fault!" she cried defensively. "What are you doing following me around, anyhow?"

His scowl grew terrible.

"I have every right to come to town," he said, in a still quieter tone as if trying to make her lower hers.

A man's voice interrupted from behind her.

"This little lady's a hero," he said. "Ma'am, may I be so bold as to introduce myself? I'm Roger Timmons, your sincere admirer."

Callie turned to see the young man who'd been teaching about raising corn bow to her, sweeping off his hat.

"May I commend you for your quick action," he said with a reproving glance at Nick, whose look grew even blacker.

Callie couldn't suppress a sudden grin.

"Why, thank you, Mr. Timmons. My name is Callie Sloane."

Then she added mischievously, "This gentleman is Mr. Smith, my neighbor."

Somehow, she still didn't trust herself not to say "Nickajack." That name seemed the right one for him.

"We're the Fletchers," the man who had called out to Baxter said, as Mr. Timmons' former audience moved up to join in the socializing. "And these are our neighbors, the Sumners."

Nick shook hands with the men.

"Whereabouts is your claim, Miss Sloane?" Mrs. Sumner asked.

"Over in the Chikaskia Creek country."

"Oh! And ours, too!"

"We're all neighbors, then!"

"What great fortune that we're all here on the same day!"

When the excitement had died down, Mr. Fletcher looked down his long nose and fixed his blue eyes on Callie as if she were a possibly naughty child.

"You're a woman alone? To prove out a claim?"

Callie decided that Mrs. Fletcher's questioning look must be caused by her years of marriage to an overly inquisitive man.

And Timmons was another one.

"Miss Sloane, are you aimin' to farm?" he said.

She made her tone very firm and confident.

"No, I'm proving out a claim and building a house on it, but I plan to be a teacher."

And if that were to come about, she'd better make one thing very clear.

"Also, it's *Mrs.* Sloane. I'm a widow."

"Sorry for your loss," Mr. Fletcher said briskly, "but I reckon a widow can be a teacher same as an unmarried lady, 'specially out here, where we'd feared there'd be no teachers at all."

A great flurry of talk rose all at once, since all of them except Mr. Timmons had children— three in the Sumner household and nine in the Fletchers'—and were eager for a school.

"But ma'am, you're no bigger than a cricket," Mr. Fletcher said. "Can you make the big boys behave?"

"Yes. I raised seven brothers while my mother and Granny cooked and kept house, and I've already taught school a year back home in Kentucky."

That pleased them even more, and a few more minutes of conversation had Callie feeling that all she had to do to be a teacher was drive straight out to her claim and ring the bell. Mrs. Sumner began counting all the children she knew would be living on the nearby claims.

"Do you have any children, Mr. Smith?"

Nick, who had been silent throughout the discussion, waited a long moment.

"No, ma'am," he said finally. "I'm a bachelor."

He spoke absently, glancing at a man in a white shirt with gartered sleeves who was working his way down the line with a handful of papers. Callie looked at the man in horror. Obviously he was an official of some kind. Had he been out here all the time? Had he heard Baxter call Nickajack a Cherokee?

"That's the clerk," Mrs. Sumner said. "He comes out every so often to hand out the numbers that mark our place in line."

"I'm sure the officials will be happy to see us all registered at the end of the day," Callie said.

"Oh, they won't register us today," Mr. Sumner said. "All your number will get you inside is another paper telling you when to come back. They're trying to scatter us out some."

"Too many of us here at once," Mr. Timmons announced pompously. "We can't all register on the same day."

Callie stared at them in disbelief.

"You mean I'll have to make another trip? I won't be done today?"

"Nope. You'll have to come back on whatever day they assign you during the next three months."

Furious disappointment bloomed inside her, taking up every inch of space inside her skin. Blast it all! She had driven those monster animals of hers all this way, only to have it to do over again!

The clerk reached her, silently handed her a square of paper with the number 144 written in wide pen strokes, passed on, and gave 145 to Nick. Instinctively she swung around to watch, and thought she saw the clerk give him a strange look—maybe an appraising look for Indian blood.

As soon as Nick had his number in hand, he strode toward the Land Office as if it were a ticket to get inside. Several people muttered their surprise, and all of them watched him. The sun beat down on Callie's head like a hammer on a nail.

Where was he going? And what did she care? Hadn't he just spurned her after she'd saved his life?

Yet the sight of his snug, weathered cabin and the sweet-smelling barn flashed across her mind. He had lived there with his parents. That was his old homeplace. He loved that piece of land like she loved the mountains.

What if she had caused him to lose it to that awful Baxter?

Nick took the three steps up to the Land Office porch in one leap and cut through the people at the head of the line like Moses parting the Red Sea. He disappeared through the door.

"Wonder what he's up to?" Mr. Sumner said.

Everyone seemed to wait for Callie to answer, so she did.

"I have no idea."

"Well, I have an idea," Roger Timmons said, looking around the little circle of neighbors. "Why don't we all drive home together? That way, we won't have our single lady going alone."

Callie tried to smile, in spite of the way his use of the word "our" grated on her nerves, but she had to bite her tongue to keep from making a sharp remark in front of her future scholars' parents. What a pompous person he was! And she had thought Mr. Fletcher was nosy!

"Oh, thank you," she said, as graciously as she could, "but I have some errands to do and don't know when I'll be returning."

The other women began giving her advice about the best places to trade in town, for they had been there overnight and felt like experienced travelers. Callie tried to pay attention, although the thought of spending any more of her meager amount of money made her stomach clutch in fear. She would have to buy food all winter, and from what her neighbors were saying, the prices here were worse than she had imagined.

"There he is," Roger Timmons said.

They all turned to see Nick almost upon them.

"Mrs. Sloane, may I impose upon you to come with me for a moment? I would be much obliged for the use of your wagon to take home some supplies."

She could only stare at him.

He actually flashed a thin version of his stunning smile at her, and then at the others.

"My packhorse turned up lame this morning and I couldn't bring him," he said smoothly. "You'd be saving me from starvation."

Liar, liar, pants on fire.

But she couldn't say that with everyone watching, with Mrs. Fletcher making sympathetic noises and Mrs. Sumner, she now saw, gazing up raptly at Nickajack's handsome face. Refusing to haul his suddenly urgently needed supplies would be a serious breach of rural etiquette—one serious enough to make these people think twice about entrusting their children to her as a teacher.

What in the world was he doing? For days

he had avoided her; now he was forcing himself into her company.

"You'll have to wait until I'm ready to leave," she said, "since I wrestled my obnoxious team all those miles to register my claim, not to start a freight service."

He touched his folded number in the pocket of his shirt.

"The officials have assured me that these numbers are sufficient to hold our places in line," he said. "We'll be back in plenty of time."

"How do you know that?" Roger Timmons demanded.

"They say it'll be at least an hour until they reach number 100," Nick replied.

He laid his hand possessively against her back, as he had done when she ran to warn him, and his huge palm and every finger set fire to her skin through her dress and her shift, as if she wore nothing at all.

Her treacherous body betrayed her will every time.

"Then come with me," she said shortly, angry at herself as much as at him.

"It's been nice visiting with all of you," she said, forcing a smile for her new acquaintances.

They replied in kind and Nick escorted her out into the street. They waited for a wagon to pass in its cloud of dust.

"Now we can get home before it storms," he said.

"What are you talking about?"

"Leaving this town. Standing in line at the land office is no place to be when a storm blows through."

"What storm are you talking about? And what about our registration assignments? I'm not leaving without one."

"I got 'em," he said, moving on out between vehicles and horses, "for a week from today, the first day of actual registration."

"Both of us? How?"

"A small bribe to a government official."

She stopped in her tracks in the middle of the street until he pulled her forward.

"But that's illegal!" she cried, feeling swept away by more forces beyond her control than his strong arm. "I resent it completely. You took it upon yourself to bribe someone on my behalf and without my permission!"

He flashed her a crooked grin. He looked for all the world like a mischievous boy.

"How dare you do something that might cost me my claim!"

She jerked away from him and stood staring.

"Back home, we know better than to ever trust a federal official. You should know that, too!"

He watched her, obviously waiting for her to calm down.

"Why would you take such a chance, Nick, after what Baxter said?"

She lowered her voice.

"What if that clerk heard him?"

"Better to strike first," he said, "and let somebody know I might make it worth his while not to listen to gossip."

"But you didn't have to risk my claim! You cannot make such a presumption as to speak for me! That's unforgivable!"

"You should thank me," he said, "instead of bawling me out."

She glared up at him. "My sentiments exactly, when I kept you from being brained by a falling two-by-four."

He didn't even have the grace to look chagrined.

"I'm going right back to the Land Office this minute and tell them you had no right to speak for me!"

He didn't turn a hair. "And wait in line for two hours to get a registration date three months from now? Giving Baxter time to file before you can?"

That stopped her.

For a long time, she couldn't even speak. They stood staring at each other while people walked around them and moved up and down the street.

"You are without a doubt the most infuriating man I've ever met in my entire life."

He smiled down into her eyes, and the heat of her anger flamed into desire.

"Maybe so," he drawled. "But I'm the man you won't forget for the *rest* of your life."

Chapter 9

~~~◦~~~

Callie still could not believe Nick had said such a thing. Not even an hour later, after they'd ordered his supplies, brought her wagon to the back of the mercantile to load them, and driven down the crowded street to leave Santa Fe behind. As they took the faint trail across the prairie, she sat beside him on the wagon seat and sneaked a glance at his finely chiseled profile.

He must have meant that she would never forget him for his take-over-her-business bossiness. It was true that no one could ever be his equal in that.

But the look he'd given her, with his gray eyes hot as smoke, had said he meant something else entirely. Could he really have been feeling the same unbidden desire that she'd felt at that moment?

It was hard for her to believe. Men didn't usually feel that way about her, for she was not the kind of woman who caught their attention with a willowy way of moving, or flowing black hair and porcelain skin, or quiet, thoughtful sayings. She was quick in her ways and her talk, and had freckles dotting her nose, which was too short for her ever to be called beautiful.

She sneaked another look at him, at his hands this time, wide and brown and strong as hickory on the lines. Joe and Judy were minding him like the most perfect team in the world.

Surely that kiss when she'd fallen off Judy into his arms had been a kiss of relief. It must have been an instinctive reaction to an escape from danger for both of them—something that any man and woman in the world would have done. It had not meant anything more.

The only explanation for his constant poking about in her life and trying to take it over, the only one that made a lick of sense, was that he liked to boss a woman and took it as his right. That scary thought made her heart beat so fast and loud that he surely could hear it.

What an irony! She had traveled over a thousand miles, vowing every step of the way that no one would ever have the power over her that her daddy had had, only to fall in with Nick Smith the very first thing.

"Now, Callie, admit it," he drawled, sending her a teasing, sideways glance, "isn't this a lot more pleasant than standing in line in the sun with Roger Timmons babbling in your ear?"

She gave him a sharp look of surprise. He almost sounded a tad bit jealous of Mr. Timmons' attentions to her.

"Maybe so," she said, "but if you really did spirit me away from there because you think it'll storm, you might've warned my scholars' parents. If they all blow away, I won't have enough children for a school."

He chuckled.

"But if they don't, you've got the job. They all seemed quite taken with you."

"Until I shamelessly went running off with you at the snap of your fingers. And what are they going to think of me when I don't come back in an hour?"

"Next time we see them, we'll explain that we saw a cloud coming up and decided to worry about registering our claims another day."

We. Our claims.

Any other time, she would have challenged that in her usual blunt fashion. She would have told him how strange that sounded, coming from a man who had sneaked into her camp so he wouldn't have to see or speak to her only three days before.

But it had a companionable sound, too, and those three days had been the lonesomest time of all her eighteen years. Baxter's sudden voice behind her and his beady eyes boring into hers had been downright scary. And every time she thought about the price of beans and meal and dried jerky in the mercantile and the precious baby she had to feed through the winter, she felt even more scared.

Right now, with the far-off dark clouds beginning to roll on the horizon, *we* was a pleasant word to hear. She was a strong woman or she wouldn't be in the Cherokee Strip in the first place. She was strong enough to hold her own with Nick Smith.

Who had inexplicably bribed an official to get her out of that crowded, dusty town and out here into the rising breeze.

The thought struck her like lightning.

"Blast it! There's another debt. Nick, how much do I owe you for the bribe?"

He gave her a look that reminded her, she couldn't say how, of his kiss.

"You're paying it," he said. "Hauling my supplies."

"Don't be ridiculous!" she cried. "You never intended to buy supplies until you'd already paid . . ."

She stopped.

"Nick, you bought these supplies and asked me to haul them just so you could say that it's payment for the bribe! You can't do that—it doesn't count. I'm determined to pay my way."

"But *you* didn't bribe anyone. So you're right, it doesn't count."

She drew a long, deep breath and prepared to argue.

Nick gave her a quick, sideways smile that stayed her tongue.

He had a beautiful mouth. Gorgeous. It was strong and proud and generous all at once. And it tasted sweeter than berries and cream.

She wanted to taste it again.

Heat rose in her cheeks. If the Fletchers and the Sumners knew that she'd already shamelessly kissed her bachelor neighbor once, and was longing to do so again, they would never let her be their children's teacher. When schools hired a woman, they preferred an innocent, never-married one who didn't know any more about such doings than the children, so she couldn't corrupt them.

Panic assailed her. What had her love for Vance been, a travesty? He'd been gone such a short time, and here she was, feeling this way about another man!

To make it worse, he turned to look full at her and his gaze slowly left her eyes and drifted down to her lips. She felt the heat of it all the way down to her toes.

Never had there lived a more aggravating, arrogant man—and she actually felt this way about him!

"You needn't sit so close," she snapped, and scooted even more toward her end of the seat. "There's plenty of room here."

"Pretty soon there will be," he drawled, "because you'll be off in the dirt if you run away from me any more." The chuckle in his voice made her face even hotter.

"I am not running away from you!"

To prove it, she slid toward him again and accidentally overdid it, ending up with her thigh pressed to his for a moment. Just that brief touch set her blood on fire. His muscles were like living iron, incredibly unyielding and powerful. Like the compelling look in his eyes.

It gave her a craving to taste his wide, sensual mouth again—which was all his fault. That kiss had been the sneakiest thing he'd ever done—including creeping into her camp to return the wheel without one word.

"I want you to take me seriously," she said, primly sitting away from him again. "How much do I owe you for the bribe?"

He slanted a long, slow look at her.

"Let's wait and see if it works," he said.

His eyelids grew heavier and at last he let

his gaze drift to her mouth, where it lingered.

"I do take you seriously, Callie."

His voice held the slightest edge of teasing, which irritated her.

"Is that why you followed me to town today? Do you take me so seriously that you watch my camp all the time, so you can sneak in and out when I'm not there and trail me if I go someplace?"

He grinned.

"Right. And in between I ride six or seven head of horses and do all my chores."

"Why are you riding so many every day?"

"To get them started on a useful life. To fit them to sell."

"Do you think you can sell enough to make your living?"

He nodded and glanced back at his big black horse, tied to the wagon.

"That's the plan. The Shifter and I don't want to be hitched to a plow."

"So the settlers you call intruders and always want to send to perdition will be your customers," she said. "You'll make your livelihood off them."

"Maybe," he said wryly. "But if they weren't here I could sell to the cattlemen who'd still be leasing the Strip."

"But then you wouldn't have anybody to follow around."

Anger sent a dark flush across his high cheekbones.

"I told you before, I don't want to ride up on your dead body one of these days on my way to town. That mare of yours is wild as a buck, and I didn't know whether you could keep her from running away with the wagon the way she did with you on her back."

"I told you before, I came out here to prove up a claim alone, and I can do it."

But her silly heart was beating out of her chest because he really did care if she lived or died.

He cocked his head and regarded her studiously from beneath the brim of his hat.

"You've got the try," he said, and she heard admiration in his resigned tone.

Well. Caring and admiration both in the same day.

"*You've* got the mystery," she said. "You don't speak to me for days, not even when you bring back my wheel, but then you worry about me enough to follow me."

"I reckon I was bound not to speak to you if you didn't want me to," he said. "I haven't forgotten that silent ride taking you home from my place, which you wanted to leave so bad that you couldn't even stay until your clothes got dry."

Nick heard those words come out of his mouth, he knew it was his voice saying them, but he still couldn't believe he had spoken his feelings right out loud. What had come over him?

Callie gave him a sharp look.

"I didn't mean to hurt your feelings," she said. "But I was . . . torn up by my memories that day."

Great. Not only had he sounded like a whiny child, he had reminded her of her dead husband when she hadn't been thinking about him at all.

"My feelings weren't hurt," he said quickly.

"Why not? I hardly said a word to you all the way to my place."

"I didn't wait to see you when I brought back your wheel because I was ashamed for letting you take that Judy home without me putting a few days on her," he improvised.

"That's not your responsibility," she said. "But if you're still willing to do that, when I get my school I'll pay you to teach her to behave."

That made him feel like a lazy skinflint.

"I'll do it for free," he said quickly.

"Why?"

That was Callie, always cutting to the quick.

"Because she's a mighty challenge," he said, and they both laughed.

Because I never knew anyone like you. Because I'd want to kill myself if that horse hurt you.

"Then why did you let me bring her back?"

To keep from getting tied to you. To keep from seeing you and talking to you and wanting to hear your voice.

To keep from wanting to kiss you again.

"So you could go somewhere if you wanted to. Ol' Joe probably couldn't pull this wagon all by himself."

Sudden darkness fell as a cloud blew across the sun.

Callie examined the sky. "You may be right," she said. "I think it'll storm."

"You can bet I'm right. But if you listen to me and do what I say, you'll be all right."

She laughed and turned her face away from the rising wind.

"Oh, sure, and who saved *you* from a two-by-four slamming into your head?"

He chuckled. "You'll never let me forget about it, will you?"

"Never."

Now, why had he said that? It sounded as if they planned to be together for months—or years—when that could never be true.

He scanned the sky, noting the gray-blue cloud layers building a wall in the southwest, feeling the heaviness of the air and the new moisture it held. The wind rattled his hat on his head.

"We may have to hunt a hole," he said. "It's hot enough to brew up a big one."

"Big what?"

"Dancing devil, my daddy called them. Cyclone, the white folks say."

"Would your daddy ever have thrown you off your homeplace—for any reason?"

The question sliced at his heart because of the hurt she tried to hide in her carefully calm tone.

"Only if I *really* crossed the line in a big way," he said. "If I hit my mother or set fire to the barn or ruined a horse on purpose."

He held his breath, paralyzed by the sudden, sharp need to know more about her.

"Did your . . ."

The word came slow to his tongue. Because he hated to think of her with another man.

". . . Husband's people run him off, too, when you married?"

She opened her mouth, then hesitated. She laid her hand on her belly.

He waited.

Thunder sounded, way in the distance. Judy pricked her ears toward the sound, lifted her head and tossed it, then tried her best to bolt, kicking at Joe as an afterthought. Nick got her back in line and still Callie hadn't answered.

Did you husband love you? Did he treat you right? What kind of a man was he, Callie?

"You know, Callie," he said, trying for a light tone to get him out of this, "that's what you need. A husband. Then you'd never have to drive this pair of knotheads again."

The instant the words left his lips, he wished for them back. How idiotically cruel! She was *grieving* for her husband. Or was she?

"Well, *you* need a wife," she said sharply. "So why don't you worry about that before you start faunching around about my not having a husband?"

Thank God she got prickly instead of sad.

"There's no comparison," he said.

She whooped with laughter, grabbing at her bonnet as the wind grew even stronger.

"There most certainly is! You're saying a wife isn't as necessary as a husband?"

"I can cook enough not to starve and I can clean my own cabin."

"And that's all a wife is good for?"

Instantly she clamped her mouth shut, regretting the words.

He smiled, enjoying her discomfiture, turning full on to give her a look. She blushed deep pink.

"Well," he drawled, one eyebrow raised, "I didn't say that."

She would be a little hellion of a wife, that was for sure. A man would never be bored.

He couldn't resist teasing her some more.

"And I'm not saying a woman doesn't need a husband for more than putting rims back on wagon wheels and driving a team."

He let the words lie between them.

She turned to him, a little bit embarrassed,

but the look she gave him was bold as brass.

"That's very broad-minded of you," she said, and then added, "and it's true, as I found during my marriage."

He nodded.

"Few women would admit to that for fear of not being considered a lady."

"I say what I think. It makes me feel better." Then she frowned and added, "Whether it changes anything or not."

"I'm for anything that makes for feeling better."

"No, you're not. You rarely say what you think."

That made him laugh out loud.

"How do you know what I think?"

She smiled up at him.

"I can read it in your eyes," she said, with such authority that it made him laugh again.

The wind gave a sudden gust so strong that it blew away the sound and made them turn to look at the cloud. It was huge, growing blacker by the second, and rushing toward them, taking over the whole sky. Callie's skin turned to chalk.

"Callie, would you go back there and close the canvas? I'd hate for those sacks of grain to get wet."

He tried to keep the tension out of his voice but near-panic surged through him. How could he have been so utterly foolish, so stupid, as to flirt and fool around and forget to watch the storm? Was he going to get them both killed?

She leapt up and started into the wagon.

"I can't close it," she said. "The flap's gone. But I have an oilskin I bought in Arkansas City."

"Hang on—we'll have to run for it!" he yelled and slapped the lines down on the backs of the team, who were only waiting for a chance to bolt.

With the wagon swaying and rocking, they raced across the prairie, heading for an arroyo he knew that was deeper than most. After that first, distant rumble of thunder the storm had been quiet, but now lightning cracked the sky and thunder shook the earth. Joe and Judy ran as if they had wings on their heels.

Nick glanced back over his shoulder. Sure enough, the wall cloud had begun to drop long tendrils toward the ground, reaching fingers that tried to touch the earth, wanted to grab anything in their path.

They stood out like evil monsters against the narrow strip of daylight that ran along the edge of the earth. Then, as he watched, it, too, vanished.

The day turned as black as the Shifter, who was having no trouble keeping up. The stallion could outrun even this fast pair on his worst day and over any terrain, and Nick wanted him cut loose. Anything could happen, and the horse had sense enough to take care of himself.

He had no hope of doing that now, though, and no chance of making Callie hear him over the rattling, creaking wagon and the pounding hooves. All he could do was get them into the cut in the earth that was the only shelter for miles, before the dancing devils grabbed them up to fandango with the wind.

Oh, God, he didn't want Callie to die. If she did it would be on his head, for he had brought her out here just in time for the storm.

The sudden rain hit like a wall of ice water and blinded him completely. His finger froze on the lines and his arms felt like lead, and he guided the wild team through sheer will in a direction he knew only by instinct.

Finally, a jagged strike of lightning lit the sky and he saw they were almost upon the arroyo. He pulled them at an angle to the right, and they surged down an old trail into the bottom of the dry creek bed. If the rain kept up like this it wouldn't be dry for long, but they'd get out of it as soon as the cyclones had passed overhead.

He drove up the creek a little farther, urged the team in closer to the bank, both for protection and to have it slow and then stop their wild race, then dived over the back of the seat and underneath the canvas cover as the storm came upon them with a roar.

"Callie!"

A terrible shaft of lightning cracked with a sound like the end of the world, and he saw her bent over the grain sacks trying to tuck the oilskin in. The blackness rushed behind the lightning, ready to devour them.

The cyclone was upon them, like a train bearing down on somebody trapped on the tracks. The dancing devil sucked every drop of air from his lungs.

He threw himself half the length of the wagon onto Callie and locked his hands behind his head, digging his elbows into the grain sacks on each side of her. Lying over her, praying for breath and for the cyclone to pass.

But it was just arriving. A shrill whistling tortured his ears, the whole atmosphere lifted, the wagon surged upward, and for an endless time he couldn't think of anything except the incredible force pulling them off the face of Mother Earth.

Just when he knew they were goners, the vehicle dropped back, rocking onto its wheels. With a last whooshing roar, the air came back into his lungs and hailstones began to beat against his back.

Unbelievably, Callie was breathing beneath him.

He sucked in all the air he could hold and

shouted through the noises of hail and rain, *"Shapeshifter!"*

The answering whinny made him sag with relief.

Ice lashed at his skin, the wind-driven rain poured through his clothes to chill his bones, but Callie's warm shape wouldn't let him freeze.

Callie—warm and soft and alive beneath him.

He laid his cheek against hers and wrapped her in his arms.

Chapter 10

The canvas wagon cover was gone, Nick realized dimly. It was the only explanation for the icy rain slashing at them and the wind stinging their skins. His mind struggled to think what to do next, but Callie was in his arms, turning to throw her arms around his neck. She clung endearingly, as if he were her only hope.

He cupped her head in his hands, her hair like wet silk under his palms, and tried to shield her as best he could. Faraway lightning showed him her face—her eyes wide and looking to him, her lips slightly parted. With a choked cry, he kissed her.

He drank in the hot honey of her mouth, let

it flow into his blood and trickle through his veins as if it were life itself, let it stream right straight into his heart without even a memory of the wall he'd built there. The dancing devil storm had left him on the earth, but this new Callie cyclone lifted him right up into the maelstrom.

All he knew was that his lungs lost all air and she gave it back to him. His mind lost all thought but she gave him his body, which had been half-dead for so long. She gave him all he needed—this sweetness and this trust, this heat from her soft arms against his neck, this closeness of his hands melded to her and his tongue entwined with hers. He would never need more than Callie's kiss.

Yet he did need to hold the soft breasts now glued against his chest by the rain. He deepened the kiss and dragged his hands desperately over the shape of her—molded her delicate jaw and long, graceful neck, slick with rain, explored the hollows of her collarbone and the curves of her shoulders, until his palms cradled her breasts and his thumbs found their tips, thrusting up to him through the thin cloth that barred his way.

He left her lips and began a hot trail of kisses down her throat to one of the hard buds that tortured him. Then he took it into his mouth and held her trembling against him while he suckled it. Vaguely, he heard her gasp.

"Nickajack!"

She thrust her fingers into his hair and held him to her so he wouldn't stop.

Her whole body was trembling, her heart galloping in rhythm with his. Her scent made him dizzy with desire; her hand stroked the back of his neck while she arched up to him.

It made him crazy with wanting her. He reached up under her rumpled, sodden skirts and stroked her silken thigh.

She stiffened and he let go of her breast. She grasped his face in her small hands and pulled it back up to hers.

"No," she gasped, "no . . . Nick, we have to stop . . . we must stop . . ."

He lowered his mouth and dragged his parted lips across hers and she answered with a sharp, quick thrust of her tongue that captured his in its sweet trap. They fell to kissing again as if they'd been born only for that purpose, for such a precious long heartbeat that his head went thick with pounding desire. Suddenly, with a cry that chilled him, she tore her mouth away.

Her breath was ragged, but her words rang clear.

"I can't. I can't do such a thing with you, Nick. I will never love anyone but Vance."

Even that awful declaration couldn't take

the sweetness out of the way she said, "You, Nick." Her voice was like the silver sound of a bell in the quiet of the night.

"Why not?" he blurted, amazing himself again by speaking his feelings aloud. "You said Vance is dead, Callie."

She winced.

"He is," she said hesitantly, "and I'm just as guilty as he was, but I'm alive . . . so I have to make our homestead dream come true."

"Guilty of what?"

Again she hesitated.

"Of loving each other. Of . . . being with . . . of marrying someone on the other side of the feud."

"From what you said, the two of you had nothing to do with starting that feud. You don't even know what it was about."

"I know. But I shouldn't have ever met him in the woods in secret that very first time he asked me to. I caused him to lose his life."

"I don't agree with that."

"It's true! He wouldn't't've been working so hard, wouldn't even have needed any money if he'd been with some other girl and planning to stay in the mountains."

"That was his decision, Callie."

"Mine, too," she said stubbornly. "I have to keep his memory alive."

Quick, hard anger at that hopeless line of reasoning surged through Nick. He bit his lip to keep from arguing with her. This was her business and none of his.

"The storm's gone," he said, and started to move away from her.

"Thanks to you," she said.

He laughed, he actually laughed, as he tried to rack his breathing back to normal.

"I didn't make it go away," he said.

"No, but you saved us from going with it," she said.

"Couldn't save your wagon cover, though."

The calm way he spoke, the cool, unhurried moves he made while untangling himself and getting to his feet, amazed him as much as the pain when she'd spoken of Vance. He was losing his sanity just because they'd had a narrow escape.

Well, he'd lived through many a brush with disaster and never gone *loco* before. His lonesome body was just making his imagination run wild because he hadn't held a woman for so long. It was disappointment he felt. Frustration. Thwarted physical desire. That was all.

Nick stood and reached down to help her to her feet, and Callie felt a whole new heat race through her. His mouth had already melted her bones; now the touch of his hard, strong hand turned her knees to jelly.

But he let her go as soon as she stood steady, and acted as if nothing had happened but the storm.

Finally, the last thing he'd said soaked into her addled brain.

"My wagon cover!"

She looked up into the lightening sky, into the growing patches of sunlight that showed between the curved ribs that usually held the cover. The reality hit her in the pit of the stomach.

"My shelter! This wagon's all the shelter I have. What if another storm comes?"

All the starch began to drain out of her spine. Dear Lord, she couldn't survive out in the open—and certainly not with this baby inside her.

The sun came out full strength right then, seemingly determined to show her the light. She'd already seen it. How could she hope to be self-sufficient now?

Nick went to the tailgate and jumped down. Even that small separation made her feel bereft, which made her furious with herself. She was *not* going to depend on him!

"My cabin's plenty big enough for two," he said, and went to hug the neck of his big black horse.

Fear sliced through her like a hot knife.

How could she ever push him away from her again? She'd used up all her fortitude, all her character . . . all her moral courage when she'd stopped him just now. Never, in her whole life, had she wanted anyone as much as she'd wanted him. Just imagining making love with him had set her on fire.

She certainly couldn't share his cabin with him and hold onto her virtue or her independence.

Then Judy gave a high, impassioned squeal and Joe roared back at her. Callie climbed toward the front of the wagon as Nick ran to the team, too.

Judy had managed to get one leg over onto Joe's side, astraddle of the shaft, and was kicking sideways at him even while she lurched back and forth, struggling to bring her leg back under her.

"Even a cyclone can't scare them into good behavior," Callie said, climbing down over the wheel. "When I'm a rich schoolteacher, I'm going to buy a real team. A good team. A well-trained team."

"Right now, I'd say trade them for a team of monkeys if monkeys could pull this wagon." Nick motioned for her to stand at Joe's head while he got Judy straightened out.

He did it so smoothly Callie hardly saw it happen. Of course, maybe she hardly saw it because she was looking at him, instead of what he was doing. The rain had plastered his thin shirt to his flexing muscles, and with sunshine spilling across the prairie and the darkness vanishing with the storm to the east, every powerful inch of him was highlighted just for her eyes.

She shouldn't be wanting him like this; shouldn't be wishing for another kiss, another touch, another time with his mouth on her breast ...

Fury with her faithless self washed through her.

Dear Lord, she was carrying Vance's baby! What would it think about having such a disgraceful, shameless mother?

And how dishonest that was toward Nick, who had saved her life and the baby's, he had staked her claim for her, and now was making her stubborn beasts behave. She could never repay him.

He straightened up and walked all the way around Judy, then Joe, checking every bit of the harness, running his hands down their legs and lifting their feet to look for damage from the storm. She had never seen a man move the way he did, with such a fluid power. She could watch him all day long.

Many, many women must have loved him. Had he ever loved any of them in return?

Maybe her kisses didn't touch his heart at all. Maybe he cared nothing about her as a person.

Her little voice of truth contradicted that at once. Hadn't he shielded her from the pounding hail? Hadn't he offered to share his shelter with her?

There was the thought that made her heart flee. She couldn't do that. She must not.

"They'll do," Nick decreed, coming around to help her back up into the wagon. "We'd better get moving."

"I need to go to my place."

But I want to go to yours.

The sun was full out now, lower in the sky but not near setting, and it bathed the prairie in a yellow glow. The wet grass smelled sweet and peaceful. For the first time since she'd come into the Strip, the daytime wind felt cool. It'd be a true comfort even to be on the same claim, in the same place with another human being, to enjoy this night. Her whole body and mind felt sore from fighting the loneliness.

"Why yours?" he said. "You can't stay there."

He jumped into the back of the wagon and stepped around and over her wet belongings to reach the seat.

"Yes, I can. I'll tie my oilskin between two trees for a roof until I get my soddy done."

But oh, how horrid it was to even think of it. She'd blistered her hands and made every muscle in her body sore for the dubious re- ward of half a wall on one side only. It would take her weeks to get all four walls high enough to hold a roof. Then how would she make that roof?

A terrible tiredness took her. At home, there had always been a dozen pairs of hands to help her. Now every one of her kin was a thousand miles away.

She reached for the lines, tried to take them from Nick's hard, strong fingers. But there was as much chance of that happening as of her sprouting wings to fly.

And just touching those warm hands that had brought her such pleasure made her weak to the core with desperate desire.

Panic sprang to life in her belly but she didn't dare acknowledge it.

"I can take care of myself," she snapped. "I can *drive* this team. I got to town, didn't I?"

"By the grace of God," he drawled.

"Well, then."

He clucked to the team and got them going, then turned them around to head back up out of the dry creekbed he'd called an arroyo.

"Well, then, what?"

"I. Can. Take. Care. Of. Myself," she said, through gritted teeth.

Her heart was pounding so hard she thought she could hear it.

"Of course you can," he said, "within reason. But not even gritty, no-obligations Callie Sloane from Kentucky can magically create a roof over her head tonight."

No roof meant no shelter from the sun to-morrow, when she rested from working on her house. No roof meant no protection if it hailed. No roof meant nothing at all between her and another cyclone sweeping out of the south-western sky.

The team came up out of the arroyo and headed out in the direction of their claims. Callie glanced at Nick. The western sunlight turned his skin to copper and threw his hand-some bones into sharp relief. The only flaw in his entire perfect face was a small, slightly bleeding cut on one cheekbone.

It struck her heart. The hail had cut him while he protected her. She wanted to touch the wound, to fix it, to kiss it away. She wanted that so fiercely, it scared her even more than the thought of depending on him.

Turning away, she dragged in a long, rag-ged breath. She had to think. She had to get away from him and think.

"I have some ointment," she muttered, scrambling up to go find it. "The hail cut your cheek."

"Forget it," he called, but she hurried into the back of the lurching wagon anyway.

In a moment she was back with the small jar.

"That storm was unbelievably precise," she said, "I just realized it took the cover and left everything else. Even the oilcloth is still over the grain."

He raised his eyebrow and gave her a look.

"We were on top of the oilcloth, if you recall."

He held her gaze while she felt her face grow hot. Yes, dear goodness, they had been on top of the oilcloth, clinging to each other with a passion. Truly a passion.

"Let me doctor that wound," she said, and her voice came out only a little bit shaky.

He turned to glance at the team quickly as if he, too, sensed the danger in that look.

"It doesn't need medicine."

"You sound like my six-year-old brother Jasper," she said a bit more steadily. "He's afraid every medicine will sting and burn."

He tried to ignore her but she waited. Finally, he shook the lines at the team and sped them up a little.

"All right. I'll prove I'm braver than a six-year-old."

Callie took the top off the jar, dipped her finger in the ointment, and reached up to him, willing her hand not to shake. The wagon lurched, Nickajack swayed toward her, and her finger pressed against his cheekbone harder than she'd intended.

"Oh, I'm sorry," she said, "I didn't want to hurt you."

His piercing gray eyes met hers.

"You can't hurt me," he said.

At that instant, she believed him. He looked as hard as this land he loved.

"Did you leave anything at your camp?"

This was the time to make him take her home. If she stayed at his place even one night, she'd be wanting to stay all the time. Just the words *your camp* sounded lonely.

"My plow."

"It'll keep."

"It might not," she made herself say. "Somebody might steal it."

"There's an old one in my barn. You can borrow it if yours disappears."

Why hadn't she told him she'd left something that she urgently needed? But what would that be?

She wrapped her arms around herself to try to stop the shivering caused by the wind hitting her wet clothes. Maybe fear was making her shake.

Her thigh lay perilously close to his, its long saddle muscles obvious under the worn, wet fabric of his tight jeans. She ripped her gaze away from it and stared straight ahead at the pricked ears of her team.

"Listen here to me, Nick," she said, clenching her jaw to stop the chattering of her teeth. "I cannot go to your place to stay. Not even for one night. I will not. I'm already obligated to you way past my capacity to repay."

It hit him wrong and made him furious—
somehow she knew that without even looking
at him. She knew, too, suddenly, that she'd
said it for that purpose.

"No, Callie, you listen to me," he growled,
anger vibrating in his low voice. "Think about
your own sermons you've preached to me:
sometimes you have to help your neighbors
and accept help from them."

"I don't need help."

She felt the disgust in the look he gave her.

"No. Of course not."

Callie turned on him.

"I'm not going to owe you any more than I
already do!"

His face flushed darker.

"I have never seen anyone so terrified of the
slightest obligation," he said, biting off every
word with a vengeance. "Do you trust me that
little? What are you afraid of, anyhow?"

You. Of my feelings for you.

"I told you. My father . . ."

"You told me," he snapped. "Does that
mean that you expect I'll find a way to throw
you out of your home the way he did?"

"No!"

"How could I? Your land will be registered
in your name."

"I know that! But anytime a person owes
debts, it puts his or her possessions in jeopardy."

He gave a bitter bark of a laugh.

"Oh, sure. I'm keeping a tally of every bit of help I give you and I plan to demand an acre of your land for each favor."

It did sound ridiculous, but she didn't care. This was what she'd wanted. Now they didn't feel close anymore. Now they had a wall of anger between them, and she intended to keep it there.

"Look," she said harshly, "just take me home."

"I should," he said. "Maybe the next hailstorm could knock some sense into your stubborn, hard head."

"I insist that you do."

"I'll regret that I didn't."

"Then take me home."

"Not until you have shelter."

"You are not responsible for me! How many times do I have to tell you?"

"I took you out of town and into the storm," he snapped. "I am responsible for the loss of your wagon top."

"I forgive you."

He turned on her, his gray eyes blazing.

"Look here, Callie, do you think I want you at my place, in my house? Do you think I want to sleep in the barn? What I want is to be alone with my horses without another human being in a hundred miles . . . and that includes you."

A sudden knot rose in her throat. How

could it hurt so much for him to say that to her? But it did.

They sat there on the seat in silence and drove across the fresh-washed land for mile after mile, with the creaking of the wagon and the jingling of the harness the only human sounds. The wind sighed and moaned against the rocks, and up ahead, birds Callie couldn't name called to each other. And all she wanted was to lay down and cry.

Why did she care if Nickajack didn't want her in his house? She didn't want to be there. Why did she feel this awful attraction to him?

But it wasn't attraction—it was only lust. Even now she could taste his lips on hers; even now she wanted to move closer so her thigh would be touching his. That proved it was only lust, because she would never be attracted to an ill-tempered man who didn't want her around.

She got up and went back to take Granny's quilt from her trunk. The storm had lowered the temperature twenty degrees at least, and wind kept making her shiver.

"I'll take you home right after morning chores," he said abruptly, when she returned to the seat wrapped in the quilt. "I'll leave you my buckboard until you can get a wagon cover."

"That'll be next week on registration day," she said, just as curtly. "In the meantime, I doubt it'll rain. I'll take the wagon."

"I'll see to it that your supplies dry out," he went on, as if she hadn't spoken a word, "and I'll bring them to you when you have a roof."

"If you're worried that I'll be so contented at your house that I'll never leave," she sniped, "set your mind at ease. I'm just as anxious to be rid of you as you are of me."

"Good."

Finally, when dusk was just beginning to fall, they reached the mouth of his canyon and drove up into it, following the curves of the creek, now filled with rushing water. The air smelled fresh as spring, washed clean of its dust, and it smelled soft, like a summer twilight. Yet there was nothing soft about this land or the man who lived here.

The canyon still called out to her spirit. Distant as it was from her mountains, it somehow felt a little bit like home with its walls folding closer around them the farther they drove.

They had been quiet too long, she realized. The air between them felt almost peaceful.

"You know you're kidnapping me," she said haughtily, as he drove into the yard of the weathered cabin.

"*You* know you're provoking me past all endurance," he snapped. "You're the most ungrateful roofless person I've ever met."

"I won't be roofless for long."

"It'll take at least three walls to hold one

up," he said dryly, and whoaed the team.

"I'll have three walls before registration day," she said. "You needn't worry about me."

A rude snort was his only answer. He dropped the lines, jumped down to the ground, and came to help her climb over the wheel, Granny's quilt thrown over her shoulder. She tried to keep her distance, tried to ignore the brief touch of his hand at her back, but the hot print of it went right through her clothes to her skin, before he pulled it away as if *she* were the one burning *him*.

The surge of desire rose in her again and briefly she pictured herself scrambling back up to the seat and driving away before he knew what she meant to do. If she had a grain of good sense, she would.

"Go on in and stir up the fire," he said, his deep voice so close she didn't dare turn her head. "Get a dry shirt from the cupboard. I'll see to the team."

She would stay here tonight for the baby's sake. After all, her feet squished in her shoes and her underthings were still soaked beneath her half-dry outer garments. She couldn't afford to get sick from wearing wet clothes for too long, now that the air was so much cooler. It would take more than an hour to drive back to her place, start a fire from scratch, and build it up big enough to do her any good.

When she started toward the house she

dared a glance at him. He was staring at two horses in a pen beside the canyon wall and seemed to have forgotten she was there.

"You were lucky," she said, "they don't seem to be hurt."

He answered with an irritable grunt and turned to lead the team to the barn lot. Callie climbed the steps to the porch, her legs a little unsteady. She hadn't eaten since breakfast, she realized suddenly. No wonder she felt weak.

She crossed the plank porch, pushed open the door, and closed it behind her to keep out the wind. Instantly, the house folded its arms around her, and she drew in a long, shuddery breath.

Her nostrils filled with the homey scents of woodfire and cedar, every pore in her skin opened to this space closed off from the wind. For the first time since leaving the train, she stood under the roof of a house.

Coals glowed deep inside the fireplace which took up most of one wall. The wide hearth held wood stacked at one end of it, next to an iron stove that sat in the corner.

She stood still for a moment, letting the quiet move over her, listening to the wind blow around the corners of the cabin. Then she spread the damp quilt over a rocking chair and went to build up the fire. Her wet shift stuck to her skin as she knelt and reached for the poker. As soon as she had the fire going, she'd run to the wagon for a change of her own clothes.

The thought stayed her hand in the air. She had no dry clothes! Her few extra garments were in a carpetbag, which was so full, it stood open to the sky. Everything in it was bound to be soaked, since the quilt had gotten damp in the trunk.

Her books! Oh, dear goodness, her books might be ruined—although the carpetbag had been wedged in on top of that box. She stood up, intending to run out to see to her things, but then she turned back to the fire. That would be the fastest way to get some things dry tonight.

As she stirred up the coals, she had a terrible realization. This was the very first time since the storm that she'd given serious thought to her possessions. They were all she owned in the entire world, all of them entirely necessary to her survival, yet Nick had filled her mind and driven them out.

Dear Lord above, she should never have agreed to stay here, not even for one night.

Desperately, she looked around her, searching for distraction, but everything she saw spoke of Nick. He was neat and orderly in his house, as in his barn, and everything in the room was either useful or beautiful or both.

She found kindling in a basket near the stack of wood and concentrated on making some flames flare up and grow. Stretching out her hands to the fire, she soaked in the warmth, ignoring her growling stomach, for she was shivering in earnest, now that she'd thrown aside the quilt.

She'd have to get dry and warm, or shake herself to death. The baby was the one she'd better be thinking about, instead of her arrogant, bossy host. As soon as the fire had caught and would keep on burning, she would do as he'd said and find one of his shirts to wear. He was so big, it would cover her completely.

The blaze settled into a steady crackling, so Callie turned to cross this main room. Her gaze clung to the oil lamp and the writing supplies laid out on the small oak table that stood against the wall. It was the paper and pen that called to her.

What she would give to sit down there and pour out on paper all the wild emotions of this day. Maybe if she could see them set down in black and white, if she could *read* them, she could make sense of them.

Near the table was a slat-backed rocker. That was something she'd need after the baby came—something she'd forgotten until now. She was walking through luxury here, compared to the way she'd been living.

She shivered again and resumed her search

for the shirt, but at the door of Nick's bedroom, she stopped short.

He had spread the coverlet straight on his bed before he'd headed for town. A tall, beautifully plain cupboard in the corner that must hold his clothes glowed reddish brown in the twilight streaming in at the double windows. A matching chest had nothing on its gleaming surface except one large eagle feather and a woven basket.

Callie made herself go straight to the cupboard, although she wanted to look at and touch every beautiful object. He was such a private person that she felt like an invader, but he *had* told her to do this. Otherwise, she'd be naked when he came in.

The thought made her blush. It also brought to mind a picture of what *he* might look like without any clothes at all, and to her chagrin, a strong surge of desire began to heat her skin from the inside. All the feelings of the kiss came back, and more.

She opened the double doors on the top half of the cupboard, grabbed a shirt off one of the two low, carefully folded stacks she found there, took a towel from the shelf below, and hurried back into the main room. In the corner she'd glimpsed stairs going up to a loft, so she'd change there in case Nick came in. She ran up the narrow stairs.

Hastily, standing in the darkest corner, she

stripped, toweled the dampness from her skin with the big, rough towel, and pulled Nick's shirt over her head. It fell to her knees, so she was decently covered, yet she was scandalously bare beneath, for she couldn't stand the thought of putting on her damp pantaloons again. Fortunately, this was a heavy shirt he couldn't see through.

Feeling infinitely better just to be dry, she gathered her wet clothes and held them at arm's length as she went back down the stairs. The table with the inkwell and papers was straight below her; in the late-afternoon light she could see that the top page was a letter. It began, *Cousin, I hope this finds you well.*

Oh, how she would love a letter from one of her cousins right now! Better yet, if she could receive even the shortest note from Mama . . .

Then the black scrawl leapt up at her from the white page again and she forgot about herself.

I take pen in hand to warn you that any return of yours to the Nation would be as much as your life is worth. Also, watch your back where you are.

The words *life* and *watch your back* had been darkly underlined twice. Slowly, Callie descended, her feet feeling for each next step, her eyes paralyzed moving on to the next paragraph.

There is talk that maybe you're at your old home in the Strip and some have sworn to hunt you there. They are naming you childkiller and traitor, even putting a price on your head. Few say aloud anymore that Goingsnake is a Raven. Instead, they say that you deliberately put the boys between those bullets and yourself.

Abruptly, the message was signed, *Fox.*

She reached the wide plank floor and ran to the desk, hoping that she had read wrong. Lifting the glass chimney from the lamp, using one of the lucifers lying beside it, she lit it quickly and picked up the page.

Dear God, protect him. Protect him.

Nick couldn't die, like Vance. She couldn't bear it.

Nick stood at the front door, not wanting to enter. No, wanting too much to enter.

If seeing the glow of light through the window had made him have visions of Callie moving around in his house, tending the fire, lighting the lamps, waiting for him, the actual sight of her would pull at him like the Shifter to a mare. It had been all he could do not to take her right there in the wagon in the middle of a driving storm.

It was time he got hold of himself. He had lived alone for a long, long time, he didn't need anyone else—especially not a woman. Particularly not a woman in love with her dead husband. They could be friends as well as neighbors, but nothing more. He must remember that.

He reached out, pushed open the door, and stepped through it.

His blood turned to a river of ice. He had thought he could trust Callie, of all women, but there it was—Fox's letter shaking in her hand.

"You would read my mail, Callie?"

The words came out in a harsh, croaking voice he'd never heard before.

She looked up, her green eyes wide and filled with panic, her face so pale the freckles stood out plain. Oh, God, after reading the letter, now she was afraid of him. She believed what people were saying about him.

"Who are these people calling you a child-killer?" she demanded, fierce as a she-bear with cub. "How *dare* they say such a thing about you?"

He stared at her, unable to believe it was anger, not fear, in her voice. But her eyes flashed green fire; she was ready to fight.

This must be his imagination at work. *He*

was the one who was angry because she was prying into his private business. But no, *she* was furious—not afraid, not embarrassed; so incensed that she didn't even care that he'd caught her going through his papers.

"Anyone who has met you, even anyone who has *seen* you, would know this is pure slander. Do you think they'll really come here to try to . . . hurt you?"

She *didn't* believe it. She wasn't afraid of him—she was taking his part!

A shaft of sweet happiness went straight to his core.

She was worried about him; she feared for his safety. Callie cared about him.

The cold stone that was his heart finally cracked beneath the heat in her eyes and her voice.

Chapter 11

~~~ᴗᴗᴗ~~~

He felt he was falling into a hole with no bottom.

Her eyes *blazed* on his behalf. When had anyone ever stood up to champion him? Not since his long-ago days as Goingsnake.

Her anger gave way to worry.

"Would they really come here to try to kill you, Nickajack?"

Her voice broke over his name; her green eyes glistened with sudden moisture. Just the question alone was enough to set his blood beating through his body in a wild dance of excitement. Just the sound of his real name, his whole name, on her lips set his heart racing.

He wanted to go to her, to hold her, to hold onto her.

When had anyone ever cared, to the point of tears, whether he lived or died? Not since he was seventeen and the ague had felled his mother.

He had to make her stop looking at him that way or he'd be lost forever, falling in love with her!

But that was the one thing he must never do. Callie could still betray him as Matilda had done—there was plenty of time left for that. Less than one moon past, he had never even met Callie Sloane from the Cumberland Mountains of Kentucky—and one moon from now he might find out that she was not as honest as she looked.

He needn't worry, though—not really. He couldn't love anybody. A loner never could.

Yet her concerned question was playing like music in his ears, and the crack in his hard heart opened a little bit wider.

"Who knows?" he answered. "People are hard to predict."

"But you would never hide behind anyone!"

"Those parents are sick with sorrow," he said. "And after all, I *am* a child-killer."

She stared at him wide-eyed, as if she hadn't understood the words.

"No! That's not true!"

He forced his legs to move, to carry him on into the room.

"I'm the cause of two fine boys dying long before their time. Their families and their friends want to kill me, and who can fault them for that?"

He meant to keep on walking, to turn his back on Callie and go stir up the fire. Her eyes held him, though, so wide and intense that looking away would seem cowardly.

"So you knew somebody was going to shoot at you at that exact place and time."

Good. Now she was starting to believe the worst. If she hated him, maybe he would no longer be drawn to her.

Yet it hurt so much to lose her faith that his breath stopped. He finally dragged in enough air to speak, but not enough courage to tell her the lie that might end everything between them.

"I led them into an ambush."

"Oh," she said, and the faint tinge of sarcasm in her tone came through loud and clear.

It had been there in her earlier statement too, he suddenly realized. He'd guessed wrong about her again.

"So," she said, prim as the schoolmarm she wanted to be, "you rode ahead of, or behind, those two fine boys and forced them into a spot between you and the bullets that were about to fly—a spot where you knew they'd be killed and you'd be protected."

She was taking up for him again, and everything in his soul warmed and reached for more. He had to put a stop to this.

"They would've followed me to the gates of hell and through them. It was my call."

He had to turn away from that fierce championship in her eyes. As soon as he could, he would.

"Did you *know* the ambush would be there?"

"No," he snapped. "Then it wouldn't have been an ambush, would it?"

He tore his gaze from hers and strode to the fireplace, then grabbed up the poker like a man possessed.

God help him, he caught her scent of flowers right behind him. He didn't turn around.

"Goingsnake was a killer? A killer of his own men?"

Paper crackled; she must be waving the letter in the air.

He wheeled to face her.

A mistake. A terrible mistake. His body ignored the fears bombarding his mind. It filled with desire at the sight she made, standing there barefoot in what must be nothing but her skin and his big shirt that fell all the way to her knees, her hair still damp and tousled around her face, its color catching all the lights of the fire.

Clothed only in his shirt and her indignation on his behalf.

"You have no right to read my letter," he said, miraculously making his voice come out low and cold in a tone that usually made grown men quail, "much less to question me about it. Put that back where you found it."

"What's a Raven?"

"A hero, someone who's done great things. Which Goingsnake did not."

"Several people must have thought he did, if he was called that at one time."

"They never should have called him that."

"Because he couldn't save those boys?"

"And because he couldn't stop the Board of Governors from selling the Strip."

He hated her for making him speak, for pulling those words out of him against his will, facing off with him as if they were old, sworn enemies. And he loved her for standing there so passionately on his side as if they were old, faithful lovers, for making him want to reach out and pull her body to his.

His arms, his legs ached to do it. Only three steps separated them.

She wouldn't let go of him. Her burning gaze held his, her lips, parted with the passion of her cause, called to his own. He ought to kiss her to shut her up.

But a kiss would be only the beginning, this time. This time he would take her completely, and that would make him lost forever in loving her. And what if she turned out to be as treacherous as Matilda?

"So the Board of Governors kept you from getting one of the Indian allotments in the Strip? Your love for this whole land caused you to lose your part of it?"

"You sound like a Pinkerton man."

She didn't sound—or look—like any man on this earth. She was all woman, a woman determined to defend him.

"Is that what happened?"

She waited for a lifetime, holding him fast with her eyes.

Finally, he answered.

"Ironic, isn't it?"

"How much danger are you in?"

He scowled.

"You sound like you're buckin' for a job," he snapped. "I can watch my own back."

"Not the night of the Run, you couldn't."

"That was only an excuse to make sure no claim jumper came and jerked up your flag," he said nastily, knowing how hard she had striven to be independent. "If I'd realized then that you're brave enough to hire out as a bodyguard, I wouldn't have worried about you."

Hurt flashed across her face and she held

her breath, silent for a minute as she searched his eyes. He felt like a low-down liar because she had helped him that night, too. It was a lie for a good cause, though. *Something* had to make her turn against him, or he'd be a goner.

"But I'm not the one with a *bounty* on my head."

He ignored that and dropped to his haunches in front of the fire, turning his back on her.

"I wonder how much they're offering," she said thoughtfully. "And who I should notify if I decide to turn you in."

He threw her a quick glance over his shoulder.

She laughed.

"Oh, Nickajack, you're acting just like my brothers, being all hateful, trying to shut me up."

Then her whole tone changed and he felt her come closer.

"When you went by the name of Going-snake, you were putting actions to the feelings of your heart. That's the most heroic thing any human being can do. That's why people gave you the title of Raven."

The words, the soft way she said them, tore like a tornado right through his body. God help him, he wanted to turn and pull her to him, into his lap, to bury his head in her breast. He wanted her in his arms, here on the hearth rug in front of the fire. He wanted his mouth on hers . . .

But then he would *really* love her, and she would still be in love with her dead husband. As if it mattered. He didn't *want* anyone to live with, ever.

"Yes," he snarled, "I knew selling it would be to our eternal shame. Ignorant settlers like you will tear out the heart of this land and for no profit. You'll never survive here, Callie."

He hated himself for going for her jugular, but desperate times called for desperate measures and he was only telling the truth. He had encouraged her in her fantasy for too long. He threw down the poker, stood up, and left the room without looking at her again.

"I'll sleep in the barn," he said, when he returned from the bedroom with a blanket.

He kept his face turned away from her all the way to the door, but stopped after he'd opened it.

"There's food in the springhouse and in the pie safe," he told her, without turning around. "Help yourself."

Her light, silvery mountain voice thrilled him as if it were her hand on his skin.

"How much danger are you in, Nick? Are the families of those boys or some money-hungry old enemies likely to come here?"

"No," he said. "Those families hated losing the Strip as much as I did, and their grief's not as fresh now. Fox's message is two seasons old."

He needed to leave her, he had to leave her—but not so that he'd be lying out there in the barn awake all night, imagining her here in the house with her heart full of support for him. Here was his last chance to destroy this insidious bond between them, and these insane emotions pulling at his heart.

"I'm the one who told Matilda where we'd be that day," he said, "after they all followed my orders and kept the secret. I am the one who killed them."

He turned away from her then, toward the new, cool night coming on, and forced himself to walk, not run, out of the house, across the porch, and all the way to the barn. Never, not even in the ambush, had he been in worse danger: all he wanted was to stay with her and take her into his arms.

Callie dug her toes into the braids of the rug to keep from going after him. He had a price on his head. No wonder he wanted to keep people off his place and away from him.

A flood of caring almost overwhelmed her. He was banished, too. He was hurting as much as she had been the day she'd walked out of the Sloane Valley knowing she could never return.

A wild tangle of feelings seized her and drew her several steps toward the door with the letter still in her hand. Partly, she needed to see him that instant; partly, she wanted fiercely to comfort him. With a touch.

Her little voice of truth demanded more.

With a kiss. She wanted to comfort him with a kiss.

She could still see his face—jaw hard, mouth set, his look completely expressionless except for the pain he couldn't quite keep out of his shadowed eyes. All she wanted was to see them heavy-lidded and focused on her lips, then glazed and dreamy from her kiss.

Wanting it so badly took her all the way to the door. She caught herself as she reached for the latch.

She must be losing her mind. This deep, wrenching feeling wasn't all sympathy and understanding for him; she had always hated injustice, that was it.

No doubt she would feel this same way about anyone else in his situation. It was just as unjust for Nick to have a price on his head for standing up for what he believed in, as for her to be banished from home for loving Vance, the man destiny had sent to cross her path on top of the mountain that long-ago day.

But Nick still lived in *his* home! The thought brought a welcome anger that she reached for and nourished. And she was in as much danger of starving to death—or more—as he was of being killed by old enemies in the faraway

Cherokee Nation. Why should she feel so sympathetic to him?

She did, though. He must have left that letter lying on top of that table for two seasons to punish himself, to remind him every time he walked past that those boys had died in his care.

Trying her best, she recovered some of her anger as she turned back into the room. He'd had no reason to say such horrible, discouraging things to her. In fact, he was a greedy pig, because one claim was all he needed and he was coveting the whole huge Strip. She hadn't had one inch of land until she'd staked her claim.

Ungrateful wretch! If this hateful treatment was the thanks she got for being sympathetic with him, then tomorrow she would tell him what a miserable ingrate he was. After that, she'd go to her own place and stay away from him. She would put all her energy toward survival for herself and her baby, instead of toward sympathy for him, and that would take care of these crazy feelings of desire.

They probably stemmed from her condition, anyway. Ever since she'd been with child her feelings had run away with her in a heartbeat, whether they were sad or happy or angry or mean. No, she didn't really care about Nick Smith, and she felt attracted to him only because she had been lonely too long.

Callie deliberately filled her mind with memories of times spent with Vance while she put the letter back where she'd found it and tended to the fire. She thought about his soft blue eyes and his curly brown hair.

Try as she would, though, she couldn't quite get his face clear in her mind when she finally dropped, exhausted, onto Nickajack's bed.

For all the nights they waited for their assigned day to return to town and register, they lived like that—she in the house, he in the barn. During the days, they stayed apart on their separate claims. Nick wanted to help her with her soddy, but she absolutely would not hear of that.

Callie protested mightily about moving back to her own place for the nights, too, but her things were spread all over his barn to dry, there was absolutely no shelter on her claim except for the few trees which would attract lightning in any storm, and the awful memory of the cyclone was too fresh to forget. Her safety was the baby's safety, so she must stay under Nick's roof until she had her own. Another hard thunderstorm came through in the middle of the week and proved that a wise decision.

Every morning Callie cooked Nick's breakfast to pay for her bed, refused his offer to help her build her house, packed herself a jug of water, two biscuits, and some jerky, then drove to her claim and resumed the endless chore of cutting sod bricks and stacking them into walls. It took every ounce of her perseverance to even dream of having a roof up before winter, every scrap of hope in her heart to keep on with the monotonous, backbreaking labor, but she did it.

On the second day, when the morning sickness came down on her again and she spent what seemed an hour doubled over, throwing up into the sand, she had to literally force herself to go on. It continued every day thereafter, even stronger than at the very beginning of her pregnancy.

She learned to endure it, though the sun was halfway up in the sky every morning before she managed to make much progress. She worked and tried to think of things to be thankful for, while she sweated and ached and watched her walls grow one or two levels of bricks in a day. It made her glad that she hadn't let Nick help her and, therefore, find out about the baby. She was thankful she could keep her suppers down, and the meager snacks at noon, so the baby wouldn't starve. And she was relieved Joe and Judy had been more tractable ever since the tornado. Joe was even pulling the plow to cut the soil!

She was grateful, too, that she still had strength left at night to cook Nick's supper to pay for the shelter he gave her. After the second day, he gave up protesting that she needn't do that and she gave up feeling she would owe him her life before she ever got started proving up her claim.

So, every afternoon she drove up the draw back to his cabin before he quit working for the day—he hardly ever quit riding until dark. Each time, she found him astride a young horse in the shady catch pen or working with it from the ground. He had a half-dozen of them fenced with brush into a long, narrow meadow at the top of the canyon, horses he had taken from the wild and was starting.

Besides all those horses, he had a smokehouse full of curing venison and turkey strung from the beams, and a small herd of cattle grazing among the timber. Nick had been back here long enough to prepare so that he was already nearly self-sufficient for the winter.

She must get ready for winter.

That had been the chant in her head that kept her cutting sod bricks and stacking them all morning and half the afternoon, but now it had lost its power. Her legs were shaking, her arms were going limp, and her stomach was roiling from the heat and no food because she hadn't taken time to eat even a bit of jerky at noon time. She hadn't rested then, either, not more than ten or fifteen minutes. There simply had not been time, for her walls were nowhere near high enough to stand up in after the roof was on, though she'd been working steadily for almost a week.

Reality struck her in the heart. After all this pain and agony, all those hours in the sun, she had built only half-walls, breast-high to her short stature. She couldn't afford to take time out to rest, no matter what.

Yet she had to, or fall face down on the ground. The heat shimmered off the rocks and hung in the dust like a curtain. It was pressing in on her from all directions, even through her hat. It was making her dizzy. She had to stop for a while and rest.

Yet she couldn't. She wouldn't. She absolutely would not because winter would come and she and her baby could not survive without shelter. She would not depend on Nick any longer than necessary.

She swiped with her sleeve at the sweat running down beneath the handkerchief she'd rolled and tied around her forehead below her hat. Then, with a deep, shivery sigh to try to steady herself, she picked up her plow again and tried to stick it into the ground. To her dismay, when Joe started walking, it only slid along the surface and raised a cloud of dust.

It was taking too much of her precious water to soften the sod enough for cutting. She was trying to *save* water, for heaven's sake— but she reached for the full dipper on the wall anyway. The earth she hadn't yet watered was simply too hard. She would haul some more water from Nick's in the morning.

Her whole arm shook, but she ignored that. "Callie!"

She stopped, the trembling dipper raised, and tilted her head to listen.

Hoofbeats.

Her heart clutched. Was it Nick? Had she really heard her name or not?

She poured the water and then straightened to shade her eyes and watch for whoever was coming. In truth, she should go get the gun from her wagon but her legs didn't have the strength. Really, truly, she thought it was Nick.

"Hey, Callie!"

It was.

Nick rode over the horizon, astride a tan horse with black legs and mane and tail that he called ol' Dun, in spite of the fact that the horse was only a three-year-old. Ol' Dun's training had just begun and he was jumping around, apparently trying to buck.

Nick sat him easily, his expression unconcerned, his eyes focused on her.

"No wonder he's trying to throw you ..." Callie said, but the words came out as a hoarse whisper that she herself could hardly hear.

The dizziness hit her again, and she leaned on the handles of her plow.

Nick rode up, swept one quick glance over her, and swung down out of the saddle. He had canteens and tools and bags of things tied across the horse, front and back, flopping against the animal's sweaty sides, which was the point she'd been trying to make when she lost her voice.

"Time to go to the shade, Miss Sunshine," he said, taking her by the arm before she could open her mouth to protest.

She shook her head.

"Not yet . . ."

This time, even less sound came out.

He looked at her sharply. When he saw that she really couldn't speak above a wheezing whisper, a flicker of irritation showed in his eyes but he didn't let it into his voice.

"Remember tomorrow's the last day before registration day," he said, "so you'll need to quit early then. I just thought I'd ride over and help you make up for that lost time today."

"What a pitiful excuse! You came because you thought I didn't have enough sense to come in out of the sun," she croaked painfully.

He raised one eyebrow.

"We-e-ll," he drawled, giving her a significant look, "you said it. I didn't."

She opened her mouth to protest, but her throat felt like cotton and this time she couldn't get out any more than a dry wheezing sound.

"Over here," he said, speaking with cheerful authority as if she were a child for whom he was responsible. "You just sit right down here in the shade of this old cedar tree and let me get you a cool drink."

He brought ol' Dun into the shade with her, took down one of the canteens, removed the cap, sank onto his haunches beside her, and held it to her lips, although she reached for it.

"Let me," he said, with irritating censure creeping into his voice. "I happened to notice you're a little shaky right now."

She let him tilt her head back into the palm of his big hand, and drank the cool water that slid down her throat as sweet as nectar. After a bit, he lowered the canteen and set it down on the ground beside him. Then he took off her hat and untied the handkerchief from around her head.

His touch was heavenly and, even in the state she was in, she wanted more. Wanted him to stroke her cheek with his long, strong fingers, wanted him to cup her face in both his huge hands . . . wanted him to kiss her now that he was so close . . .

But he was all business. He poured water on her handkerchief and washed her face, then wet it again and held it to her forehead.

"You nearly got your stubborn mountain self too hot out here on the prairie," he said.

This time he didn't even try to conceal his annoyance.

"How many times this week have I told you to go to the shade for a while at least twice, morning and afternoon?"

She wouldn't take a chance on her voice quite yet, so she had to content herself with making a face at him.

"So," he said disapprovingly, as if he were the teacher of the two of them, "you haven't been following my orders. Have you?"

Callie couldn't help but smile.

"I wouldn't think of disobeying you, Nick," she said in a whisper, "You know that."

"Sure. That's why I had to ride over here to see what you were doing. When you drove in last evening, your face was red as the sunset."

"Only because Judy was misbehaving," she rasped, holding out the handkerchief for him to wet it again. "I was red because I was embarrassed."

"You'll be dead if you don't listen to me," he snapped, with a worried frown. "Damn it, Callie . . ."

"It's all right, it's all right," she soothed. "I've learned my lesson, Nick, really I have. I was getting woozy right before you came. I won't do it again."

He looked at her long and hard.

"I promise," she said, lifting one still slightly shaky hand.

"All right," he growled, his tone doubtful. "Sit here and rest awhile. Drink some more in a minute."

She did as he said and didn't even protest when he got up, took down another canteen, and strode to her plow with his long-reaching, free-flowing gait. Then he stripped off his shirt.

It was soaked with sweat and clinging to him, showing clearly how his big muscles rippled beneath it and how his broad shoulders tapered to his taut, slim waist and hips. He peeled it off and threw it over one of her pitifully short walls of sod.

"I don't know why you want more bricks anyway," he called in a teasing tone. "You've got four walls up. Why not slap on a roof?"

She laughed and managed to call back with her voice only slightly trembly now.

"That was my plan, until I realized I'd have to walk on my knees all the time."

He laughed, too, then picked up the lines, threw them over his shoulders, and took hold of the handles of the plow. He called to Joe, and the mule pricked his ears and moved out as if he knew a masterful voice when he heard one.

Nick's back gleamed with sweat in the sunlight, which turned his skin to such a rich copper color it looked as hot as his kiss had been.

That was the wrong line of thinking. She

could remember exactly how his lips felt and how they tasted, and the memory filled her with such deep longing that she couldn't look away from him.

He was the most magnificent man she'd ever met.

Vance had been muscular and handsome, yes, but . . .

The disloyalty of the thought made her mind jerk away from it. She was friends with Nick. Friendship was all that would ever be between them; she didn't want any more, and neither did he.

But Nick was the strongest man she'd ever met.

To keep the plowpoint cutting in a straight line, which she was never able to do, he held the handles firmly in front of him and the point upright. That took considerable power, and made the muscles across his shoulders and back flex and tighten beneath his glistening skin.

Callie couldn't take her eyes away. She couldn't get her breath. She couldn't think anymore.

If she couldn't get up and go to him and run the palms of her hands over his shoulders, and follow that trickle of sweat down his spine with her fingertips, then she had to hear his voice, had to meet his eyes.

She took another drink of water and called to him.

"For somebody so scornful of farmers, you seem pretty handy with a plow."

He laughed, turned Joe, and started back toward her.

"Careful with the insults," he called back. "Don't bite the hand that feeds you."

At that moment she didn't care that he was feeding her; she didn't care that she was obligated to him for food and shelter and for this work. She was too mesmerized to tell him to stop. All she cared about was listening to the low, easy tone of his voice, and watching the way a lock of his hair fell across his forehead.

This would be a memory to warm her this winter.

Chapter 12

The next day Callie did quit early—
because of Nick's suggestion, she told
herself. Because she was excited that tomorrow would be registration day, a day free from
this monotonous toil, this backbreaking work!

Or maybe, her little voice of truth said, it
was because she wanted to get back to Nick.

Whatever the reason, she stopped stacking
bricks when the sun was only halfway down
the afternoon sky, put away her tools, hitched
the team to the wagon again, climbed into it,
and took the lines, hoping she wouldn't have
to pull on them much since she had new blisters on her hands. She got her wish. The drive
back to Nick's place was peaceful and more

enjoyable than usual, since she wasn't quite so tired.

When she came into the yard and drove past his training pen into the barnlot, they exchanged waves but she didn't linger. Last night and this morning she had made herself maintain her distance, although that incredible pull she felt toward him had grown stronger and stronger ever since he had come to see if she was working too hard in the heat.

She climbed down, unhitched her team, turned them out into what Nick called the pony pasture, and started toward the house. It'd be much better for them both if she kept up the routine they'd had all week, mainly spending time together only at meals.

But her feet felt leaden, her skin hot, and there was a pleasant, almost cooling breeze springing up. The shade of the trees surrounding his corral beckoned like an oasis in the desert, so she went in that direction, instead of the cabin.

But it wasn't just the breeze. Right now she had to have the comfort of a little human companionship, or die. Right now she needed to talk to Nick.

He was riding with his head cocked to one side, looking down at the young yellow horse, completely absorbed in its movements—a random circle here, a figure-eight there. It must be following Nick's commands, but she couldn't see him giving any.

Callie walked into the shade, sweeping her hat off to fan herself with the wide brim. The corral fence was old and stout, built of peeled logs. Nick's father must have built it.

She climbed up and sat on the top log, unable to tear her gaze away from Nick. His pale blue shirt clung to him, the dark V of sweat between his shoulder blades showed the flexing of his muscles almost as clearly as no shirt at all. And the powerful way he sat, the proud way he held his head, made her breath catch in her throat.

His long legs held the colt and guided him, the muscles of his thighs controlling the thousand-pound animal with an easy strength that looked like magic. A new-old longing came over her, powerful as the waterfall on the north side of Sloane Mountain. It made her weak in the knees and the sweet spice of his mouth came onto her tongue. She let the hat fall.

She wanted him to ride over here, reach up and pull her down onto the horse with him; wanted him to hold her close, close, so she could turn her face up for his kiss . . .

But she might as well be back in Kentucky, for all he knew. He had the horse sauntering around the other side of the corral and they were absorbed in each other as if they were the only two creatures on earth.

Sudden jealousy of an *animal*, of all things, shocked her to consciousness. What was she thinking? She still loved Vance, no matter how much she admired Nick. She did, didn't she? She couldn't be starting to love Nick.

He came around the circle of the fence, his head still cocked, still watching and listening for messages from the horse. While she watched, a sudden, terrible premonition that he was in danger made the hairs on the back of her neck stand up. A rifleman from the Nation, bent on revenge, could be in the trees anywhere. He could be within a stone's throw and Nick wouldn't know it, wrapped up in that horse as he was.

She opened her mouth to call to him, then shut it again, not knowing what to say that he wouldn't ridicule. As he rode closer, she straddled the fence—awkwardly in her skirts—and thrust her feet in between two of its logs so she could stand up to scan the grove of trees and the sides of the canyon above and behind him. The feeling faded, though, instead of getting stronger. It must have meant nothing.

"You'll fall off that fence if you're not careful."

He was directly in front of her, murmuring "Whoa," to the horse, relaxing in the saddle to let his reins cross at the horn while he pushed back his hat. But falling was all she wanted to do—right into his arms.

He stroked the horse's shiny neck and she remembered the feel of his hard, calloused hand. Oh, how she longed to feel it again! It made her feel weak just to think of it, made her skin, her whole body ache for it.

She looked into his gray eyes, smiling at her with a twinkle she'd never seen before.

"You're the one needs to be careful," she said, trying to keep her tone light, yet warn him.

"See what happens when you read somebody else's mail?" he said. "You start harping on somebody else's worries. Carrying on like that's liable to keep you from sleeping at night."

"I'm not harping," she said, sitting back down. "For it to be harping, I'd have to say it a dozen times or more."

She couldn't tear her gaze away from his. His eyes gleamed with a look that made her hot, hot as working in the sun all day.

"Have you, Callie?"

"Have I what?"

"Been sleeping."

Warmth rushed into her cheeks and color with it, she knew.

"That's a rather personal question," she said.

"Not for a person sleeping in my bed."

He held her gaze relentlessly. The heat spread all through her body just as mercilessly.

"If it's your bed, you ought to know if it's comfortable or not."

"It is," he said, nodding judiciously.

She managed to draw in a breath.

"Then why did you ask me that?"

They looked at each other for a long time.

"I've been having a little trouble sleeping, myself," he drawled, "thought it might be something in the air."

Her bones were melting, her whole body tilted toward him.

"Come here," he said and reached up for her. "This filly needs to learn to carry double and you need to learn how to ride."

He swung her down into his lap and she couldn't find it in her to resist.

"Don't worry, Yellow Girl's some gentler than Judy," he said. "But not gentle enough for me to sit behind and get out of the stirrups."

"That's . . . fine," she said.

No, it wasn't fine. It was downright dangerous, was what it was. Even through her clothes she could feel the hard bulge of his manhood against her.

"She'll make a good mount. I'm pleased with her," Nick said.

"So that's why you're in such a good

mood," she said, trying not to sound as breathless as she felt. "I thought it was because we don't have to work tomorrow and you're excited about going into town and maybe seeing some of your neighbors."

"Wouldn't miss it," he said. "I'm just hoping my man's still working at the Land Office in case there's any question I'm Cherokee."

"If you keep paying bribes, you'll have paid a premium for your claim," she said, glancing back over her shoulder. "That's not fair."

He held her gaze with his.

"Nothing is."

She smiled.

"Probably not."

"That first bribe was worth the money, though," he said, in his low, sensual voice. "It got us out in open country in time for the storm."

Her breath became too shallow for a laugh, too fast for her to speak. He, too, remembered that kiss, those caresses. He, too, had felt the hot thrills in his blood beneath the cold, slashing rain.

The next instant, the horse shied from a glimpse of Callie's flapping skirt and nearly jumped out from under them. Callie screamed and grabbed the saddle horn, but Nick only tightened his arms around her and sat back a little. After another crowhop or two, the filly settled and fell into a long trot.

They floated around the pen.

"Now what do you think?" Nick said, and Callie smiled at the pride in his voice. "Isn't she a smooth ride?"

"I hope she doesn't take another fit of bucking and throw us," Callie said.

Nick bent his head beside hers and tucked her into the curve of his body. He smelled of sweat and leather and horse and of his own man-scent. She would recognize the fragrance of him if he rode past her at a gallop on the blackest, windiest night.

"If she tries anything else, relax and hold onto me," he said.

"Relax!"

She turned an indignant look on him. Their eyes locked. He was giving her that crooked grin that charmed her so. His lips came perilously close to brushing her cheek, his eyes came disastrously close to melting her where she sat.

Callie had to force herself to look away so she wouldn't reach up and touch his face.

"Yellow Girl isn't going to dump us in the dirt," he said. "She's only teasing. She's come a long, long way in these last few days."

His satisfaction-filled voice made Callie smile again. How curious that she was no longer jealous of the filly when she sat in Nick's lap.

She leaned against his hard-muscled arm.

"This filly is smarter than most people," he bragged. "And she's got the heart to try anything."

"You should get a good price for her."

He was silent for a minute, as if he hadn't thought of that.

"I don't know that I'll sell her."

It was her turn to laugh.

"Nick, how can you make a living out of horses if you don't sell them?"

"I'll sell most of them."

His tone was so confiding, so leisurely, it was as if they were friends, all of a sudden. It felt strange and incredibly satisfying after seven days of avoiding each other, of eating their meals quickly so they could go about their separate tasks and be apart, so they could escape the pull of these feelings that were winding around their hearts.

Now, neither one of them was trying to escape. Her pulse quickened, her breath came shorter still.

What would happen? Would Nick kiss her again?

She wanted him to. She was afraid for him to. Oh, Lord, she should've clung to the fence with both hands—she should never have let him pull her down onto this horse with him!

Yellow Girl slowed and then stopped. Callie gasped as Nick tightened one arm around her and reached for the gate latch with the other.

"A trip to the pond and back ought to be about right," he said, his voice low and rough.

He was feeling the same desire she was. It wasn't just in his voice but in his body, in every inch that was touching her. Her heart thundered in her chest.

Oh, dear God, another kiss would only make them want a whole lot more.

He pressed his leg against the filly's side, and she moved sideways through the gate. Nick left it open and turned her toward the pond, then pulled Callie closer against his chest.

"We'll let her out a little," he said, and Callie thought she felt his lips pressed briefly to her hair.

She was afraid to turn and look at him for fear of offering her mouth up for his kiss.

They began to fly instead of float above the ground, and she loved it. She wasn't even afraid. She let her body melt against Nick's.

He bent down and pressed his mouth to her ear.

"You could learn to ride this mare," he said. "I'll teach you."

She nodded. He laid his cheek against hers for the space of a heartbeat.

Soon, way too soon, she felt the filly begin to slow and realized that they were almost to the pond. They rode into the trees on its west side, and when they reached the water Nick signaled Yellow Girl to stop. She stood quietly, blowing a little.

"Callie," he said. "Look at me."

Her blood raced as fast as Yellow Girl had carried them, but her breath came slow, too slow. She didn't have enough air and she couldn't seem to get any more. She turned and looked up into his burning gray eyes, powerful as stars against his coppery skin.

He tilted her face upward with the tip of one finger and started to lower his mouth for a kiss. Suddenly he stiffened.

"Listen!"

Dimly, she understood what the word meant; finally she managed to use one of her senses for something besides being with him. She could hear hooves striking rocks, branches breaking.

"Horses coming up the draw," he said, speaking low but in a voice as hard as stone. "Get down, Callie, quick. Whoever it is, I've got to keep them from seeing my set-up."

"No. I'll go with you."

He was already lifting her out of the saddle, though.

"Damn!" he muttered. "Double damn! And me without a weapon."

He set her to the ground in an instant, at the side of the filly.

"Over there," he said. "In that thicket of cottonwoods. Don't make a sound. If they're dangerous, I can't protect you against that many."

Callie was as befuddled as if she'd just waked from sleep, with his arms gone from around her now and her blood roaring with wanting them back again.

"They're close," he said, his voice cracking like a whip. "Go!"

She turned and ran for the trees and he rode toward the mouth of the draw.

Nick rode out and stopped the intruders before they got to the pond. Callie watched through an opening in the brush and tried to catch her breath.

Nick had more nerve than anyone she'd ever known. He sat the yellow filly with the air of a king in an old story song and faced down six riders—to her best count, but there could be more behind them. The evening was growing dusky dark, so the yellow filly was the plainest thing she could see at this distance.

"You're under arrest!" one of the strange men boomed.

"What the hell for?" Nick shot back, using his tone of voice as the only weapon he had.

"Robbing the bank in Santa Fe," the man answered. "We done found the money where you dropped it at the edge of town, but I aim to make an example of you."

"Who are you to make such a brag as that?"

"Sheriff Cap Williams, duly appointed until the e-lection."

"When was the robbery?"

"This noon—as if you didn't know. We got a witness seen you; he knowed where your claim was."

"Your witness is mistaken."

"Description fits you to a T. Big black stud horse, fine-tooled saddle."

"Does this look like a black horse to you?"

His accuser gave a short laugh.

"Same saddle."

"I haven't been to Santa Fe *since* last week."

"Yore name Nick Smith?"

"Yes. Who's your witness?"

"Man name of Baxter."

"He's a lying son-of-a-bitch," Nick said. "He's wanted this claim since the Run."

"We're taking you in," Cap Williams ordered.

Guns drawn, the men surrounded him.

"No!" Callie screamed. "Listen to me!"

She ran, crashing through the dry leaves and twigs, darting in and out through the brush, fighting it away from her face with both hands. Nearly breathless, she burst out of it closer to the band of vigilantes that had taken Nick, but they were already riding away.

"I've been with him all day," she yelled. "He hasn't been to Santa Fe."

"Yeah, sure," Cap Williams called, barely

turning in his saddle to take note of her. "Next time, get you a man who won't drop the money in the road."

All of them guffawed at that.

They urged the horses toward the mouth of the draw, moving so fast Callie soon couldn't see them in the dusk—not even Nickajack's pale shirt above the yellow mare.

Callie drove up to the small limestone building marked JAIL shortly before noon the next day, parked the wagon, and wrapped the lines around the brake handle. She'd never imagined, when she saw the little place last week, that she'd be rushing to get to it today with her heart in her throat.

She climbed down over the wheel and stood for a moment, brushing the dust from her person. If she looked as nice and as respectable as possible, Williams would take her as seriously as possible. Surely he would, despite the way he had treated her the day before.

Also, she wanted to look nice for Nickajack—to help give him hope.

It would show him, too, that she was capable and self-sufficient and not falling apart without him. That would keep him from worrying about her.

She practiced smiling a time or two, wishing she had a mirror so she could tell whether she was succeeding. But never, since they brought her the news of Vance's death, had she felt less like smiling. Ever since she'd risen from Nick's bed before first light, she'd had that shivery, scared feeling all the way into her bones that she used to get whenever Mama woke her in the middle of the night for the start of a journey or to harvest the oats ahead of a rain.

But this time there was no excitement or anticipation underneath the uncertainty, no deep security of kinfolk surrounding her. Only fear like she'd never known.

It wasn't worry for herself, though, that had kept her awake all night. It was worry for Nick. She was going to get him out of this jail if it was the last thing she ever did.

She crossed the short distance to the door, which stood open as a concession to the heat of the day, and stepped into the one small room. Nick sat behind a row of rough iron bars that reached from the wood floor to the low ceiling, his long legs stretched out before him on the narrow bed, his hands clasped behind his head, looking as if he hadn't a care in the world.

His eyes told a different story, though—she caught a glimpse of mute despair before he saw her. His eyelids half-closed and his lips curved in the ghost of his rare smile.

The look made her heart ache and her blood run hotter.

"You don't appear surprised to see me."

"I knew you'd come," he said, in a low voice that touched her, deep inside. "After all, ain't you the buggy boss of that whole country out there around Chikaskia Creek?"

He got up and walked to the row of bars that divided the small room in half.

"No-o-o," she said, moving to meet him as helplessly as a moth to a flame. "I drive a wagon."

That made him actually smile, although barely.

"Wagon boss is another name for it."

"Well, I'm not any kind of boss at all or you wouldn't be . . . in there."

She, who was so blunt by nature, couldn't bring herself to say "in that cell" or "behind bars." It physically made her heart hurt in her chest to see him helplessly trapped, when he should be astride his big, black horse riding freely across the vast prairie.

"I'm furious Williams wouldn't listen to me when I told him you hadn't been to town yesterday."

"He thinks you're my wife, so you'd lie for me."

His gaze held hers.

"I would lie for you," she said, "but he won't even believe me when I'm telling the truth."

"Like the truth that you were with me all day yesterday?"

That made her smile.

"Yes. For all the good it did."

"Exactly," he said, his voice suddenly sharp with worry. "I told you to stay hidden."

His gaze lingered on hers.

"I couldn't," she said, lifting both hands to wrap them around the bars, wishing she was strong enough to rip them out of their sockets. "Where's the High Sheriff?"

"Across the street to get my breakfast. Said he can keep an eye on the door from there."

"As if you could break these bars. Or go through those thick stone walls."

She glanced around, aching to get the feel of those words off her tongue and the sound of them out of her head. He followed her gaze. Despair for him filled her, for he hated to be inside, much less locked in. It was already hot as sin in there.

"Another irony of the selling of the Strip," he said dryly. "This is an old line cabin of the Circle N, the outfit that leased this graze. I used it some when I rode for them."

Callie tried to imagine that.

"But it surely didn't already have *bars* across it?"

He gave a bitter chuckle.

"Nope. But Cap Williams gets things done, even if the town is only three weeks old. He's a lawman on fire to lock up the bad men, so he's gotta have a cage to put 'em in."

He sobered and looked at her straight.

"He's a good politician, too, is our Cap. You better be gone before he comes back. Running out of the trees to defend me last night and now, hanging around the jail talking friendly with the big *bandido*, might be enough to keep you out of your school."

"I'm here to talk to *him*. To tell him that we've been together for the last week, and that I know where you've been and that you couldn't have robbed the bank."

That brought a glint of amusement before he gave her a stern, warning look.

"Then you *really* won't get a school. Surely you don't think he'd believe I've been living alone in the barn for a week."

His sleepy-looking lids lowered, and his eyes told her he wished he hadn't been. For a minute, that look held her and she wished the same. The feel of his arms around her aboard the yellow filly flowed through her. When he got out and came home . . . if he still looked at her that way . . .

"You might as well be whistling "Dixie," anyhow, Callie. The man's happy as a hyena about catching himself a bank robber. He won't take anybody's word to let me go."

"Then I'll find somebody to contradict Baxter! You know he can't be the only one who saw the robber, right here in town!"

"You go register your land description, is

what you do," he said fiercely. "Of all days for me to be locked up! I could kill the claim-jumping . . ."

"I brought your permit," she said, opening her reticule to take out the folded paper and pen and ink she'd wrapped together. "I thought if you'd sign it, they might let me register for you, too."

A bleak hope flashed in his eyes.

"Give it here."

As he took it, he gave her a slow grin.

"Going through my papers again, hmm?"

She felt herself blush a little.

"How'd you get a permit, anyhow?" she asked, to change the subject while she held the ink for him to dip the pen. "A bribe?"

"A visit to a registration booth," he said, with a chuckle, "and then a ride back home, keeping to the draws and off the ridges. I saw several other Sooners on the way."

He motioned for her to turn and let him prop the paper against her back. One of his big hands held it flat, feeling like a brand to her skin. She wanted it to stay there forever. What if he could never touch her again? What if she could never touch him again?

"If they won't let you do this, don't worry," he said. "I'll try again when all this is over."

Her heart dropped again.

"How will you ever get out?" she whispered.

"I may have to break out," he said. "If I hit the owl-hoot trail, stay at my place and take care of my horses."

"I will."

After she said that, her voice was gone.

"Try to go to the bald-headed clerk that took my bribe," Nick said, and touched her shoulder so she'd turn to face him again.

She did, fighting tears with all her might.

His light gray eyes blazed at her from his dark face.

"Callie . . ."

He put his hands on the bars then, too, over hers, and the heat they held shot through her whole body. It was a thrill and a comfort, both. It gave her strength and took the very starch from her bones at the same time.

She waited, holding her breath.

". . . Be careful."

It wasn't what he had first meant to say, and she knew it. But another moment and she'd be sobbing like a child, trying to separate the bars to get to him, never mind letting him out.

"Go," he said.

Slowly, he removed his hands from hers and let them fall to his sides.

She tore her gaze from his, turned, and ran for her wagon.

It was only after she'd driven all the way through town, past loud saloons and rearing horses and a fight or two, and had left her team and wagon at the livery stable, that she could even think about anything but Nick. The registration. Today was the day he'd paid good money to get, and she couldn't let that go to waste. The line was already more than a dozen people long, even with the method of assigning days. She must get this done, and then she'd try to find someone else who'd seen the robber running from the bank.

"Hey, there, home-steadin' widder-woman!"

The shout stopped her in her tracks because her body recognized Baxter's voice before her mind did. She turned to see him crossing the street, waving at her, hurrying to get to her before a line of freight wagons reached him.

Her fear of him didn't even have a chance of overcoming her anger. He'd lied about Nick and tried to ruin him, he accosted her every time she came to town, he—

But wait. He was just the man she needed to see.

She pretended to ignore him and walked on to take her place in line at the Land Office, which had become the most significant spot in her life. Well, today would be the last time because she—and Nick, she was determined to believe—would be registered and she wouldn't have to come here for another five years, when she'd proved up her claim and earned final title to it.

This slow-moving line at the Land Office would be dear to her heart forever, if she could gain Nick's freedom here. If she could challenge Baxter and then bribe him to change his story, this ugly Land Office shack would even be beautiful.

"Well, well," Baxter called, gaining her side of the street, "my reckoning was you'd be coming to town to see about yore man."

"No," Callie said sweetly, turning on her heel to face him, "I came to town to see you, Mr. Baxter. And you certainly cannot be called 'my man.' "

She held herself to her full height and waited for him to come to her. Frowning, he did so, his eyes glinting bright as they bored into hers.

"Then you found me, little lady."

"You know you lied about who robbed the bank," she said. "Mr. Smith wasn't in town yesterday."

"Wal, now, I'll grant you that if anybody's liable to know where that Injun's at, you're the one," he said, "but I can't deny what I seen with my own eyes."

"But you *can* deny that the robber was Mr. Smith if you think it over and realize that you were mistaken."

He shrugged.

"Tall man, well built," he said flatly. "Black hat, big black stud horse."

Every word he spoke in that self-righteous tone and every satisfied look he gave her fanned the flames of her fury, but she refused to let him see that.

"That could describe a lot of people."

"Th' Injun's nothing special, true," he said derisively, "but that black horse is a humdinger. Couldn't miss that good-lookin' sucker in a coal mine at midnight."

Suddenly it struck her. He hadn't had Nick thrown in jail and then hailed her on the street to taunt her for revenge. He wanted something.

Callie's heart soared. In the middle of the night, she had realized that he probably could be bribed. Of course he could! He had all those children to support, didn't he?

This was the reason he had falsely accused Nick. He'd seen Nick's fine horse twice, he'd seen his nice saddle last week in town, and he'd decided he was tired of riding a mule. The Baxters had nothing as a result of the Run, and he believed Nick had staked two claims . . .

Panic trailed cold fingers down the length of her spine. No. Surely not. Surely something smaller would do.

Chapter 13

~~~◦◯◦~~~

Baxter must have very little money. Surely he would take something much smaller than a claim.

"Perhaps I could offer you some compensation for your time to think again about what you saw yesterday," she said softly, grateful that her voice held steady. "It's such a gross injustice that Mr. Smith is sitting in jail when he is innocent and the real robber outlaw is running free."

He stroked his beard with a slow gesture that seemed somehow both insolent and menacing.

"If that's true, it's a shame," he said. "And it might be that I have possibly misspoke about him. In what way do you think to compensate me?"

She did a quick calculation in her head.

"You understand that I'm limited to my own resources only," she said. "If Mr. Smith knew about this conversation, he would be out for your blood rather than your good will."

A little threat couldn't hurt; maybe it would even help keep the price down.

"Maybe so," he said, "but I ain't worried about losing my hair."

So. Here was a second threat. Nick would never be able to register his claim if the government found out he was a member of the Cherokee Nation.

"What are you offering, lady?"

His voice had gone cold as stone.

"Twenty-five dollars," she said. "It's all I have."

That wasn't quite true, but it was close enough. Without that amount, she'd be on Nick's charity for food this winter.

He laughed. He threw back his shaggy head and laughed long and loud. Then his laughter stopped.

"Your claim," he said.

Even though she had expected those words, Callie cringed.

"I have to have a place to live," she said. "We must come to some other agreement."

He watched her silently with his shrewd,

malevolent gaze. When she had held her breath forever, he spoke.

"No deal."

"Thirty dollars."

"Your claim."

In the middle of the night, she had worked out a whole list of possible bribes. She'd have to bring out her best offer because she could not, would not, give up her land.

"Mr. Baxter, I will be teaching the Chikaskia Valley School when it opens," she said, amazed that she could speak so calmly. "And for the first few years at least, the parents will have to pay a subscription. The first time we met, you mentioned that you have several children and so does your brother. I could give a reduced rate to your and your brothers' children."

If he bargained with her and asked for free subscriptions, she would give them. Surely that and thirty dollars would persuade him to withdraw his false accusation.

Instead, Baxter roared out an oath. "All them children may go to school or they may not, but they are gonna work a farm for me," he said tightly. "They've got to pay for their raising somehow."

"They can do more for you if I teach them to read and cipher . . ."

"Your *claim*," he roared. "That's the end of it."

And it was. Her heart sank and she wanted desperately to try again, but she knew that he would take nothing less.

She had to give him her claim.

Suddenly the sky felt huge above her and the land stretching beneath it even more vast, while, small and pitiably weak, she stood in Baxter's trap giving in to his highway robbery. The town seemed to close around her, close enough to choke her.

No one could help her, and she couldn't help herself.

Never, not even when she'd left the mountains, knowing that she wouldn't see her family again as long as she lived, had she felt so helpless.

It ain't jist a feelin', girl, it's the hard-down truth. Ain't nothin' you kin do.

It was Granny's voice speaking in her ear: all-seeing, all-knowing Granny, who never failed to get to the heart of any matter. Once again, Granny was right.

Fury at the injustice of it came surging into her soul, mixed with fear. A terrible fear of what might happen to her and her baby.

A terrible shaking came over her inside and she fought not to let it show on the outside.

They would have no place to live! She'd have no place to be when the baby came!

Oh, and all her whole week of hot, miserable drudgery cutting and stacking sod bricks—all her four, hard won half-walls that were going to be her home—would go to Baxter! He would come with all his kin and live on her land.

And with this one tiny baby who was now her only kin, where would she go?

Granny would tell her to take it one day at a time and trust to the Lord to provide. And both Granny and the Lord would stand behind her in doing anything to get Nick out of jail. After all he'd done for her, she'd never sleep well again if she left him there in order to keep her land.

"Baxter, you listen to me," she said, clenching her teeth so that her chin wouldn't tremble, "you had better not mention the word *Indian* or make any reference to it ever again."

"I wouldn't think of it," he purred, with an evil grin that she longed to slap right off his face.

But there, too, she was helpless. If only she were a man! Then she'd . . .

Callie forced herself to turn her back on the despicable Baxter and to turn her thoughts, too. No sense working herself up into a froth over him; this was the way it was and it couldn't be helped.

She must calm down and think this through.

While they stood in line waiting to get into the Land Office door, she wracked her brain for something, anything, she could do so as not to feel so helpless. That feeling was dragging her down toward real despair and she had to fight it. She also had to deal with this horrid fear that Baxter still would make trouble about Nick's being Cherokee once they stood in front of the clerk. That way, he might end up with her claim and Nick's, too.

As a few more claimants left the small building, some more crowded in, and she and Baxter moved a few steps forward. She turned to him.

"When it's our turn, if you breathe a word about Indians or Cherokees or even hint at it, I'll not sign my claim over to you, understand?" she said. "I'm registering Nick's claim for him first. Then when that's done, and if you've made no trouble, I'll sign mine over to you. *Only* then."

"If you refuse to sign it over, your big redskinned buck will still be sitting in jail. He might even hang. Have you thought of that?"

"It won't matter," she said, willing the calm authority to hold firm in her voice. "If he loses his claim, he'd rather be in jail or dead."

He scowled.

"Think about it," she said. "Call him an Indian in there, make him lose his land, and I won't sign mine over to you. The only way you'll ever get it is through the law, and that would cost you a fortune."

Baxter thought about it.

"All *right*," he growled. "Let's just get this done."

Callie still felt shaky, but at least she had some bit of leverage, which comforted her a little.

When she saw a man going up and down the line handing out sheets of newspaper, a faint hope rose in her heart. Ned Adams, the publisher of Santa Fe's new newspaper, *The Prairie Fire*, was giving away sample sheets of that day's edition. While Baxter stood breathing down her neck like some greedy, malevolent monster, Callie asked Mr. Adams if he had investigated the story he had printed about the bank robbery. He assured her that he had done so very thoroughly, and that no one, not even those coming and going from the busy restaurant tent next to the bank yesterday, had claimed to have seen the robber's escape.

The bank's tent was jammed onto a small lot that people frequently cut across to avoid the traffic in the street, so all the robber needed to do was let the bandanna used as his mask fall from his face to his neck, and he would've looked like anyone else hurrying about his noontime business, carrying a bag of possessions in hand.

The clerk, too, had described him as black-hatted, tall, and well-built. He had ducked into the bank from beneath one canvas wall and had departed the same way.

Callie's heart sank as Adams tipped his hat and moved on, calling out his headline about the bank robber. He had only one or two takers in the line; most people were too wrapped up in trying to get registered to want to read.

Almost everyone there had his life hanging by a thread, with no money in the bank, and had more interest in his own survival than the bank's.

And now she was one of the ones hanging by a thread, as if she hadn't been before. She would have to move into this teeming town with its ugly Hell's Acre and try to find a job she could hold until the baby began to show. Or stay at Nick's place.

Quickly, she closed her mind to all the visions that came to mind. The brave, reckless part of her wanted that more than she wanted air to breathe—which scared her half to death.

She couldn't even think now. All she could do was feel, and all she could feel was a bone-wrenching regret that her baby would have no homeplace after all, no land to roam and to call his own and pass on to his children, no big space to run and play, no creeks to splash in or rocks to climb. That was how it would be if she moved to town.

The sun was high now and heating up the prairie with a vengeance, and from time to time her stomach roiled. Once or twice she thought she might even faint. She closed her mind to everything but Nick sitting behind bars. In only a few minutes she'd be able to see the terrible despair disappear from his eyes.

Suddenly, she just couldn't stand there any longer. She turned to Baxter.

"We could walk quickly up to the jail before our turn comes, and you could tell Sheriff Williams that you've made a mistake with the identification . . ."

"Yore nowhere near wily enough to fool this old possum," he said coldly. "Don't even try. Sign the claim to me first, and *then* I'll get your lover out of jail."

She looked at him, letting the cold blade of her fury shine sharp in her eyes.

"If you know what's good for your health, you will do exactly that," she said. "If you try to walk away from me after my claim is in your name, I will see to it that you die. I don't care if you have a *hundred* children to feed."

Her heartfelt words astonished her as much as they did him—for the first time ever she saw his narrow eyes widen in surprise.

"I'm a man of my word," he said, with a gruff defensiveness that was almost laughable.

She kept looking him straight in the eye.

"Yes," she said sarcastically, "except when you're a witness to a robbery."

"I am," he said, taking a step forward as the line moved again. "Didn't I tell you the first time I ever seen you that I'd have my name on that there piece of land you was claimin'? And ain't that what we're gittin' done right now?"

The truth of that made her sick to her stomach but she marched on, climbing the steps of the Land Office with the triumphant Baxter right beside her. The blisters tingled in the palms of her hands. She had worked like a man, day after day, to build a shelter for her baby, only to give it to him. There wasn't a blessed thing she could do.

"And my word has held up in another way, too: when I said you and that Injun is a pair," he said, with a disgusting smugness. "You wouldn't be doin' this for him if you wasn't his woman."

The phrase sent a waterfall of fear cascading through her. Any woman who became Nick's woman would be placing her heart in reckless jeopardy. Nick Smith didn't want any lasting companionship or sharing of his life.

"His name is Smith," she snapped. "And you'd better not refer to him as 'the Injun' again, if you don't want to be branded a liar right there in this Land Office, because then I'll have nothing to lose. Be quiet and you can walk out of here in ten minutes' time with a claim of your own."

They arrived at the door and stepped inside the shack. Baxter stepped right in behind her, breathing down her neck, but at least he was silent, thank God. The air inside the building was sweltering and too thick to breathe. There were four clerks and at least one customer in front of each one.

Callie squared her shoulders and held her thoughts to the moment, to this one instant and then to the next, so that she wouldn't make any mistakes. The rest of Nick's whole life, maybe even his life itself, depended on her doing this right.

Then it was her turn and, as luck would have it, the bald government clerk beckoned to her. She pulled out and unfolded Nick's registration permit.

"I'm registering this claim," she said. "And then I have another to sign off on a sale to this man behind me, Mr. Baxter."

"Very well," the clerk said, and took the paper from her. "Your full legal name?"

"Mrs. Calladonia Sloane."

The clerk wrote that down, then looked at Nick's permit.

"There's a note on the back," Callie murmured.

He turned it over and read what Nick had written.

"Hmmn, Nick Smith," he said heartily. "I remember Mr. Smith."

"Maybe that's because his skin's a little bit *redder* than usual," said a man's voice.

Callie's blood froze in her veins. She stiffened, then whirled to look for the speaker as she realized it wasn't Baxter.

It was a man she didn't recognize who was in line across from her at the next clerk's table. When their eyes met, he spoke directly to her.

"I seen you last week with a man they said was named Nick-a-jack Smith who nearly got hit by a flying board," he said flatly. "I'd say they was right calling him a Cherokee."

Silence fell in the little room.

The interfering busybody held her gaze and said vehemently, "From the looks of him, I'd say he is."

Several people had turned to look at her, and a burly man just inside the door spoke out loudly. "You mean you're in here registering a claim for a Indian? I thought th' U. S. Government paid the Indians good money to get this land away from them so godfearing white men could farm it."

Callie's heart stopped. What could she do? How could she offer this clerk another bribe, right here in front of everyone? How had Nick done it? Oh, Lord, what could she do?

"Damn straight that's what she's doing," the man at the next table said. "I seen her with him. Redskin blanket's what I'm talkin' about—I seen 'im with my own eyes and I've seen a passel of Indians in my time."

"My grown son didn't get no claim," the burly man roared. "And he was *in* the Run. He's a white man, too."

Another man stepped out of line. "My brother lost out, too," he said.

"Now let's just see about this," another one said, stepping out of line and moving toward Callie. His hard gaze was fixed on the clerk who was helping her.

A general muttering began to rise.

The bald clerk raised both hands as a peacemaking gesture toward the men who were advancing on him now from three directions.

"Calm down now, folks, calm down. There's no conflict here," he said smoothly. "Mrs. Sloane did not say that she was registering the claim *for Mr. Smith.*"

He rustled the paper in front of him.

"According to these records, Mr. Smith's claim has already been contested by her, Mrs. Calladonia Sloane, and she has won. The land in question will be registered to her, in her name, and, as you can all plainly see, she is white as a lily."

His tone and assured way of speaking soothed the protesters instantly. Callie stood stunned—and silent—as his pen began to scratch across the page of his ledger.

He was putting Nick's claim in her name— and she dared not stop him! She could say nothing, absolutely nothing, or she would lose his claim forever.

She took a deep breath to steady herself and realized that it was all right. A few months from now, when all the furor died down, she could sign it over to him.

The clerk seemed to take a year to finish with his notations in the ledgers, but finally he handed her a deed made out in her name. Then she gave him her own certificate.

"And what is your full legal name, sir?" the clerk asked Baxter, starting the whole process all over again.

It took only seconds, it seemed, to sign away what had taken her months of dreaming, weeks of hard traveling, and days of unspeakable work to achieve. Her mind skittered away from that, and from the thought of her baby growing up in town in rented quarters.

Right now, she had to concentrate on the present. She had to pray that Baxter would keep his word so she wouldn't have to kill him with her bare hands, and go to jail with Nick instead of getting him out.

"You should know that I carry a purse gun," Callie said to Baxter, as they left the Land Office. "And that I'm a dead shot. Don't try to get away from me and don't try to tell that Cap Williams again that he's got the right man locked up."

Baxter cast her a scornful, sidelong glance.

"Ain't I done *told* you my word is good? Ain't I kept ever' promise I ever made to you, girl? I got my name on that claim like I said that first day, didn't I?"

Callie walked faster, practically running, wondering how quickly she could get the gun out of her purse if Baxter tried to slip away into the dusty, crowded street. He walked beside her like the honorable man he claimed to be, however, and gave no sign of any troublesome intentions.

When they reached the jail, she stepped back to make sure he went inside, but that wasn't necessary. He stepped right in ahead of her and hailed Cap Williams, who was sitting at the battered table in one corner.

"Sheriff, I need to talk to you."

"Mr. Baxter! What can I do for you today?"

Nick leapt to his feet and, as she followed Baxter in, he strode to the bars. His eyes met hers with a look so intense it made her shiver.

"I've come to set somethin' straight," Baxter said, never once looking at Nick. "This here ain't your bank robber, so you'll have to turn him loose."

Cap Williams turned red.

"What are you talking about, man? You're changing your story?" he asked angrily.

"Yep. I reckon I done made a mistake."

"How can that be? How come you've not realized that 'til now?"

"All of a sudden, you might say," Baxter drawled, not the least perturbed by Williams' bluster.

"Got t' thinkin' about it," he said. "Got t' recollectin' how it was. That yahoo I seen runnin' acrost the bank lot to th' big black horse was a lot older rascal than Smith here, hair as white as my old grandpa's. His hat like to blowed off when he come past me, an' he had to jam it back on his head."

"You sent me to arrest a black-haired man."

"Don't recall that I ever said *that*. I give you his location, yes, but then I never seen Smith without his hat 'til I walked past the jail this mornin', and it jist hit me like a streak o' lightning that the robber's hair was white."

Cap Williams clearly ached to rip Baxter limb from limb.

"As if you can't tell what color hair a man has in spite of his hat!"

"Not always," Baxter said, solemnly shaking his head.

"So you say now Smith is innocent."

"I do. To a posse, to a judge, to whatever powers that be."

"You'll swear it?"

"On a stack o' Bibles. I remember now, clear as ringin' a bell. This here Smith is not your man."

"Baxter, you son-of-a-bitch, I don't know what kind of game you're playing—"

Baxter pulled himself up indignantly.

"I'm dead serious, Williams. Tryin' to do my citizen's duty."

"Why am I thinkin' I even *want* to run for this office in the election," Williams grumbled, "when I get this kind of grief? Somethin' stinks in this deal, and I aim to find out what it is."

"Help yourself," Baxter retorted. "But don't forget I'm a voting citizen of K County."

He walked to the door, then turned and looked back at Nick.

"Matter of fact," he said, "I'll be homesteadin' out near the Chikaskia Creek."

Nick stared back without flickering an eyelid at that news.

"*Neighbor*," Baxter said to him, "I'll be seein' ya."

He flashed a grin at Callie and disappeared onto the street.

Cap Williams, fuming and muttering, went to unlock the cell.

"I've got no reason to hold you now," he said.

"You never did," Nick said.

He stepped out as the door swung open, grabbed his hat from the wall peg, and crossed the tiny room to Callie.

"Next time you set yourself up as the law and take out your posse," he said to Cap Williams, "don't believe everything you hear."

He put on his hat and pulled it down in a quick, hard gesture.

The next thing Callie knew, they were outside, Nick's big hand around her arm, bringing her along beside him so fast it seemed her feet were off the ground. He didn't stop until they were around the corner of the livery stable and in the quiet shade of the big cottonwood.

"Now," he said fiercely, turning her back to its trunk and stepping close as if to hold her captive, "what did you give Baxter to take back his lie?"

He sounded furious. He *looked* furious.

"*Give* him? I *traded* him, if you haven't noticed. Has it occurred to you that you are now out of jail?"

"At what price?"

His imperious tone deepened her anger.

"I didn't expect you to throw yourself at my feet in gratitude, but isn't it just a little rude for you to bite my head off?"

"Callie," he said in his dangerous tone, taking hold of her other arm, "tell me what you did to make him change his story."

"I signed over my claim."

Saying it out loud suddenly made it *really* real. She sagged back against the huge tree as all the strength left her legs, and the helpless, despairing feeling came over her again.

Nick stared at her, his eyes blazing pale fire from beneath the brim of his hat.

"No."

"I had to. It was what he'd planned. Accusing you of the robbery was only meant to get Baxter a homestead, that's all."

His eyes narrowed until his long black lashes almost touched.

"So you played right into his hands. Did exactly what he wanted you to do."

"For *you*! To set you free! You saw what a crazy zealot Cap Williams is; he'd never have found *any* evidence to help you. Why, he would accuse his own grandmother to say he'd caught an outlaw!"

A terrible desolation swept through her, body and soul. She felt nearly too shaky to stand.

"What choice did I have?" she cried. "There was no other way to get you out. Nickajack, you might've *hanged*!"

But he didn't give so much as a flicker of acknowledgment that that was true. His face had set like a stone carving.

"You didn't have to do it," he said, his voice like a lash. "You foolishly walked into Baxter's ambush. I could've escaped—"

She began to shake all over."And *then* what would you do? Live on the run? Never see your cabin and your horses again? Look over your shoulder every minute?"

"That was none of your concern."

Somehow, that hurt her sharply.

"The devil you say! I couldn't have lived with myself if I'd walked away and left you there."

"And now you have nothing. No home. No land."

Her body turned to jelly. Oh, dear Lord, that was so. She tried to push the truth out of her mind, but it grew and filled her with an inescapable feeling of doom.

"I have my honor. You've helped me more than once, and risked your life to stake my claim in the first place. My honor demanded that I help you."

He let go of her and she felt as if she'd collapse in a heap on the ground. Snatching off his hat, he frantically ran his fingers through his hair, and then slammed it back on.

"Dammit all, Callie, you didn't have to do this."

A paralyzing dizziness came over her. She reached for the tree to hold her up and dug her nails into its bark.

"Yes, I did. I've sacrificed my homeplace, my lover's dream, but I *did* have to do it."

Her lover's dream.

Those words quivered in his heart like a thrown knife.

Nickajack stared down into her stricken face and could barely feel sorry for her, he was so full of fury. What a trap corral to run him into! He'd known the sodbusters would ruin the country, but he hadn't known they'd ruin his own personal life, too.

"Why didn't you tell me?" he said, although his jaw felt so cold and locked-up he didn't know how he could talk. "Why didn't you come back to the jail and tell me what he wanted?"

She lifted her head and looked at him, her green eyes huge, her face white as an antelope's flag, and his heart broke. He couldn't let her see that.

"You had no right to be hornin' in on my—"

Her beautiful mouth turned down, and for an awful minute he thought he'd made her cry.

"Well, you needn't worry about that for another minute," she said, in a dry, tight voice he'd never heard before, "because from now on you need never lay eyes on me again."

"From now on I'll lay eyes on you every day," he snapped. "What do you think I am?"

He had to fight to keep from yelling.

"You've sacrificed your dream for me, and you think I'll let you live here in town, alone, with it full of rowdies and holdup men and pimps and drunks and chiselers and rounders of all kinds?"

He thought a glint of laughter flashed across the misery in her eyes.

"It's not funny," he said. "I'll have to split my claim with you."

Her eyes narrowed and she looked as if she could've cheerfully shot him.

"You don't have to do one blessed thing but step back and get out of my way."

He was standing so close she'd have to climb the tree to get away from him. Still, he didn't move an inch.

"What I have to do is marry you," he said. "We might just as well find a preacher and get it done so we can get home before dark."

Chapter 14

The look on her face almost shocked him out of his anger, and now *he* wanted to laugh. All of this was craziness, all the *loco* feelings warring through him. But the moment the words came off his tongue, he knew they were right. She'd put him so far in debt to her he had no choice.

Well, that wasn't all of it, but what did anything else matter? Maybe he did care about her, some, but she loved a dead man and he could never fully trust any woman, ever again.

"Have you lost your mind?" she cried. "I won't marry you! What a cold idea to even think of!"

"Well, you don't have to be so scornful about it!"

He felt anything but cold. The idea filled him with a hot, raging fury mixed with fright. What if he started loving her when he lived with her every day? She made him lose control of his feelings more than anyone he'd ever known. Right now he was more furious than any other person had ever made him, man *or* woman.

"Let me tell you, Nick," she began, her chin stuck up in the air.

"Look," he interrupted in a ruthless tone, unable to keep from taking hold of her by both arms again, "you'll have to live with me. If we aren't married, you'll never get a school to teach."

Her stubborn little jaw thrust out. He had to hand it to her—she had sand. She'd dealt with Baxter alone and gotten him out of jail, even if she had done it the wrong way.

"I'll get a room in town," she said, in that new, strangled voice. "I'll find work."

"Where? How many of these businesses can afford to hire help?"

She hesitated.

"Somebody can."

"No. You'd be a woman alone. I can't be responsible for that."

She glared a hole through him.

"You *aren't* responsible. You didn't kill my

... Vance. You didn't drive me away from the Sloane Valley. I was a woman alone before I ever met you."

"You have preached nothing but no-obligations to me since the minute we met," he said. "I'm of that same mind. I won't be obligated to you for my freedom, not when you've paid such a price."

"I won't marry you."

Now she sounded scared.

"You talk about honor," he said. "I have to split my claim with you, I can't be responsible for what might happen to you alone in town, and I can't take time now from the horses to build you a separate shelter and be riding over there to see about you when the snow flies."

That was the truth. Those were the reasons. He mustn't let himself care for her. He had probably imagined that feeling, anyhow.

Callie leaned into his grip as if it were a crutch, because if she didn't, she would fall down. She didn't have the strength any more even to move without help. She would collapse in a heap on the ground if he didn't hold her up.

She had failed. The knowledge washed over her in an overwhelming wave.

Vance's dream was gone, after all she'd suffered to try to make it come true. She had failed him. She had lost him forever, except for the baby.

The baby. How could she take care of it now? The very thought filled her with fear. She had failed everyone she loved, from her parents to Vance to this precious baby. If she took him into danger, if she lost him, she wouldn't want to live. She *couldn't* live.

The gun she carried made it possible for her to defend herself, but in town, with a Hell's Acre full of desperate, unsavory characters and no law yet except for the ambitious Mr. Williams, she would have to be on guard all the time. In her present state of exhaustion, that was impossible to imagine after working twelve hours or more in a café or a store.

If she could find steady work. Not even in town would there be a school until months had passed, and she didn't have enough money to wait.

If she could get the school when it opened.

Never in all her life had she felt so abject, so hopeless, so helpless.

"When spring comes, I'll build you a cabin on your half of my place," Nick said. "And I'll not lay claim to a husband's rights, nor expect you to behave like a wife. So you can hold onto at least one of your dreams."

That touched her like nothing else ever had. His tone was so tender it brought tears to her eyes.

What difference would it make, except that she'd still be a respectable woman worthy of a school to teach? What difference, except that she'd have a real roof and real walls instead of a tent to protect her and her baby during the fall storms and winter blizzards? What difference, except that she and her baby wouldn't be alone in this ugly, noisy town crowded with strangers, some of them definitely dangerous?

Besides, out at the claim she knew Mrs. Peck, and Nick could go for her to help when her birthing time drew near.

The thought gave her strength. She would earn her keep at Nick's. He had a safe, secure nest with plenty of supplies for the winter, and his companionship, once they got used to this arrangement, would be a great balm to her loneliness.

He wouldn't really be her husband. This wouldn't be a betrayal of her love for Vance—it would be an arrangement, only for show. And it would offer her baby more protection than she could ever provide.

She looked up. Nick's eyes held a mix of impatience and anger and ... whatever had been in them that evening when he caught her reading the note from his cousin. Caring. He did care about her as a friend.

"All right," she said hoarsely, "I'll marry you, Nick."

*   *   *

But when she stood in the middle of the tent with the cross on top, surrounded by Nick, the preacher, the preacher's wife, and the preacher's wife's mother, Callie could not believe she had agreed to such a thing. What in the *world* was she doing here?

"Do you, Calladonia Sloane, take this man, Nick Smith, to be your lawfully wedded husband?"

It should have been *this man, Vance Harlan.* Except that that was a long time ago, and Vance was fading from her memory. But without love between her and Nick, this was all wrong, a travesty—a wanton, cruel injustice of life.

She didn't reply for such a long time that Nickajack placed his hand at the small of her back. Its warmth gave her strength, somehow.

"I do," she whispered.

Nick made his vows in a strong voice, as if he had already come to terms with the fact that they meant nothing.

The preacher declared them man and wife. "You may kiss your bride."

Her heart gave a double beat as Nick bent his head to hers, but he gave her only a chaste peck on the lips.

She had to suppress the grievous disappointment that threatened to overcome her. The little peck of a kiss was fine. She only needed comfort and reassurance, not passion, from a man who was marrying her out of duty. Hadn't he said they wouldn't really behave as if they were married?

"Please sign these documents for me," the preacher said. "For each marriage I conduct, I make one for my own records and one for yours."

Callie sat down while the kindly preacher drew up two identical certificates of marriage in his beautiful penmanship. Nick folded one and put it in his pocket, then she was on her feet again and they were accepting the good man's good wishes and those of his wife and mother-in-law.

In what seemed only an instant after that, she found herself and Nick walking back down the street. *Man and wife.* Those were the only words of the whole ceremony she could remember, and they kept ringing in her ears.

The whole world was a hot blur of dust and glaring sunlight that sapped the life out of her, and all Callie wanted was some shade and a stretch of grass where she could lay her body down. Lay down and not think at all.

"You're exhausted," Nick said, as she stumbled.

She felt his sharp, sideways glance as he put his arm around her waist to steady her.

"Have you eaten anything today?"

She tried to remember.

"No. I guess not. I ... didn't feel too good this morning ..."

"Sit down right here."

They were passing the open-air cafe and he guided her into the shade of its canvas side, rigged to make a roof instead of a wall in the heat. After Callie dropped into the rickety chair he pulled out for her, he made his way through the scattered mid-afternoon customers at the boards-on-sawhorses tables to the serving counter in the back by the big cast-iron stove.

He moved like a mountain lion, with all the grace and power of an animal that ruled where he roamed. But Nick didn't want to rule; he didn't even want to be bothered with anyone else. He loved his solitude. He didn't want her on his place, yet he had taken her in for the winter.

Even though—no, *because* he was obligated to her. What an irony, for them to be married today with their friendship ruined, when only yesterday they'd been good companions! She felt the heat rise into her face. Yesterday, when all this trouble had started, they'd been in each other's arms. Now they were married, and that would never happen again.

Dear Lord, she was *married* to him—to that handsome stranger over there who was buying food for her because now she was his wife—when what he really wanted was to walk off and leave her where she sat. How had she let this happen?

And he didn't even know about the baby. Oh, dear Lord, would he throw her out for not telling him beforehand? How would he feel when he found out he'd taken on still another mouth to feed?

Vance's baby wouldn't come until spring, though, and by then she'd be moving out of Nick's house. It wouldn't be right to take half his land or let him build her her own cabin, but at the moment she wouldn't argue with him. If he could help her survive through the winter, that would be all she could accept from him.

Once the baby had come and the Chikaskia school, which she really believed would be hers, had been assigned, she would make other plans. Surely six months or so of providing for her would fulfill his sense of obligation.

Soon he was at her side again, carrying a small cloth sack full of food and a canteen, pulling her out into the sun again, striding off toward the livery stable. He seemed to be growing more tense by the minute.

"Everybody was all right when you left this morning?"

"I don't know," she said, hurrying to keep up with him. "I threw hay to the young ones, but it was too dark for me to really look them over or see any of the mares in among the trees."

She stood in the shade while he collected her team and wagon and the yellow filly, paid the man, tied his young horse to the wagon, and drove to her. Exhausted, she nevertheless tried to climb up over the wheel by herself, but he got down to help her. Then he handed her the sack of food and slapped the lines down on the backs of her team.

She ought to insist that he ride his horse and let her drive her wagon, but the very thought made her know that she was stretched to the limits of her endurance. Her arms ached and her head hurt, and if she had to use them to try to control Judy and Joe, she would break into a million pieces. Or into tears.

"Eat," Nick said.

Pulling at the drawstring, she opened the sack. The fragrance of buttermilk biscuits and fried ham floated up to her and her stomach growled. She didn't feel hungry, though. She felt sick, and so defeated she could die.

The baby had to have food, though, so she forced herself to choke one sandwich down. Nick slid the strap off his shoulder and held the canteen out to her.

She drank long and deep, also for the baby, and then put the food on the floor and stood up.

"I have to rest," she said, and went back into the box of the wagon.

She wouldn't be able to sleep, but she had to lie down because she couldn't hold her body upright anymore. Never had she felt so broken and drawn down. She felt bent toward the earth as if she were dying. She had done just what she'd sworn not to do: she'd given up the only land she'd probably ever own.

It didn't count that she'd also broken her vow not to give a man power over her life. Nick didn't want it. All he wanted was for her to be gone—but she had no place else to go.

The stars were out when she woke, the wagon stood still and Nick was gone. Quickly, her mind panicking, she sat up.

He was in the pen with the young horses, talking to them in a low, sweet tone that blended his words into the sultry air. Home. They were home.

Her heartbeat slowed upon seeing he was safe, then picked up again. How could she think of Nick's cabin as home when she'd only been staying here for a few days, when it didn't belong to her and it never would?

Now she had no home.

The back of this wagon, right here, where she sat all covered in grimy dust and dried sweat, was the closest thing to a home that she owned.

The knot in her throat grew huge and threatened to choke her. She scrambled down off the wagon, forcing her stiff arms and legs to work, and flew into the house, grabbed some towels, then a pitcher from the kitchen, and ran out the back door. When she reached the spring, she stripped down to her skin and poured the cool water over her grimy body, head to toe, over and over again.

It shocked her hot skin and woke her completely, but it did nothing to wash away the battering day just past or to cool her feverish heart.

Nick would do the chores before he ate, Callie knew, so by the time he came in through the back door carrying his boots, with his hair slicked back, his shirt off, and his wet jeans clinging to his skin, she had fresh, cool water poured into mugs and a semblance of a supper laid out on the table. She would earn her keep; she would maintain her independence; she would manage her life separate from Nick's.

In spite of the fact that the sight of his copper skin gleaming in the lamplight made her want to stare at him for the rest of the evening. His skin called so relentlessly to her hands that she ached to touch him.

She turned her back and moved things around on the table.

The nap in the wagon had unsettled her,

that was all it was. This whole, long day she had been torn apart by too many emotions that ran too deep, and now she didn't know what to feel or how because her plans were gone and her life was raging out of control.

From the corner of her eye, she glanced at Nick, to see whether he was ready to be called to the table. His wet pants clung so tightly to the powerful muscles in his thighs that she couldn't look away.

He really made her furious. If they weren't going to behave as husband and wife, then why was he walking around half-naked in front of her? Was he planning to do this all the time?

"Helps to wash off the dust, doesn't it?"

His low voice was as calm as if this had been just any old day like any other.

The ragged edges of her feelings tore a little more.

"Yes," she said sharply, barely keeping her voice steady, "we were probably the grimiest bride and groom that preacher ever married."

He chuckled and bent to set his boots down beside the door. His arms and shoulders rippled with muscles, and her palms itched to slide over them. Oh, how she needed to feel his warm arms around her!

"You were a beautiful bride, Callie. The dust didn't show on you at all."

"How can you *say* that?"

The words burst out uncontrollably as she whirled to face him, a fork in one hand, a case-knife in the other.

Startled, he walked toward her.

"Because you were," he said gently. "I thought that while we were saying our vows."

The trembly feeling inside her had never really gone away all day, not since the minute she'd waked. Now it took hold of her in a frantic grip.

"I was *not* a bride!" she cried. "Have you forgotten already what you said?"

He stopped in his tracks and stared.

"Well, did you want to be? What I said was that I wouldn't lay claim to my husband's rights. I sure as hell didn't say I wouldn't accept them if you offered."

She stared back at him, shocked speechless.

"Are you offering?"

He was looking at her tenderly, from the damp hair clinging around her face to her bare feet sticking out from under his big white shirt she'd commandeered from the cupboard in his room. It came all the way down past her knees, nearly to her ankles. She was decently covered, but his eyes said he could see her body beneath it.

"No!" she said, after a lifetime had passed.

"All right," he said, with the ghost of his smile starting to play on his lips, "I was only asking."

He strolled toward her, his feet soundless on the wood plank floor. It was all she could do not to run to meet him and throw herself into his embrace. She needed that, oh, she needed it so *bad*.

"What's the matter, Callie?"

He sounded as if he really wanted to know.

But he was only going to make love to her if she offered. What man wouldn't take any willing woman?

"I'm not beautiful, either, besides not being a bride," she cried, as the tears that had been threatening began to pour from her eyes. "I've never been beautiful or my looks considered womanly—*never!*"

"Then there must be something about the fine air of the Cherokee Strip that suits you right down to the bone," he said softly, and at the sound her very bones began to melt.

She cast about desperately for a defense.

"If our ... marriage ... is going to be in name only," she said, trying to sound properly indignant, "you need to put on some clothes, Nick."

He stood directly in front of her now, looking down at her, searching her face. Then he gave her that rare, crooked grin of his that would charm the birds from the trees.

"Let me take your weapons," he drawled. "And I will."

He lifted the utensils from her upraised

hands and reached around her with both arms to lay them on the table behind her.

His body pressed against hers, wet and cooling, yet full of heat. Hard heat. He enveloped her in it. He was almost holding her.

His scent made her drunk. He smelled of the fresh spring water and the night air, and his wet jeans held the fragrance of horses and dust and hay. But it was the aroma of his skin that made her dizzy—the man-scent that belonged only to Nickajack.

She wanted to kiss the hollow in the middle of his chest. It was all she could do not to press her lips against his smooth skin.

But that would be too dangerous. He already thought she was asking him to truly make her his wife. She'd already given him the wrong impression, and she needed to set him straight.

Try as she might, though, she couldn't remember what they'd been talking about.

"You will do what?" she said slowly, managing to recall his last words.

"Put on some clothes."

He took his arms from around her.

She felt abandoned, forsaken, lost.

Until he lifted his hands to the top button of his shirt, which she'd fastened just above her breasts, and began, slowly, to undo it.

"Nick . . . ?"

She tilted her head back to look into his eyes.

"You tell me to stop if you want to, Callie," he said, "and I will."

But how could she? She was mesmerized. He was weaving a spell with his nimble, callused fingertips brushing fire into her skin.

He moved on to the next button.

"I meant put on some . . . clothes . . . of your own," she said, taking in a deep draught of air, as his hands moved against the swells of her breasts.

"I am. This is my shirt."

"I meant . . . a shirt of yours . . . that I wasn't wearing," she said, gasping each time he touched her.

He leaned back to see her face and raised his eyebrows, feigning great surprise. With one fingertip, he traced a wandering, tantalizing line from the hollow of her collarbone down and down, in between her bare breasts, his knuckles barely brushing one, then the other. A shivering thrill raced through her.

"Oh?" he teased. "Well, then, why didn't you say that to begin with?"

She couldn't even frame a reply, much less speak.

He unfastened another button.

She had to stop him. He had said she only had to say the word.

Stop. She must say it, *Stop*.

The shirt was hanging open now. Soon it would be all undone, and he'd see she was wearing nothing underneath. His scent and his touch and his handsomeness were making her shameless, and she didn't even care.

Her little voice of truth flashed the warning of danger—if she made love with this man who wasn't really her husband, she would want to again and again, just as she always wanted more of his kisses. And when spring came he'd be lost to her, because she'd be gone from this claim which also wasn't really her own.

She must push him away.

He undid the last button of the shirt and stood back with his head cocked to look at her. The breeze from the window lifted one side of the shirt, then let it fall.

Nick's eyes never left hers. He intended to know every thought, every feeling inside her, they said. He was searching to see what she wanted and he wasn't going to quit until she showed him.

She must not let him learn she desired him so desperately that she couldn't breathe anymore. She must keep that a secret, or be lost.

His wet, black hair glinted blue sparks in the dim light, and clung endearingly to the noble shape of his head. She couldn't help herself, she reached up and smoothed it back with her palm.

He leaned into her hand.

That tiny, beguiling, unguarded gesture, so unlike him, broke her heart.

She didn't care about next spring. She didn't care about tomorrow. She needed Nickajack—only Nickajack.

"All right," he drawled, "what do you say? Are you going to give me back my shirt?"

"N-o-o," she managed to say, mimicking him, "I'm not. You'll have to take it."

Chapter 15

His gray eyes warmed to the color of smoke and a smile played around the corner of his lips.

She thought he was bending to kiss her, but he scooped her up into his arms, held her nestled against him, where she fit like a dream, lifted the lamp chimney with one hand, and blew out the light. A trembling came over her and she had to wind her arms around his neck and press her cheek against his chest.

It was broad and hard and warm. She wanted more; she wanted all of him. She stroked his neck, his shoulders, and he held her closer until he laid her down.

"Do I have to give your bed back, too?" she

said, breathlessly teasing him. "First it's your shirt, then . . ."

"We're sharing this bed," he said firmly. "From now on, we're sleeping here together."

From now on . . .

Instead of scaring her, that thrilled her. A reckless abandon was growing inside her.

She pulled him back down when he started to let her go.

"We'll have everything sopping," he muttered, but he said it against her lips and then took her mouth in a kiss that plundered her soul.

In the kitchen, there by the table, she'd thought that she wanted him. She had honestly, secretly thought that she'd wanted him the first time they'd kissed.

But she had not known what wanting was.

Wanting took hold of her like a swirling tornado and ripped her right up off the earth. No gravity pulled at her anymore, no connection held her to the planet. Her only bond was to Nickajack, and he was creating it with his hot mouth and his tormenting tongue and his unbridled lips.

Heaven help her. Now she wanted more and more, wanted him to do she didn't even know what, wanted him never to stop this . . .

She felt his hands leave her and go to the buttons of his jeans, but she wouldn't let him move away; she couldn't live without his mouth. Shameless, she sat up and moved with him, took his head in her hands so as not to break the kiss, then tried to help him peel away the stiff, wet, heavy cloth.

She wanted all barriers away from between them. Then she wanted Nickajack inside her and around her and *with* her, skin to skin.

She pulled her mouth from his only long enough to whisper one word against his lips.

"Hurry."

He groaned and kissed her again, quick and hard, dragging his tongue along the seam of her lips as he turned away to peel down his jeans. Then, as she knelt up to reach for him, to run her hands over his back, his slim waist, and brazenly down onto his hard bottom, he caught her hands in his and held them away from his body as he turned to her.

She gasped.

In the moonlight, he was magnificent. She could not take her eyes from his hard manhood, which looked huge and ready and . . .

"I want to see you, Callie."

There were no curtains at the long windows. The moon was rising fuller and brighter by the minute and its light poured in, falling across the bed like the dawn.

He sat down beside her and cradled her head in both his big hands, but he didn't kiss her. Slowly, he stroked the sides of her neck and her shoulders, ran his hands down over her arms. Even through her sleeves, his touch set her on fire.

And then his hands came together at the front of the shirt, parted it, and gently, gently drew it down over her shoulders and off. Nothing lay between them now.

Tenderly, he laid her down again, pushing the pillow beneath her head.

Nick caressed her with his gaze and she felt it as warm as the stroking of his hand would be on her skin. Some small corner of her mind marveled that she felt so easy about it, so truly comfortable with something so new and bold as this.

"You *are* beautiful, Callie," he said hoarsely. "You're the most beautiful woman I have ever seen."

Tears sprang into her eyes.

"Ah, Nick," she said, and held out her arms, "come here to me."

And he did. He came to her and enfolded her; he kissed her senseless and then pulled back to look at her again, laying one hand on her hipbone as if it were a brand.

By then she was writhing beneath him, ready to beg but unable to form words. Only one. Nick. That was all she could say.

"Nick," she whispered, reaching for his hard shaft, "Nick."

He groaned pitifully as she took him into her hand, and rolled over on top of her. He pushed her legs apart with his knee, then thrust into her with a fierce need that matched her own. His mouth and hers fit together again with an old, familiar passion. Inside the magic circle of his arms was where she was meant to be.

Everything about them was meant to be.

They moved together to the rhythm of their deep, wild heartbeats. She clung to him, digging her nails into his back so as not to go flying off into the universe—yielding, then demanding, then incredulous that pleasure could be so strong, so all-consuming. She had known nothing before this. Nothing.

Then the pleasure built and built into a whole new storm that grew wilder yet. Nick swept her into it and through it to the peak of a mountain of joy, where lightning struck her, heart and soul. She could not think, she could only feel, as he collapsed with his face against hers and his ragged breath against her ear.

With her primal instincts, she knew one thing: never, ever would she be the same.

The dawn light, the earliest pale shadings of gray, told her *how* it was that she would never be the same. They lay entwined, her head on Nick's shoulder, her leg thrown over his, his hand cupping her bottom.

She smiled. Yesterday at dawn she had been scared half to death that she could never get him out of jail and he'd be hanged. Today she rested, peaceful, in his arms.

Well, that just went to prove a person shouldn't faunch and worry about what might happen, because there was no way of knowing. Never, *ever*, not even at noon yesterday, had she dreamed she'd wake up married to him this morning.

Why in the world had she done such a thing? She could've scrabbled out a living in town somehow. She could've left the Cherokee Strip, for that matter! After all, she didn't have a claim anymore.

But, like a stranger to herself, she had married Nickajack. It wasn't all for the baby's sake, she didn't think.

It was because she'd been so lonesome. Probably because she needed to be kin to someone, since she'd never been away from kin during her whole life. Yes, it was the comfort of being tied to someone, even if it was only temporary, to salve the awful wounds of the heart she'd carried away from Kentucky.

She idly stroked her palm against Nickajack's warm skin, let it slide up and over his shoulder.

No, she had married him for some more mysterious reason.

It came to her with the gray light in the sky turning to rose. She loved him. She was still the same person, no matter how far from home, and Calladonia Sloane would never marry a man she didn't love.

Nickajack Smith had been a part of her blood and her breath since the minute he rode up to her on the day of the Run. That was why that passion had always been there, lurking, ready to reach out and pull them together at the slightest provocation.

Loving Nick was the reason Vance's memory had slipped away from her. One reason she had been trying so hard to hang onto it was so she *wouldn't* love another man. Look what loving Vance had done to her: it had hurt her like poison when he died, it had destroyed her whole life, it had scared her all the way to her soul to be alone in the world with the baby and without him. Something in her had been afraid of facing all those dangers again if she loved a man and lost him.

Against her will, Nick had made her trust him. And love him. She loved him with all her heart.

She had Nick back here at home now, and she would never lose him.

She smiled as she drifted back to sleep, her hand over his heart as if she were staking her claim. She'd never known what passion was until Nick—and the same was true of love.

Nickajack finally brewed some coffee, just to have something to do with his hands besides start stroking Callie's porcelain skin and making love to her all over again. It wouldn't be fair to wake her up when she was sleeping so soundly, her face open and innocent as a child's.

Plainly she was exhausted, and who wouldn't be? Yesterday had been a day for the tally book.

He sat on his haunches, opened the door of the old cookstove, and punched up the fire under the coffeepot. Yet it'd be such a wonder and a release to him if he could just go crawl back into bed with her and hold her, just hold her, and tell her that he loved her.

It felt so strange, so unlike his usual self, to be bursting to tell his feelings to someone else. He couldn't help it, though—it seemed like such a miracle. He had never told any woman that he loved her, and now he knew that if he had, it would've been a lie.

He heard the coffee begin to boil, closed the stove, and crossed the room to the open front door to lean against its frame. The chores were done, the horses shifted from one pen to another; it was time to ride. The sun was halfway up the sky.

But he couldn't make himself get to work, couldn't make himself leave the cabin. Not until he saw Callie awake this morning.

He smiled to himself as he watched the young horses start a game, running in a bunch from one side of the round corral to the other. The smile wasn't for them, though; it was for Callie.

Who would've thought a slip of a girl like her could have stuck in there and wrestled that crazy team of hers to town, found Baxter, made a deal, and got him out of jail in time to get home in time for evening chores? He shouldn't have bawled her out for trading off her claim—plainly she'd had no choice, since that was what Baxter'd been after all along.

The deal had just scared him because he'd known in his gut that if they lived in the same house, they'd be in the same bed before long. Last night had proved him right. Thank God, she had wanted it as much as he had, and if actions really did speak louder than words, he had a feeling that one of these days, she'd be telling him that she loved him, too.

The thought made his heart clench in his chest. If *that* dream came true, he'd have no right to ever expect anything more, in this life or the hereafter.

An incoherent choking sound made him turn around.

Callie raced past him, one hand over her mouth, heading for the back door with her other hand holding the sheet wrapped around her. He stared, then dashed after her.

She ran out through the back door and into the yard, but she couldn't make it past the cottonwood tree. All she could do was latch onto it for support as she bent double to throw up what little was in her stomach.

Nickajack turned back into the house, grabbed the first cloth he saw and the pitcher of water, then ran toward her while he wetted it. She tried frantically to wave him away and hold up the sheet at the same time but he went to her, anyway.

Pitifully, she shook her head at him, then doubled over again.

"You haven't eaten for hours," he said. "You're throwing up nothing but bile. Here, let me hold this cold rag . . ."

She blushed beet red, as if this were the most embarrassing situation he could ever find her in.

"No!" she gasped, flapping her hand at him weakly. "Go away . . ."

Then she was retching again.

He held her head, he put the cloth on it, he wet it again, and finally led her to the back porch, where he sat her down on the steps.

"Callie, what has made you sick? It can't be what little you ate on the way home . . ."

She took the cloth from her forehead and held it out while he poured more cold water over it. Then she slumped back against the porch post and stared at him with her huge, green eyes.

"The smell of coffee makes me sick," she said.

"It does? Why didn't you tell..."

She shook her head and the look on her face shut him up instantly.

"What I didn't tell you is a whole lot more than that, Nickajack," she said baldly. "Come spring, I'll be having a baby."

He couldn't quite take in the meaning of her words. He searched her face, as if they'd been written there for him to read and refresh his memory.

But his memory wasn't the problem; he remembered what she'd said, all right. He thought he knew her. How could he not know such a big thing as this?

He shook his head to try to clear it.

"You never said..."

"I never said it because you'd have tried even harder to send me back home or into town," she said wearily. "Don't you see? You'd have jumped on that fact like a dog on a bone. You'd have lectured me from now to kingdom come about how a woman with child could never prove up a claim."

He didn't even try to respond to that. All he could do was let every time he'd been with her since that day of the Run flash back through his head.

Had he been wrong about her openness, her bluntness, her honesty?

Yet, why should she tell him all her secrets?

This was a big piece of information, though—one that would soon be visible. Obviously, she didn't feel as close to him as he did to her.

"What were you going to do? Let me find out along with the rest of the world? You could've told me, Callie. You *should* have told me—why, you wouldn't even let me help with your soddy!"

Hurt and anger held his jaw so tight he could barely get the words out.

"My soddy isn't . . . wasn't . . . your responsibility."

An even more horrifying thought hit him.

"And last night! We might've damaged the baby . . . good God, Callie, I had a right to know!"

She paled even more, so the freckles across her nose stood out like tiny brown specks on snow. Her eyes filled with pain and regret but he didn't feel sorry for her.

"You have a right to know something else, too," she said, clearly fighting to keep her voice from shaking.

He could see that it was all she could do to hold his gaze and not look away, but she did it.

"What?"

"You're my first husband. Vance and I were never married."

That rocked him back on his heels. All he could do was stare at her.

Her eyes filled with tears. He didn't care.

"I never figured you for a liar."

Or a betrayer, like Matilda.

"I'm not!"

"It would be fair to say that you are, *Mrs.* Sloane."

"What did you expect me to tell people?" she cried, throwing up her hands in despair.

Every line of her body pleaded with him.

"I want to teach school. I'm going to have a baby. No one way out here would ever know the difference—and you wouldn't have, either, if I hadn't been honest and told you!"

He turned on his heel and walked away.

Callie couldn't move. She couldn't have moved if an angry rattlesnake had uncoiled from around the post she leaned against and struck at her, fangs bared.

Nick would never love her now.

And she was *married* to him.

Worse, she loved him.

She ought to get up, pack up, and leave.

She ought to drive her wagon straight to Arkansas City and find a place to live and a job. It was a settled town; she'd be safe enough there.

That thought held firm for a moment, but

then it was gone. If she did that, she'd never see Nickajack again.

Her whole life, for endless days just past, had been nothing but losing people she loved whom she'd never see again. She'd endured more loneliness than she had ever imagined could exist. Only when she was with Nickajack had it eased.

One night with him had healed the terrible wound in her heart.

Callie stood up, wrapped her arms around the post, and leaned on it to steady her. The heat-blasted trees and rocks, already reflecting the early-morning sun, led her eye farther up the hollow from the house to a trailing patch of sumac turning red.

The cyclone that had stolen her wagon top had brought the only rain in months, but it must have been enough to keep the sumac alive. That one night in Nick's arms had done the same for her spirit.

She leaned her cheek against the weathered wood and looked out across the homey old place. That feeling still lingered, deep inside her somewhere—the feeling she'd had the day of the Run that this valley was where she was supposed to be.

Nickajack would get over his surprise at her news—he was a fair person, in spite of his prejudice against farmers and homesteaders. Wouldn't she be prejudiced against them, too, if a bunch of strangers had come rushing in to the Sloane Valley to carve out farms for themselves?

Yes, he would get used to the thought of the baby. Didn't men always get overexcited if they had a big shock of some sort? Wasn't that why Granny and Mama always said not to tell a man bad news or ask him for something he didn't want to give until after he'd rested a while and had his supper?

Once he'd become accustomed to the idea, he would see reason.

That thought gave her strength, and so did looking at the hard land. Those trees, that sumac, had endured for no telling how many years, and so could she. Hadn't she come this far?

Callie let go of the post and walked steadily back into the house, went straight to the stove and set the coffee off the fire. From the feel of the pot, it had half boiled away.

She was beyond getting sick from the smell. Right now, she was beyond everything but hope.

Hope sustained her during the long days and helped her go to sleep each night. Nick spoke very little.

"What are you doing, trying to prove I need a wife?" he had said on that first day at supper, when she'd covered the table with a fresh apple pie from the drought-stunted fruit in his orchard, a venison roast from his smokehouse, potatoes from his cellar, and shucky beans and jelly from her own meager stores.

"You've got one whether you need me or not," she'd retorted.

He had raised a wry eyebrow at that and she imagined she saw his ghost of a smile.

The next day he did come in to eat at noon, which he had not done the day before. Callie had spent the morning baking yeast bread and cleaning the main room of the cabin to a gleaming shine.

"Now, look here," he said, glancing around the room as he sat down to hot bread, butter, and sliced leftover venison, "cooking is enough. It's not your place to clean up after me."

"It's not your place to sleep in the barn, either," she said.

"This marriage is in name only," he snapped. "I told you that from the start."

The hurt that stabbed through her surprised her with its strength.

"I intend to earn my keep," she snapped back. "But you needn't worry about my baby's. I'll be gone before he comes."

She looked down at her plate and steeled herself.

Then go now. I want you off my place. I never want to see you again. I wish I'd never thought of

*marrying you. A marriage in name only can easily
be undone.*

But he said none of that. He ate his food,
looked her in the eye when he thanked her for
the meal, pushed back his chair, then got up
and strode out to the round pen. Callie
couldn't stop herself. She rose from the table,
crossed the room, and stood just inside the
door, watching him.

Desire moved through her in a surging
wave, desire for more than the pleasure he'd
given to her body. His arms had held comfort,
a comfort so splendid.

Ever since the moment he'd ridden up to
her during the Run, his eyes had searched hers
and seen into her heart. Surely he would get
over being angry that she'd kept the baby a
secret.

But when should she try to talk to him? He
had to give her a chance or she had to make
one.

If he wasn't going to forgive her, she didn't
know if she could stay.

Even as the thought came to her, though,
she realized she had no choice. He had merely
looked straight into her eyes and had let his
gaze linger for the first time in two days, and
she was wanting desperately for him to take
her into his arms. One look every *thirty* days
would most likely do the trick just as well. She
was as trapped by her own desires as if he'd

built a gate at the mouth of the canyon to keep her here.

Callie went back to the table and started clearing away the food. She had just finished wrapping tea towels around the leftovers and putting the jelly into the pie safe when she heard the thunder of hooves.

"Callie!"

He hadn't called her by her name since she'd made her confession.

"Callie!"

She was already running toward the front door and out.

"Go and stand down there by those trees," he called, pointing toward the pond and the creek which eventually led to the mouth of the draw. "If they come that way, don't let them past. Get in front of them and wave your arms until they turn."

Blindly, she ran toward the spot where he'd sent her.

Once there, she turned to see that Nick had ridden the colt he was training around the house, toward the oncoming hoofbeats, and was waiting to the right of the horses' path as they ran down the draw.

"I can slow them and probably haze them into a circle," he called to her. "Don't worry if they come toward you, though—a horse won't run over a person."

Her heart was beating fast. What if these

horses didn't know that rule? She wasn't a very *big* person—what if they didn't even see her?

Instinctively, she laid her hand on her belly as if to protect the baby.

"We'll jump out of the way if they get too close," she told him. "Nick can do without three more horses."

Yet she wasn't scared, she realized. She was excited—because she trusted Nick. He wouldn't put her in a spot that was dangerous.

He began to move his horse in beside the three running ones as they came on. Pushing his mount close to the nearest, a tall bay, he began to guide them off the path onto the grass at the front of the house. They started to slow, then gradually turned in a circle. A steadily slowing circle.

"Come on up this way, Callie," he called. "Keep to that side of the bunch and we'll drive them into the corral."

She saw then that he had left the wide gate open on the pen where he'd been riding.

"They're tired," he said, as she walked toward him, "they must've been running all over the hill up there."

Callie laughed.

"That's not a hill. I haven't seen a hill since I got here."

Nick flashed her a quick smile. Her heart lifted.

"These are the three young ones I brought from the Nation as weanlings," he called, in a soothing, sing-song tone meant to calm the slowing horses. "They're pretty gentle, but they're young, too. Somehow they let themselves out of the brush pen I built up the canyon."

She took in a deep, long breath. Nick was talking to her again. Maybe it was for the horses' benefit, but he was talking to her again.

Working together, with Nick directing her with words and hand signals, they guided the horses in through the gate. Nick closed it from horseback, then he dismounted and stood beside her as she watched the three nose around inside the pen.

"They know they've been naughty," she said. He laughed.

"Maybe so, but they wouldn't hesitate to do the same thing again," he said. "We'll keep them here for a few days while I fix that fence on the south pen. They can benefit from some human attention."

Callie hardly listened to what he said, only to the sound of his low, rich voice. They stood there, leaning on the fence, looking at the horses for a moment more, and then he swung back up into the saddle.

"I'll take this one down the creek a ways," he said. "Thanks for your help."

She watched him go and remembered the last time he took that trail with her in the saddle in front of him. When he was out of sight she walked slowly back to the house. Maybe those renegade horses had given her her chance.

Chapter 16

Nick was still friendly and talked some at supper, so when a cool breeze sprang up afterward and he went out to sit on the porch that ran across the front of the house, Callie joined him.

Suddenly, though, as she sat down in the old rocker handwoven from strips of bark that sat opposite his, she resented needing to explain anything to him at all. Any man ought to understand that a woman wouldn't simply blurt out the news of her condition to a man. And any man ought to understand the powerful pull of a person's body toward someone she loved.

Maybe that was it. Maybe Nick was judging

her for not being married to Vance.

"Nickajack, do you think I'm a loose woman?"

He whipped his head around to look at her. "What did you say?"

"You heard me. Are you thinking bad of me because I was with Vance without being married to him?"

"No!"

He looked genuinely shocked. "That's nobody's business but yours. What riled me was the silent lie of not telling me about your baby." He shrugged. "Call yourself 'Mrs.' for the sake of a school, if you want to, but tell me the truth about what I need to know."

"Have you told me all *your* secrets?"

His only answer was a long, straight, angry look, his eyes full of pale fire in the gathering dusk.

"Well, I'm glad you're not judging me for Vance, anyway. I can't bear to think what I'd do without this baby."

Nickajack couldn't stop looking at her. She had turned away to stare out across the yard with her determined chin lifted just a little to prove she was right.

"What you'd better be doing is thinking what you'll do *with* this baby." His voice came out hard as stone.

She whirled around to look at him.

"What do you mean? That I can't stay here

after he's born? I *told* you I'd leave in the spring."

"No," he snapped. "I'm telling you that you can't take care of a baby and hold school at the same time."

"Oh, yes, I can."

Her belligerent tone made him want to smile but he didn't. He wanted her to know he meant what he said.

Suddenly the thought of her baby became real and he wanted to see it, wondered if it would have huge, green eyes like its mother. Her gaze held his, wouldn't let go.

"What are you thinking?" she demanded.

"Reckon that baby will have a stubborn chin like its mama's?"

She frowned at him, then smiled.

"Yes," she said, "and lots of sand. This is a baby who made the Cherokee Strip Land Run."

Her smile widened into that big, brilliant one that lit up her face and the whole world besides. The smile that could break the heart of the meanest man.

Any woman with a smile like that surely could be trusted. Any woman blunt enough to walk out on the porch and ask straight out if he considered her a loose woman surely was honest enough to be trusted.

Somehow it seemed comforting, the thought of having a baby around. And interesting. He had always loved being with his young cousins in the Nation.

He couldn't let her go, once the winter was over. Yes, he'd told her he'd build her her own cabin on half his claim, but she couldn't go there and have the baby alone!

But, oh, Lord, she certainly couldn't stay here and have it with him. He'd not know how to help her; couldn't bear to hold those two lives in his hands.

Terror trickled like icy water into his veins. He was losing his mind, because the gravity of this situation had just now hit him.

"Here, now," he said, too roughly, "who's going to help you when your time comes?"

She bristled.

"You don't have to worry," she said sharply. "I've told you more than once that I'd be gone as soon as winter's over. *Before* my time comes. I'll keep my word."

She was so appealing, glaring at him with the high color rising just beneath her fine skin. He ached all over his body, he longed to reach out and pull her into his arms, but he would die before he let her see that.

Because she might not feel the same way about him. She must not, or she wouldn't be constantly talking about leaving. She'd be hoping that their marriage might somehow turn out to be real—like he was, much as he hated to admit it.

She had cared for him, for his safety at least, when she found Fox's letter. That was no sign that she *loved* him, though. And she'd never told him so.

Except with her body, all of one whole night.

But who could say? The way she'd so carefully kept her baby secret, despite how close he'd felt to her . . .

Look, Smith, she's carrying another man's baby. She loved that other man, she told you so, and she still loves him. So get a hold on your runaway feelings.

And, knowing Callie and her honor and her sense of obligation, she might've been merely pleasuring his body on their wedding night, doing it out of a feeling that she owed that to him for offering her a place to winter. She was bound to be scared—out here alone with no place of her own now and a baby to provide for, come spring.

If he had a grain of sense, he'd take her somewhere else right now and make her go back to civilization, where she'd have help with the baby—before he really fell in love . . .

But it was too late for that. Way too late.

"Callie," he said, his throat tight with wanting her, every muscle in him tense with wishing he never had to let her go, "maybe you should think about a school in town."

She stood up and brushed the dust from the back of her skirt, clearly too touchy tonight to consider a sensible suggestion. One from him, at any rate.

"Nickajack, I told you. You will not have to do one single thing concerning this baby. I'll take care of it. There's no need to start trying to run my life again, either—soon we'll both be out of your hair."

She sounded very adamant and very sure. Callie knew what she wanted; she always did.

He sat there like a bump on a log and let her walk away from him. She stopped at the door.

"I hate to put you out of your bed," she said, "but I know you won't hear to anything else. Let me know if you change your mind."

Then she went inside, huffy as could be.

It made him smile in spite of the mixed-up emotions roiling in his heart. Yes, she was bound to be scared about taking care of a baby, and yes, she had no claim anymore and she had worked all those days on her soddy only to hand it over to Baxter, but she still had her tough spirit—none of her trials had dampened her fire. If anybody could hold school and take care of a baby at the same time, Callie Sloane could.

Callie *Smith*. According to that preacher's piece of paper, she was Callie Smith now.

He sat there, looking out across the wide yard sloping down to the dry creekbed, watching the mares move about in their pasture and the young horses in theirs as they all settled quieter and quieter beneath the night, falling dusky and sweet from the east while the sundown claimed the sky in the west. He could feel the faintest hint of coolness in the air. After all, it was October.

This might be one of those years when October passed hot and dry as one of the summer moons, and then November blew in cold and wet as sudden winter. It was a good thing Callie had given up her claim, much as he'd hated for her to do it for him. She and a baby couldn't survive over there without a man to haul water and cut wood and make a shelter that would protect them when the blizzards blew.

Finally, the moon began to rise. He needed sleep. He needed to get away from the house and to his bed in the barn. He needed to stay away from Callie until he knew her true feelings about him.

That made him smile. He sounded like some prissy woman demanding to know if a man's intentions were honorable.

He stood up, and the chair rocked back and gently thumped the wall. One of the colts raised his head and whinnied at the moon, which was full and bright and beautiful coming out to ride the sky.

But instead of walking through its mellow light toward his bed in the barn, as he intended, he turned to the door of the house. Callie had had plenty of time to wash up, go to bed, and get to sleep. He wouldn't wake her.

Silently, he stepped inside the big room. Callie had made it look like a real home again, the way it had when his mother was alive. Callie was a whole lot like his mother, except for her blunt openness. His mother had kept her own counsel.

Something drew him to the table-desk, and he stood in front of it before he realized that what he wanted was to look at that marriage certificate again. He'd barely glanced at it when he and Callie had signed it.

He felt sheepish but he picked it up, anyway. Callie had thrown it and the registration papers for the claim there at some point—he'd noticed that in passing to get his clothes from his room.

He needed to put the papers into the tin box hidden in one log wall behind a weaving his Cherokee grandmother had made. But first he really wanted to look at the marriage paper. Somehow, he needed to look at its words and Callie's handwriting, although it was all meaningless if she didn't love him, too.

Her bedroom door was open for the breeze, so he left the lamp unlit and silently crossed the room to the light of the low fire. He sat on his haunches in front of it and stirred the coals until some small flames leapt up.

The registration paper slipped from his fingers and fell onto the floor.

Calladonia Sloane.

That was the only name on the front of it.

He picked it up, unfolded it, and read it rapidly, front and back.

Calladonia Sloane was the only name on it anywhere. The legal land description was the correct one for his claim.

A flash fire burst up the back of his neck and that whole half of his scalp began to burn.

He let out a roar so terrible that it nearly tore out his throat.

Callie leapt from the bed reaching for a weapon, for anything to fight with. *What was it? It was in the house!* She tried to yell for Nickajack, but was so wildly scared that not one sound would come out.

A panther? No, it wasn't that scream. A bear? How could a bear get into this house without making a sound?

"*Goddammit*, Callie, get out here!"

Her toes grabbed the wood planks of the floor.

Nickajack?

Her heart raced at a gallop.

What in the world was he doing, terrifying her like this?

He filled the doorway, his face awful in the moonlight.

"What the *hell* did you think you were doing?"

His voice was anguished now but it was that same roar.

He waved pieces of paper in both hands.

She couldn't speak, couldn't move, could only stand there in her night shift and stare at him while she tried to hold her heart in her chest with both hands.

"So this is how you get a home for your baby," he snarled. "You planned it all along, didn't you? Were you and Baxter in league? Or did you see your chance and take it when you saw me sitting helpless in jail?"

Her mind was racing, doing its best to take that in, but she must've been asleep even though she thought she hadn't. Not one word of this made the slightest bit of sense.

Gradually, though, her pounding blood began to slow. This was Nickajack and he wasn't attacking her. Not physically, so the baby wasn't in danger. She wasn't in danger—except of dying of heart's pain.

How could he talk this way to her?

Her tongue felt thick as cotton wool, her lips stiff as the paper he was brandishing in her face.

"What?"

She finally managed to get that one word out of her mouth.

"You've stolen my claim, that's what! *My* land, *my* homeplace, where my mother's bones are buried. If you think you can get away with this . . ."

Just as suddenly as he'd appeared in the door, he thrust past her and staggered to the bed. He dropped onto it as if someone had knocked his knees out from under him.

"You *can* get away with it, though, can't you? And you know it. All you have to do is side with Baxter and shout to the world that I'm Cherokee."

Finally, at last, her brain began to work again. So did her legs.

She ran to him in spite of the fact that his eyes were burning the skin off her face.

"That's why I had to do it, don't you see?"

The words came out in an anguished cry.

He stared at her, shaking his head, uncomprehending.

"Baxter was in the Land Office with me— he was talking about you being Indian, and the other people were speaking up about their white relatives that didn't get any claims," she said desperately. "There was going to be big trouble over it, but your bald-headed clerk saved the day."

"By giving my claim to you?" Sarcasm dripped from the words.

"*Yes.* He pretended that your note on the permit was to sign your claim over to me and he passed it off that way. I couldn't say anything in front of everyone, and I knew I could deed it over to you when all the excitement had passed."

"But the excitement's just beginning, isn't it?" he said with that biting sarcasm meant to wither her.

Reckless, irresistible fury wiped out her fear.

"You do not trust me at all," she said. "After all we've been through, after I signed away *my* homeplace, the only legacy I could have for my baby, to get you out of jail, you ungrateful, abominable *wretch*, you do not trust me at all!"

A flash of startlement showed in his eyes.

But he stood up and towered over her like an avenging angel.

"I don't trust any woman," he said, in a dead voice. "After Matilda, I should've known better than to put any faith in you."

Callie stepped back so she could look him in the eye. The devastation she saw in his soul broke her heart.

She certainly hadn't put it there. She had done him no wrong, if he would stop jumping to conclusions long enough to realize it.

"I don't know Matilda, I have no connection to Matilda, and I resent being compared to Matilda," she said firmly.

"Matilda betrayed me for her own ambitions," he said with a furious look that said, *As you did, too*.

"*I* haven't betrayed you, Nick."

She waited patiently, but he appeared not to have heard her.

"Matilda told my enemies where I'd be so they could set up the ambush," he said. "But you didn't need to do that, since Baxter already knew I was locked up in jail."

All her pity burned away in the fire of her anger.

"Stop comparing me to Matilda!"

"She taught me not to trust even the *word* 'love'."

"Coming from *her*," she cried, before she could stop herself.

What was she doing? Getting ready to say he could trust her, Callie, if she said she loved him? She could never tell him that—he hated her now. He didn't trust her any farther than he could throw this cabin they stood in.

And if he didn't leave her this instant, she was going to throw herself at him and beat his chest with her fists until her bones broke. If he didn't trust her, he didn't love her.

Woe to her, she loved him anyway, in spite of all—and she could not bear to be near him another instant.

"All right," she snapped. "Fine. You've learned your lessons about life. Leave me now so I can get dressed."

* * *

Callie decided to wait until daylight to leave. She marveled that she could have that much control, because all she wanted was to run to her wagon and drive Joe and Judy away as fast as they could gallop. Nickajack didn't love her. The thought sliced a wound across her heart that would never heal.

Not only did he not love her, he didn't know her. He didn't even *want* to know her.

After all their adventures, after she'd showed her loyalty by buying him out of *jail*, for heaven's sake, he didn't even know she was herself, Callie Sloane—no, Callie *Smith*, to her own everlasting regret—and not that Matilda from his past. That woman must have been an awful person and he was lumping them together, saying they were peas in a pod.

The hurt of his words hung in the air around her like a fog clinging to a river. She needed to get out from under it more than she needed her belongings in his house and barn—but she needed her baby even more, and the danger of wrecking the wagon in a ravine in the dark was too real. Never, in a million years, should she have started that trip to rescue Nick from Cap Williams in the jolting, scary dark.

"As things turned out, it wasn't worth the risk, was it?" she muttered to the baby.

Never, since she'd boarded the train that

carried her out of the mountains forever, had she felt so alone.

She dressed quickly, just to be able to get out of Nick's bedroom, wrapped her things in her nightgown, and carried them out into the big room. He wouldn't come back into the cabin until she was gone. He didn't want to see her any more than she wanted to see him.

The cut across her heart widened a little. She had thought she had a friend for life. A husband in name only, maybe, but a friend. Now he was gone because he had no faith in her at all.

If she needed any proof of that, she had it. On his way out, he had thrown the marriage certificate and the claim registration to the floor.

As she crossed to the kitchen, they mocked her, those two stiff pieces of paper, their edges blowing gravely back and forth in the breeze from the open door like winged ghosts, shining white in the night gloom. They *were* ghosts—the ghosts of her dreams.

Trying not to think, she went to get her favorite iron skillet and the cloth sack of shucky beans. She would need every scrap of everything to eat until she could get a job in Arkansas City.

When she had looked around for everything that was hers, when she had tied it all into a bundle and set it beside the door, she went to

Nick's desk and lit the lamp. He could think what he wanted from now on, but he'd never be able to say she stole his place.

She longed to grab all the paper in the house and start covering it with writing, to pour out all the anguish that filled her, to hammer the truth into Nick until he had to see the light, and pelt him with every pain that she felt.

She couldn't, though. Her little voice of truth warned her that if she even looked at all her feelings, they would tear her apart.

And they would probably have no effect on him at all.

Nickajack didn't trust her. That was all that mattered. He could never love her because he didn't trust her.

Before she sat down in his chair, she went around the room and gathered the paper ghosts. She needed the land description since she didn't know it by heart.

Spreading the two crumpled pages on the table, she left the marriage certificate on top while she pulled out the drawer and took out one clean sheet of paper. Nickajack's name stood out where he'd signed it in a hand so bold and big that it brooked no contradiction.

He had spoken in that very way when he'd announced they would marry. She hadn't had a chance, really, to refuse him.

She had only agreed to marry him because of her reputation, because she needed and wanted so badly to get a school. That was the only reason.

Except for the fact that she loved him, whether she knew it or not.

She faced that fact again, let it tear through her again.

Then she banished it into the very nether regions of her mind. Next month, next year, after the baby came to fill up her arms and her life, would be soon enough to think about Nick. Until then, she had to think about what had to be done to survive.

I, Calladonia Sloane Smith . . .

She stopped and looked at that name. She would probably never write it again. As soon as she had money for a lawyer, she would find out how to get a paper of divorce.

A divorced woman would never be hired to teach school.

All right, so she would go by Sloane and stick to her story of widowhood in Kentucky. Nick certainly didn't want to be married to her and would tell no one.

She dipped the pen in the ink and continued to write.

. . . Do hereby renounce any and all claim to the tract of land in the Cherokee Strip with the legal description . . .

Finally, it was done: the closest approximation to a legally binding quit-claim deed that she could imagine how to make. It should serve. In all likelihood, Baxter wouldn't protest any more, since he had what he wanted, and Nickajack could pass for white to get the land title changed.

She blotted the page, let it dry for a moment, then placed it on top of the land registry document in the middle of the table. After a moment's fruitless search of the drawer, she got up and brought a heavy pewter mug from the kitchen to hold both pages down.

There. Nick would see that immediately when he came into the room.

The marriage certificate still lay where she'd left it, folded, to one side. Callie looked at it for a moment, then picked it up, folded it again, and put it in the pocket of her skirt.

Nickajack sat on the tallest rock at the high end of the canyon to watch the moon travel across the sky all night. The old people said that the moon was a ball thrown up against the sky in a stickball game a long time ago.

The legend went that, back in the Old Nation, which was the Center of the Earth, two towns had played each other, long and hard, and one town was about to win when the leader of the other side picked up the ball with his hand—which was not allowed in the game—and threw it toward the goal. Instead of going in, it stuck against the solid sky. It stayed fastened there to remind players never to cheat.

Callie needed to hear that legend.

His heart hurt. How could she have betrayed him so?

I knew I could deed it over to you when all the excitement had passed.

She had sounded and looked completely sincere when she said that.

But so had Matilda when she had asked which road he would take to the Board of Governors' meeting.

How could he have been so fooled, just because Callie was little and green-eyed and quick in her movements and usually blunt in speaking her mind? Matilda may have been tall and languid and dark-eyed and mysterious, but they were sisters under the skin.

I haven't betrayed you, Nick.

That had sounded even more credible because she had said it in such a sure, flat way, with that innocent light blazing at him from her eyes.

A man could be fooled, though. A man could always be fooled by a woman.

A man could never believe it when a woman said she loved him.

Hadn't he believed Matilda? And hadn't she gone out of her way to set him up to be killed?

The old, soul-racking pain tore at his heart again. Those boys never would have died if he hadn't listened to that woman. Too bad Matilda's friends had been such bad shots. He would have died with a smile on his face to have saved his young followers.

No wonder he couldn't trust even the word *love*, ever.

What was it Callie had said when he'd told her that?

Coming from her. Her.

Said with such derision. That, too, had come off her lips with all the honesty in the world.

Had she almost said that *she*, Callie, loved him and meant it?

Surely not.

Grandfather Moon began to set. The sky in the east went black, and then, so gradually that the eye could not mark it, the darkness began slowly to fade into gray over the land that he loved.

He looked at it and waited for wisdom.

When the very first wash of pink appeared, he got to his feet.

This would always be his land—no matter what the white-eyes' law said, no matter whose name was written on a piece of paper and in a book. He would not leave it.

Callie lured her team up from the pasture with grain as soon as she could glimpse gray on the horizon. She had them hitched and the wagon loaded by the time there was enough light to see as far as the spring and the pond.

Nickajack was nowhere on the place. She'd steeled herself to see him when she entered the barn, but she'd sensed instantly that he wasn't there. All the horses were, though. Where had he gone on foot?

She climbed up over the wheel and picked up the lines.

It looked to be a cloudy day. Or maybe it was still too early for streaks of pink and yellow to flare across the sky.

She brought the lines down, the team pulled against the harness, and the wagon started to move.

This morning washed across the land exactly as it had done that other time. The light seemed to float the same way it had done then. It was a gray like smoke, like the color of Nickajack's eyes. Like the warm gray they had been when she lay in his arms in the moonlight.

She would have to live on that memory for the rest of her life, but right now she couldn't bear to recall it.

She set her face toward the mouth of the draw and didn't so much as glance at the cabin as she drove past. This was not her home, and she never wanted to see it again.

Chapter 17

Nickajack moved slowly down off the rock, across the flat butte, then over the edge to descend the rough side of the canyon, feeling his way by the shape of the earth under his feet. He knew it as well as he knew the floor in the cabin. He would never leave it, not even in death.

But the thought gave him no comfort; it only hardened the rock that used to be his heart.

At the bottom, he stood still for a minute, head up, face turned to the north into the wind. Yes, it had shifted. It was coming out of the northwest.

Even that thought gave him no hope. How could this north wind bring rain, now that his petrified skin wouldn't be able to soak it in?

The faintest light of day lit the sky but it hadn't yet reached the ground, and he started down canyon by instinct. If Callie had slept at all, she was still sleeping.

And why *wouldn't* she be able to sleep? She had accomplished what she set out to do when she left Kentucky, hadn't she? She had a claim in her name, and it was one with a cabin and barn and supplies and water. She owned a place where she could have and raise her baby.

He felt a grim smile curl his lips. Whether Callie knew it or not, she also had him on her new place, since he wasn't leaving.

A juniper brushed his face, and he reached out and broke off a piece to carry with him, held it to his nose to catch the spicy scent. It still held its fragrance, but it wasn't as pungent because of the drought.

The aroma didn't give him consolation, though. It couldn't penetrate his wooden body.

Had Callie felt the slightest twinge of guilt or remorse while she was stealing his land? Had she been touched at all by regret when he had found her out last night?

An image flashed across his vision before he could stop it: Callie's shocked eyes as he roared his fury into her astonished, open face. She had looked genuinely stunned.

He would have sworn on his mother's grave that Callie had always been honest with him. Yet look what she'd done. And look what she'd kept from him when he'd thought they were friends.

Of course, he *had* kept telling her all the time that it was impossible for a woman alone to homestead. And she was right to think he'd have been even more adamant if he'd known she was carrying a child.

It was also true that a condition like that wasn't easy for a woman to talk about to a man. But he had been foolish enough to think they were close friends, that she could tell him anything. Hadn't he blabbed to her all about Matilda and every other painful thing?

A new wave of hurt swept through him, so unexpected it nearly brought him to his knees. He'd thought he was numb, that he was getting past it, yet here he was, longing to hold Callie in his arms with an ache that threatened to kill him with misery.

He came out of the upper canyon into the wider valley that held his buildings and pens just as the light broadened to show the beginning of a cloudy day. Without even a glance toward the barn or his horses and chores, he picked up his pace and strode toward the house.

No smoke came from the chimney or the stovepipe. Callie was either still asleep or she'd decided not to cook anymore, and he would bet the yellow filly that it was the former. She was bound to be exhausted—when he'd first charged into her bedroom she'd been trembling like a willow in the wind.

She had looked so truly surprised when he accused her. How could she be so deceitful, after the way she had always been?

The baby would be making her sleep, too, he'd imagine. Just the thought of it almost made him ashamed of putting that dreadful, fearful look in her eyes last night—but dammit, she had brought it on herself! What a weak story: the clerk in the Land Office had done it; she'd had no hand in registering Nick's claim for herself!

He jerked his mind from the past and fixed it on the present. What would he say to her first?

This is my place, and I'm not leaving.

She was so determined, so stubborn, that she would never leave, either.

The infuriating, downright unjust truth of it all was that he'd have to keep living in the barn, with his own house right here. He couldn't put her out now in her condition and he couldn't later because the babe would be so new.

Images flashed through his mind: Callie big with the child, her small hand resting on her huge belly. Callie with a baby in her arms, both of them looking at him with wide, sparkling green eyes.

A paralyzing thought struck him. Damn! He would be here when the baby came. No matter what Callie had done to him, he couldn't ignore her at a time like that.

As soon as winter passed, he'd have to build her another cabin somewhere else on the place—that was all there was to it. He'd pick a spot and snake some logs onto it this fall, and in the spring he'd put it up fast, working like a madman.

Which he would be by then, after having her right here beside him all winter.

I'll let you winter here with no trouble, and then I'll give you half my place if you don't tell the officials I'm Cherokee.

No, that made him sound too weak. He had to take control of this situation somehow.

He crashed through the dry leaves in the yard, bounded up the steps, and strode across the porch in a fever to get the confrontation over with. The instant he stepped in through the door, he saw it: the tall mug sitting on his desk where it had never been before.

It stopped him in his tracks. Beneath it, a sheet of white paper gleamed like a light in the dim room.

Callie was gone. That paper was a note to him.

A desolation like he'd never felt before overwhelmed him. It drew his whole body down, toward the ground, and nailed his feet to the spot where he stood.

Callie was gone.

Finally, he was able to move, to go to the door of his vacant bedroom, and then to the windows at the front of the house, where he saw that her team and wagon were no longer there.

After that, he forced his feet to carry him to the table. He moved the mug away and picked up the note.

I, Calladonia Sloane Smith, do hereby . . .

It was not a note to him. He blinked and read it again, his eyes going back twice to that name.

Dear God. At last, he read it all the way through and went back to look at her name again. She was giving him his claim.

Callie hadn't left him a note; she had left him a deed to his place.

He read it one more time before the lightning bolt hit him. At the end there was no signature. Callie had left him a deed, but she hadn't signed it.

Nick picked up the registration certificate from the Land Office that bore his land description and her name. Beneath it, the surface of the desk gleamed up at him. She must have taken the marriage certificate.

He folded the deed she'd written and

stuffed it into his pocket, left the Land Office document under the mug, and crossed to the door in a heartbeat, whistling for the Shifter as he ran to the barn.

She needn't think she could take that certificate and keep him tied to her forever! Or leave him an unsigned quit-claim deed that probably wouldn't be worth a hill of beans to the officials! What kind of game was she playing, anyhow?

He saddled the Shifter and mounted, then followed the wagon tracks he should have noticed when he came into the yard. This *loco* situation was destroying his eyesight as well as his mind.

Nick and the Shapeshifter moved out through the early morning, catching deep breaths of air sweet enough to break their hearts. The scent of rain rode on the wind and the Shifter lifted his head and whinnied toward it, welcoming the promise.

Nickajack, too, tried to wish it would rain, but at that moment even the drought and the land he loved weren't all that important. He needed to find Callie before she got too far away.

He rode with his eyes on the distance, searching the woods and the creekbed for the arching, bare ribs of the wagon. Who could say what that wild team might have done? She might even still be here, in his canyon.

When, dear God, had she hitched up and started out? Surely she hadn't been traveling in the dark—surely she hadn't gone too far.

As soon as he passed the last trees and rode out of the mouth of his draw, he saw the wagon not far out onto the open prairie. He lost all the air from his lungs. It was empty. It was standing still.

He smooched to the Shifter and raced toward it, searching the surrounding area in every direction as he went. Coming up from behind, he was nearly on the wagon before he saw Callie.

She was in between those two wild beasts of hers, straddling the shaft with her skirts hiked up, pulling in vain with both hands at the mare's firmly planted hind leg. Judy had tangled herself up again trying to kick Joe, who looked ready to retaliate any second now.

"Callie, get out of there!"

He sat back, stopped the Shifter, and leapt off.

Callie turned only far enough to flash him an angry glare.

"*You* get out," she said, and went back to her hopeless task.

He murmured to both animals, let them smell his hands, and stepped in between them, stroking their sides as he worked his way to their hindquarters. Callie kept at it.

"You heard me," he said.

"I've heard you say a lot of things you shouldn't have said."

He bent over and reached around her from behind to help just as Judy gave in and stepped daintily over the shaft. Callie, overbalanced, tumbled backward into his arms.

"There, you see?" she said breathlessly.

Nick's arms closed desperately around her, although he meant to let her go.

Yes, I see. I see that my own body will not obey me when it comes to you.

She stiffened after the fleetest moment of leaning against him. He kept one arm around her waist and backed up, reaching for Judy's head with the other.

"Come on," he said, "before this mare has another fit and stomps us both into the ground."

She came, but she was dragging her feet.

"Turn me loose! What are you doing here, interfering in my business, anyway?"

"Saving your life, looks like."

"Ha!" she said derisively.

Once safely away from the team, he let her go. She whirled to glare at him, though she didn't step back very far.

He felt as if she'd put a mile between them, however. This was ridiculous. He hadn't ridden all this way to try and hold her. Had he?

"I'm out here tending to *my* business," he said.

"Then it has nothing to do with me."

"I think it does. My marriage certificate is missing."

She widened her eyes in mock innocence.

"So? What makes you think I have it?"

"You've been meddling in my personal papers, as usual."

"As usual! Meddling! I simply sat down at your desk to write! Weren't you glad to find the deed?"

He pulled it out of his shirt pocket, fighting the sudden urge of his hands to shake as he unfolded it.

"It would be a lot more help to me if you had signed it."

The mixture of sudden feelings that crossed her face made his heart turn over. Surprise and sorrow, he was sure of them both, but then her old determination wiped them out.

He'd seen regret there, though. Hope surged to life in him—maybe he *had* ridden out here to hold her, after all.

She glanced at the bottom of the page she had written.

"My name's at the beginning."

"Yes, but it needs your signature at the end."

"Very *well*," she said irritably. "Did you bring pen and ink?"

He realized then what he had done. He had come to bring her back. To bring her home.

All along, he'd been afraid to know it.

"No."

She lifted those green eyes and looked at him. Somewhere, off far away to the southwest, thunder rumbled low behind the cloudy sky.

"I have ink and pens packed in my supplies," she said abruptly, and turned away.

Maybe he'd been wrong. Maybe she hadn't leaned into him for just one heartbeat when he had his arms around her. Maybe she would refuse to come with him.

He followed her to the wagon wheel and helped her climb up to the seat. She moved quickly, let him touch her very little. When she was in and turning toward the back, to her meager load of supplies, he couldn't take his eyes from her. He held his breath.

Thunder sounded again.

"Oh, don't go to all that trouble," he said, as she went to a stack of boxes carefully wrapped in her oilskin sheet. "Come on back to the house. It won't take long and it's a shame to tear into your boxes now."

She hesitated. A drumbeat of panic rolled through his blood. Her boxes belonged in his house. *She* belonged in his house. Oh, God, could he make her see that?

"Well," she said, turning toward the now-stronger sound of the thunder, "it might rain."

He forced his words to come out light and careless.

"It's October," he said with a shrug. "About time for the fall rains."

She glanced around at her things.

"I was going to stop in Santa Fe and buy a wagon cover."

Was. He didn't dare say a word. He waited.

"All right," she said, at last. "No sense getting everything wet before I can get to town. I'll go back and wait out the storm."

He longed to climb up to the seat and take the lines from her when she sat down and picked them up, but he couldn't, for fear of scaring her away. For fear of reaching for her too soon, before he thought of what to say.

"Good plan," he said, and vaulted up onto the Shapeshifter. The horse turned back toward home as if he'd understood every word.

"You caught up with me just in time," Callie said, as she brought the wagon around, "like you did the first time."

"First time?"

"Here's where I was driving my stake on your claim," she said matter-of-factly.

He glanced around. She was right, within a stone's throw. His pulse quickened—maybe it was a sign.

The trail up the canyon was too narrow in most places for them to travel abreast. Callie seemed lost in her own thoughts, anyway, and he wanted time to pull his together. He didn't know what to do or say, but he did know he had to convince her to stay.

The thunder sounded louder as they rode up the dry creekbed, and he began to smell rain much heavier in the air.

"Maybe it'll come a good, long rain," he called to Callie, who only nodded.

He couldn't could care less about the rain, except as it served to keep Callie with him. If only it could be a long, steady deluge that would go on all day! He might need time to convince her to stay. That was what he wanted, he knew that now, but on what terms? Was he wanting to make their marriage a real one?

Scattered drops hit them on the way past the pond, and huge fast ones began to pelt down as they drove into the yard.

"Drive on into the barn!" he called, but she was already doing so, as if she did indeed live there.

Smiling, he opened his mouth to say something about unhitching her team, then snapped it shut again. She was intending to drive on soon; she didn't know yet what he was thinking.

She might not want to know, either, but he had to try to tell her, or spend the rest of his life battling even worse regret than he was now. He knew that.

Nick rode in behind the wagon, stripped the Shifter of his bridle, and turned the horse out. All the horses were running and calling, excited by the coming storm.

"We're going to get wet!" Callie was laughing when she said it, when she ran up to him at the pasture gate.

He looked into her beautiful, open face, with the raindrops running down her cheeks like big tears.

"Do we care?"

She laughed again.

"No. At least it'll settle the awful dust."

Just then the heavens opened and it began to pour. He grabbed her hand and they raced for the shelter of the porch.

"I thought we didn't care if we got wet," she teased, as they ran up the steps.

"We don't. We're going to go right in and stir up the fire."

He opened the door and shepherded her in ahead of him. Now, suddenly, he knew what he must do. He had known it since he'd walked in here and seen that mug sitting on his table desk.

"But first," he said, "let's take care of our business."

She had headed toward the fire but she stopped.

"Yes," she said, suddenly sober, "let's."

Going toward the desk, she glanced back at

him. "Then, when the rain stops, I'll be on my way."

He didn't answer, only pulled the sheet of paper from his pocket and unfolded it. Callie sat down in his chair and opened the bottle of ink, took up the pen, and wiped it.

Spreading the page out in front of her, he bent over to hold it flat. He shouldn't have. She smelled like rain, and as always, like flowers—which should have been impossible, since there couldn't be a fragrant blossom alive within a hundred miles.

He fought the need to touch her while she dipped the pen into the ink and the rain poured down outside.

Calladonia Sloane Smith, she wrote.

He couldn't stop looking at those words. Would she ever write them again?

"There," she said briskly, in her school-teacher voice.

"Thank you."

He picked the paper up with his fingers gone stiff with fear.

"Now we'd better stir up the fire," she said. "From the sound of it, the rain won't stop for awhile."

It *was* a deluge, nothing less, water streaming from skies that had been dry for months. Years.

He walked toward the fire because he didn't know what else to do. He knew he couldn't touch her until he said something, but his tongue was tied.

How did a man get a woman past all those terrible things he'd said?

She wasn't coming along behind him; she hadn't gotten up from the chair. She wasn't making a sound.

He got to the hearth and dropped to his haunches in front of the glowing coals. Holding the deed in one hand, he reached into the kindling box with the other.

"Callie," he said, in a voice he hardly recognized, "would you be so kind as to bring me some lucifers from that box in the drawer? This has burned down pretty low."

He tucked the paper beneath the sole of one boot and kept busy arranging the kindling on top of the barely glowing pieces of old logs, while his heart beat as hard and slow as death to let him listen in between.

At last, the drawer opened and closed. The chair scraped back. Her skirts swished; her heels clicked against the planks of the floor.

"Here."

He glanced up, took them and struck one against the fireplace stone, breathing in its scent of sulphur as he held it to the kindling. A whiff of hell, they said. And if he didn't do this right, if Callie left him now, that was exactly where he'd be.

The twigs caught fire.

He half turned and cocked his head so he could look Callie in the eye.

Rocking back on his heel, he took the quit-claim deed, crumpled it in his hand, and dropped it onto the bursting flames. Then he gathered all his courage and stood up to talk to her.

"Nick! You just had me sign that!" she cried, glancing back and forth from him to the fire as if to rescue the paper. "What are you *doing?*"

As she stared at him, though, a dawning understanding mingled with the shock in her eyes. The look stripped him of fear and brought the truth to his tongue.

"Trying to prove that I trust you," he said hoarsely.

She looked at him for a long minute more, as if trying to memorize him, and then she reached up to touch his cheek with her velvet fingertips.

"I'm sorry," he rasped, "Callie, I didn't mean those things I said."

"Oh, Nick," she whispered, "you put your homeplace in my hands."

"I'm putting my *life* in your hands."

She took his face between her hands as if to prove what he said was true, then stood on tiptoe to bring her mouth to his.

He accepted the kiss and kissed her back, with a desperation he had never known before. She felt it, too. It trembled through her with the same ruthless force as through him; he could feel it in every inch of her body.

To reassure her, he stroked her back, her shoulders, her arms. Then he cupped her bottom and brought her up against him so close that nothing could ever get between them again. His tongue found hers and did the same. She thrust her fingers into his hair and pulled him down to the floor in front of the fire.

He helped her unfasten her bodice, she helped him peel out of his jeans, both of them clumsy as dolts. Lost in the magic of the kiss, they fought the endless stream of barriers they wanted gone, ripping and tearing, sending buttons flying and garments after them until they lay tangled on the solid oak planks, skin to sweet skin.

"If you'd gotten away, I'd have lost my mind," Nickajack murmured against her lips when he finally broke the kiss. "I tell you, Callie, I would have."

She gave a breathless chuckle.

"I think you have, anyway."

"I have," he said, "so get ready. I won't get up from here until I kiss every inch of your body."

"You have to do it twice," she said, tightening her arms around his neck. "I've lost my mind, too."

He froze and stared down into her eyes.

"The babe! I forgot."

She laid her finger across his lips.

"It's all right," she whispered. "It's very early yet."

Then she cradled his face in her hands again and kissed him in such a way that he forgot everything he'd ever known, even his own name. When he finally reclaimed his mouth, then kept the promise he'd made her, she cried out and arched beneath him so hotly he could barely restrain himself.

"Now, you stop that," he murmured, as she stroked her soft thigh against him. "You won't trust me unless I keep my promises. I promised to kiss every . . ."

She brushed her taut nipples against his chest.

"You are a she-devil," he rasped and shifted so that he could reach one of them with his mouth.

"That's not what you say when you want me to sign some paper or other," she purred, writhing beneath him, running restless fingers through his hair.

Her breathing went shallow and quick as he dropped a ring of kisses around the tip of her breast, but she stubbornly kept on talking.

"No-o-o. *Then* you're all polite and nice to me and it's 'Callie, you're an angel this, and Callie, you're an angel that.' "

"Will you *hush*?" he said, laughing in spite of the pain of his great, swollen manhood. "I never knew you were so silly."

"There's lots you don't know about . . ."

He took the rosebud nipple into his mouth and laved it with his tongue, and she couldn't say any more. She could only give a soft cry and tangle her fingers, hard, into his hair.

"O-o-oh, Nick."

She barely breathed his name but he heard it. He couldn't stop hearing it, said in that sweet and loving tone.

Then he moved to her other breast by marking a trail down into the fragrant valley between them and up the other side, and she could only gasp her pleasure and run her nails over his back and give little moans. His heart galloped; his body ached for release.

But he laid slow, deliberate siege to her breast and reached for the tangle of red-gold curls between her legs. He brushed his hand across there, back and forth, then slipped inside to stroke the sweet, feminine folds.

She fell to pieces.

"Please," she cried, squirming helplessly beneath him, but there was joy hidden in the plea. "Please, Nick . . ."

She arched to him, then tried to twist the other way.

"Nick, I want . . . please, Nick . . ."

He tried, he truly did try, to keep his promise, but when she stroked his back, his hip, and then reached to close her silky hand around his huge, hard rod, he gave it up and gave in to her begging. He took her small, perfect hips in his hands and entered her.

The joy pierced his spirit.

If his life had ended at that moment, he could have been transported, happy, to that bright, yellow ball of the moon. For she cried out in pleasure and held onto him as if she would never let him go, and she kissed him as if she loved him. As if she would love him and stay with him forever.

Callie was the partner he had needed all his life.

He managed to kiss the tip of her turned-up nose, and then he forgot the promise and everything else. He let himself go into the hot, wild world they created together, and when it exploded inside them, he felt that his heart had exploded as well.

It had spilled over into hers, and now it would belong to her forever.

They lay entwined for a long time afterward, just breathing into each other's ear, just feeling each other's skin, just listening to the rain come drumming down.

"I love you," he said, before he even knew he would speak.

Words he had never said to a woman before now.

"I love you, Nickajack. I always will."

He raised up on his elbow to look into her shining eyes.

"When I came into the house this morning and saw that mug sitting over there on the paper, I knew you were gone and I thought I would die."

"I took my time about leaving." She smiled her ten-thousand-dollar smile.

"I am so sorry, Callie," he said, holding her gaze with his. "I don't know how I ever could've said you were like other women, or that all women are alike."

Her smile changed to a teasing grin.

"That's all right," she said. "I know how unreasonable men can be."

As they laughed together, he had never felt so close to anyone before.

"You've left a piece of business undone," she said, stroking his shoulder slowly, slowly.

Spent as he was, desire began to stir again.

"What is it?"

"You came after me for your marriage certificate, remember?"

"Oh. Yes."

"What did you want with it, to throw it into the fire, too?"

He laughed and brushed back the curving hair from her face.

"N-o-o," he said, "I was after proof of my husbandly rights."

She traced the shape of his lips with one tantalizing finger.

"You don't need words written on a piece of paper for that," she said. "And you never will."

He kissed her again just to see if she meant it.

And she did.